SEX IN THE CITY
NEW YORK

EDITED BY

MAXIM JAKUBOWSKI

Published by Accent Press Ltd – 2010

ISBN 9781907016240

Printed and bound in the UK

Cover design by
Zipline Creative

Contents

Introduction

I AM RELIABLY INFORMED that the art and practice of sex is well-known outside of major cities too, but that's another book altogether!

Our new SEX IN THE CITY series is devoted to the unique attraction that major cities worldwide provide to lovers of all things erotic. Famous places and monuments, legendary streets and avenues, unforgettable landmarks all conjugate with our memories of loves past and present, requited and unrequited, to form a map of the heart like no other. Brief encounters, long-lasting affairs and relationships, the glimpse of a face, of hidden flesh, eyes in a crowd, everything about cities can be sexy, naughty, provocative, dangerous and exciting.

Cities are not just about monuments and museums and iconic places, they are also about people at love and play in unique surroundings. With this in mind, these anthologies of erotica will imaginatively explore the secret stories of famous cities and bring them to life, by unveiling passion and love, lust and sadness, glittering flesh and sexual temptation, the art of love and a unique sense of place.

And we thought it would be a good idea to invite some of the best writers not only of erotica, but also from the mainstream and even the crime and mystery field, to offer us specially written new stories about the hidden side of some of our favourite cities, to reveal what happens behind closed doors (and sometimes even in public). And they have delivered in trumps.

The stories you are about to read cover the whole spectrum from young love to forbidden love and every sexual variation in between. Funny, harrowing, touching, sad, joyful, every human emotion is present and how could it not be when sex and the delights of love are evoked so skilfully?

Our initial batch of four volumes takes us to London, New York, Paris and Dublin, all cities with a fascinating attraction to matters of the flesh and the heart. We hope you read them all and begin to collect them, and that we shall soon be offering you further excursions to the wild shores of erotic Los Angeles, Venice, Edinburgh, New Orleans, Sydney, Tokyo, Berlin, Rio, Moscow, Barcelona and beyond. Our authors are all raring to go and have already packed their imagination so they can offer you more sexy thrills ...

And it's cheaper than a plane ticket!

So, come and enjoy sex in the city.

Maxim Jakubowski

Gotham Sex
by Donna George Storey

First Comes Marriage

I RECEIVED MY FIRST proposal of marriage in Central Park.

I turned the guy down.

Of course, I was only eleven years old.

It wasn't the only occasion my life would take some precociously perverse detour in Gotham City. The proposal seems a fitting prologue to my New York adventures in infidelity, prostitution, voyeurism: edgy, forbidden acts that never happened to me anywhere else, not even in cities that stake their reputations on sexual sin like New Orleans or Las Vegas.

But let's return to the beginning of my corruption: Central Park, late summer 1973. My older sister and I had come down from Albany to see *No, No Nanette* featuring the great Ruby Keeler. My sister was eighteen, and for the first of many times my parents – often misguidedly as you will see – entrusted her with my care in the city of bright lights and big adventures.

The first morning of our spree was uneventful. We shopped for dresses at Macy's, ate the worst piece of pizza I ever had in my life in a midtown joint and, to compensate, bought chewy, charred soft pretzels from a street vendor.

To be honest, I didn't see much adventure in any of it.

Then, as we strolled through the park, a tall, slim black man weaved toward us. He waved at my sister's halo of hippy chick curls and said, 'You've got great hair. Will you marry me?'

'No, sorry, not today,' she replied with a smile.

'How about tomorrow?' the man pressed.

'I'm busy then, too.'

I stood at her shoulder, taking it all in. The man's Afro and colourful patterned shirt. His sinuous gestures and strange herbal smell. For a moment I conjured the unlikely picture of him standing beside my white-gowned sister in a church.

'How about her?' The young man glanced at me, but then fixed his gaze soulfully on my sister's face. 'Will *she* marry me?'

'She's not legal yet.'

The man laughed and crouched down to my level. 'Come on, honey, say you'll marry me.'

For one perverse instant I wondered what the future would bring if I said 'yes'. Of course, that was absurd, but I still had a prickle of pleasure at being desired, if only as second choice.

I shook my head.

'Well, if you change your mind when you're older, I'll be waiting.' He flashed me a knowing grin and sauntered off.

'God, he reeked of pot.' My sister took my hand and began walking quickly back toward the hotel.

Her legs were fashion-model long and I had to run to keep up with her. My heart was racing, too. Even then I sensed the proposal didn't mean a tiered cake and showers of rice, but something darker, dirtier, faster.

Like New York itself.

Brain Fuck

Seven years later my sister had graduated from barely respectable midtown hotels bankrolled by parents to staying with friends; at a very different price. On this, our second visit to the city together, she was already talking about

4

finding a way to live in New York. Only here, she said, did she feel like her true self.

I was only a few inches taller than I'd been that day in Central Park, but I was much wiser. For example, I'd finally figured out that I didn't have to wait for a stupid high school boy to ask me out. I could make my own wild times with *her* friends, grown-up men in their late twenties, who were proving ridiculously easy to seduce.

Not that I was totally confident in my new powers. When we walked into Joel's apartment in a white brick building across from the Strand Bookstore, I had no idea that within hours I'd be sprawled on his bed naked, my mouth stretched wide as he fed me his thick, swollen cock.

But first, he gave me a New York kiss on the cheek and a 'Great-to-meet-you-I've-heard-so-much-about-you.'

I'd heard a lot about him, too.

Joel was my sister's on-again-off-again boyfriend's best friend, and his very name was shorthand for brilliance and achievement. He'd graduated from Harvard Law School and now had a job in a top law firm located in the Citicorp Building. My sister told me his office had a stunning view, as if all of New York were bowing at your feet.

The promising young lawyer had just gotten home from that very office when we arrived at his apartment on a Saturday around six. Joel worked hard, but he played hard too. My sister had slept in the same bed with any number of guys without having sex with them; everyone did that in those days. But when she crashed on Joel's bed one night expecting he'd honour his friend's claim, she woke up the next morning with his erection wedged between her ass cheeks. And, being Joel, he didn't stop there.

I wasn't sure if this was a warning or a promise.

My sister also told me I was the type of woman he liked: blonde, blue-eyed, ready to start Princeton in a few short weeks. *The minute he sees you there won't be any introductions, he'll just drag you over to the sofa and start humping away ...*

It didn't happen exactly that quickly, but I did note the sparkle in his eyes when he looked at me across the table in the 'best Hunan place in Chinatown'. Joel ordered all his favourite dishes for us: twice-cooked pork, General Tso's chicken, and cold noodles tossed in spicy peanut butter sauce.

I studied him covertly as he ate, envying his culinary knowledge of the city, his shameless appetite. I was already smitten with his five o'clock shadow, his dark curls, his long, thick fingers. Barely touching the food, I realized I was really hungry for Joel himself, as if I could suck down his savvy and success along with his jism.

Back at his apartment, he fixed us gin and tonics, as a proper host should. He offered us a joint, too. My sister declined, but I accepted immediately. I knew it meant he would sit next to me on the floor and our fingers would brush as we passed the homemade cigarette between us, bathed in the rain-soaked neon glow filtering through the Venetian blinds. It also meant that when I slumped to the carpet, my skull as soft and hazy as a cloud of smoke, Joel would lean down and whisper, 'Are you all right, sweetie?'

'I'm great,' I murmured. 'This is all so New York. Thanks for everything.'

'It's my pleasure.'

Lie down next to me.

Of course, I didn't say it out loud, but some incantations need no words. Obediently, Joel made a soft sound in his throat and stretched out beside me.

Touch me. Press your dick up against my ass.

I waited. Joel remained motionless. I could feel the heat of his body, but he wasn't touching me at all. I knew he had a live-in girlfriend who was visiting her parents for the weekend, but she was just a name, a character in my sister's stories. How could such a flimsy thing come between his erection and my ass?

Unable to bear the suspense any longer, I rolled my head toward him so that our temples were pressed lightly

6

together. Still he didn't move. My scalp began to prickle. The tingle turned to a delicious, throbbing ache. Slowly my skin softened, opened, until I had a brand-new orifice, wet and hungry, pulling him inside me. I swear I could feel Joel's brilliance flooding into me through that hot crescent of skin-to-skin contact.

One of the smartest men – in a city of the smartest, most successful men in the world – was fucking my brain.

Then I felt a hand on my shoulder. It rested there a moment and began to move slowly down my arm. I imagined a man stroking a beautiful statue, willing it to come to life. My cunt muscles twitched. Now I was the one in total control. I could ignore the caress, sensing he would go no farther. I could brush his hand away, feigning innocence and indignation. Or I could reach up and squeeze his hand in a wordless 'yes'.

I touched his hand. He froze. I closed my fingers around his and squeezed. *Yes.* Through that open channel between our skulls I could feel his surprise and pleasure. *Yes.* I turned toward him and offered my lips. We kissed. His mouth was gentle, almost shy. I quickly grew tired of subtlety and thrust my tongue between his teeth.

'Slow down, sweetie, we have all night.'

Did we? I pulled away and glanced over at my sister. She had dozed off on the sofa. At least I hoped she was asleep.

'Can we go to your bedroom?'

He grinned at my audacity.

The rest would be easy, or had been with the others, but when Joel joined me on the bed he was shivering. His voice trembled, too, when he told me, 'Oh, God, you're so young, and this is so sexy. I feel like I'm back in high school.'

I bit back a smile. That's what they all said before they fucked me.

Then he asked, 'Are you a virgin?'

Strangely, I got the strong impression he hoped I'd say yes.

'No,' I replied haughtily, not admitting that I'd only gone

7

'all the way' twice. Let him think I had a cunt as busy as Grand Central Station.

I moved in to kiss him again and now I did feel it, his storied boner, hot against my thigh. I reached down and closed my fingers around the thick shaft. He tilted his hips toward me for a moment, but then suddenly pulled back.

'Wait,' he said. 'Wait right here.'

I burrowed into the sheets, my flesh humming with anticipation. Of course he was going to bring back a condom.

Two shadows appeared in the doorway.

He'd returned with my sister instead.

With an odd, almost merry little laugh, Joel helped her onto the bed as if he were handing her into a taxi. He climbed in beside her. 'Let's have a slumber party!' he announced.

Through the lingering buzz of marijuana, I struggled to make sense of this. Did he want a threesome? Then why was she in the middle? New York was for adventures, but I wasn't willing to go that far. Or maybe once he saw me naked, my tits smaller than he expected and my ass bigger, he didn't want me any more?

I didn't need to stay to find out the answer.

I rolled off the bed, grabbed his robe and retreated to the sofa. Soft voices floated out from the bedroom. I took a swig of my drink and watched the lights of his stereo wink green in the darkness, my skin still tingling with humiliation. The evening was not turning out the way I expected at all.

A few minutes later, my sister crept out of his room and snuggled next to me on the sofa. 'Hey, what's going on?'

'I thought you two were having a slumber party,' I snarled.

She laughed. 'Well, whatever you did to Joel, you sure got his motor running.'

Why did she seem so surprised? She'd predicted it – or was it all a joke at my expense? Then it occurred to me that she'd just given me some useful information. If Joel was turned on, then he was just scared to go through with it for some stupid reason like my age or the pesky girlfriend. But even if the hotshot lawyer was chicken underneath, I had enough daring and desire to make a satisfying ending for both of us.

Whenever anyone claims Bill Clinton 'took advantage' of young Monica Lewinsky, I remember how I stood in Joel's bedroom door in his bathrobe and demanded with all the indignation an ambitious eighteen-year-old girl can muster, 'Damn you, why won't you fuck me? What are you afraid of?'

Joel's head jerked back into the pillow as if I'd slapped him. Then his eyes narrowed and flashed with a steely light.

'Close the door.'

Suddenly the room was noticeably chillier. Even his voice was different; deeper, implacable. It was my turn to start in surprise. My pussy tightened in an almost painful spasm.

I closed the door.

'Take off your robe.'

I undid the belt with quivering fingers. The terrycloth fell to the floor and puddled around my ankles.

'Come over here.'

Cheeks burning, I shuffled over to the bed.

'Do you want me to fuck you? Is that what you want?'

'Yes.' How could I be so afraid, yet like it so much?

'Get into bed.'

This time there was no nostalgic hesitation in Joel's hands. He touched my flesh as if he owned it, tweaking my nipples, testing my slit to see how ready I was.

'You are a wet, horny little bitch, aren't you?'

I flinched at the words, but couldn't deny it.

'I want to suck your cock,' I whispered, not sure if this would put me back in control or lead me deeper into this intoxicating new state of submission.

'Go ahead and suck it then,' he said, his icy tone unaltered.

9

I scooted down and straddled his knees, noting how pale his sturdy thighs were under the dark, wiry hair. I imagined them hidden away in his dark suits as he talked with clients, did all those mysterious things important men did. I felt another stab of lust in my belly. I wrapped my hand around his shaft and stretched my lips over the glans. I sensed his eyes gazing down at me from above, like the lights glowing down from skyscraper windows. I began to move, taking him as far into my mouth as I could, fighting the gag reflex to show him I could do it. Joel merely watched me in silence. I pumped faster, hoping to make him arch up and moan. Instead his hand came to rest on my hair.

'That's good,' he said, 'but I want to do something else now.'

Licking my swollen lips, I waited for instructions.

'I want to watch you masturbate.'

My secret muscles clenched again. No one had ever said that naughty word in my presence. Not that I didn't play with myself, frequently, but the thought of doing it in front of him took my breath away. Showing him what I did after school, on boring Saturday afternoons, at night when I couldn't sleep – my darkest, dirtiest secret – would make me more than naked before him.

'Please, no,' I whispered.

He frowned, as if pondering whether to insist. Afterwards, in my fantasies, he always did exactly that. Only much later did I see that his command was a favour, a clever way to teach him how I liked to be touched. But it probably struck him then, as it did me, that I was way in above my head.

'Can't we fuck now?' I ventured. That always made them forget everything else.

'I don't have any condoms,' Joel said with a sigh.

'Just fuck me for a little bit and then I'll suck you again. I'm good at that, aren't I?' My voice sounded so small, so desperate for approval.

His lips stretched into a tight smile. 'Yeah, you're good.'

So I rolled onto my back and he took me with no further preliminaries. I gasped at the girth of him when he entered me, but he was well beyond tender solicitude. Each pounding stroke nudged me further up the bed until my skull knocked against the headboard. But I didn't complain. I'd gotten everything I wanted. I was embracing the night side of the city, all arrogance and selfish desire, desire that could turn on you, but take you places you'd never been before.

His thrusting grew faster, more desperate.

Lose control. Come inside me.

Foolish as it was, I craved that final conquest. But this time he didn't listen. Instead he pulled out and knelt over me, pushing his cock deep down my throat. Choking down a whimper, I sucked and sucked as if I'd be graded on it. The other men had always warned me when they were about to come, but Joel only grabbed my hair and pushed deeper, shooting his load down my throat with a groan.

It was the first time I swallowed cum.

Ever after the taste of semen reminded me of that night in the city, as bracingly bitter as a dream come true.

The Girl in the Bed

By Christmas my sister was living in a loft on the Bowery with a gay friend from college and his equally colourful band of friends. The place had all of the downtown 'amenities': a makeshift kitchen area lit by a single bare bulb, a creaky tin shower stall, and a weird W.C., perched on a stepped platform like a throne. My sister had the only salaried job as an assistant buyer at Bloomingdale's, so she scored the lone bedroom with walls tucked in the back of the loft beside the toilet. There she entertained her lovers: a string of touring punk rockers, a middle-aged artist whose work I still see in museum calendars, a journalist who wrote for a popular music magazine.

The other roommates camped out in territories along the cavernous main room. The first den on the left, draped in

11

silk scarves, belonged to Anne, a beautiful petite Parisian who worked for a high-end escort agency and dated a heroin dealer. My sister's friend, Jerry, built a nook where I often found him snuggling on a salvaged mattress with his lover of the moment, wearing pearls and a beehive wig and watching reruns of *Father Knows Best*. Golden-haired Wolfgang would have been gorgeous if he hadn't been so dangerously thin. He'd once been the boy toy of rich men in Vienna, gifted with mink coats and villa vacations, but New York called to his spirit. Now he tended bar and earned sporadic extra income from giving blowjobs in the men's room at a Soho club.

The flamboyant loft gang broke every rule and more than a few laws, but whenever I took the train up from college, I felt like the oddball, the criminal of the spirit, strangling the magic out of life with my slavish addiction to regular meals and 'A's in Chaucer. Yet I couldn't stay away. And I'd always bring back my own secret *I heart NY* memento – a studded leather cock ring I wore as a bracelet, a biker's jacket that stank of my sister's latest keyboardist – to remind myself I nurtured a darker, freer self.

Of course, I couldn't miss the loft-warming party in January, even though I was in the middle of finals and suffering from a cold. As befitted the Bowery, refreshments were simple: grain alcohol punch and cheap beer on ice. Far more energy was spent on dressing up. The boys monopolized the kitchen table with their 'make-up for men' kits, carefully drawing on eyeliner and lipstick. Anne and my sister both had their eyes on new men that night, so they chose fuck-me outfits: Fiorucci dresses, candy-coloured stockings and suede boots with punishing stiletto heels. In spite of my protests that I was just an observer, Anne insisted on dressing me up, too, in a mini-skirt, tight sweater and slinky leather jacket with a sheepskin collar.

'You never know whom you might get into bed tonight,' she purred.

By ten the guests began to arrive. One of the first was a

true south-of-14th-Street celebrity and founder of the Mudd Club, Steve Mass. The loft gang were regulars there, and my sister once sat next to Jerry Hall who, she reported, had "thick ankles". Middle-aged with long grey curls and a muddy complexion, Mass looked even more uncomfortable than I felt as he stood by the punch bowl.

'Would you like something to drink, Steve?' my sister asked with the perfect blend of cool and deference.

'I'm getting over a bladder infection,' the famous man announced in a gravelly voice. 'Do you have cranberry juice?'

Miraculously, someone found a big bottle in the ancient refrigerator, as if they were expecting plenty of partygoers with urinary tract problems. Steve sipped his virgin drink and scanned the room, obviously unimpressed by gyrating dancers, the Andy Warhol look-alikes, the squad of lesbians dressed as nurses from the 1950s.

Suddenly my own belly clenched in a painful, burning cramp. Was the great Bohemian socialite starting a fad in this, too?

The next stab of pain was so intense, it took all I had not to double over. I'd hoped at least to have some good stories to take back to my roommates, but the show would have to go on without me. I limped through the crowd to my sister's bedroom, stripped off my costume and collapsed on my sister's futon in my underwear. The party faded into a dull roar of chatter and pulsing music, dancing at the edge of my dreams.

I must have drifted off, for I was startled awake by a deep voice drifting down from heaven.

'Hey, this my kind of party. They have a girl already in bed waiting for you in the coat room.'

I slit one eye to see an angelically handsome man smiling down at me.

'Are you the kid sister from Princeton?'

I grunted.

'I'm Winston.'

I was about to tell him I'd heard a lot about him, but another spasm twisted my gut into a pretzel. Still, I had enough of my senses about me to feel a small thrill at this unexpected gift from the heavens. Winston was one of the legends of my sister's inner circle, a saxophone player who sported piercings on tender parts of his body before such things were as common as dirt. Sure enough, I glimpsed a glittering nipple ring through his unbuttoned shirt.

'Would you mind if I join you?' He wiggled his eyebrows.

'I have a really bad headache,' I managed to whisper. I didn't mention I thought I was about to vomit, too.

'Damn, they always say that,' he grinned.

Except I knew Anne still mooned over him after a fling involving lots of public sex, and that he occasionally allowed the equally smitten Wolfgang to suck his cock when he was feeling broad-minded. Everyone who was anyone leaped at the chance to fuck Winston.

'I'm sorry, it's true,' I croaked.

'Best get some sleep then,' he replied, his voice surprisingly gentle. 'But if your headache gets better, you know where to find me.' Winking mischievously, he closed the door behind him.

Even in the midst of my misery, I had to smile. Winston wouldn't have given me a second look if I hadn't been curled up on a bed at his feet like a girl in a porn magazine. I'd already gotten more attention just by lying bed than I ever would have managed cruising the party in call-girl clothes. Even Anne would be jealous. I had my good story, now I could just lie back and relax for the rest of the night.

Or so I thought.

'We can't, someone's in the bed.' An unfamiliar male voice roused me from another feverish dream.

The door clicked closed. But I was no longer alone.

'No problem. She's asleep,' said his partner. Anne.

I heard more whispers, a zipper, the rustling of cloth. The futon dipped as a weight settled onto it beside me. It sighed again as another body joined the first.

There was a feminine gasp, immediately followed by a familiar rhythmic rocking of the mattress. Was I hallucinating? No one would be rude enough to have sex in a bed right next to a stranger, asleep or not. And what kind of man would stick it in without even a kiss?

I opened my eyes a crack, my view modestly veiled by my eyelashes.

I wasn't hallucinating.

Anne was indeed stretched out beside me on the futon. An apparently fully dressed, blue-haired man was on top of her, arms extended so their bodies barely touched. Anne rested her hands on his shoulders in an odd gesture, as if she were pushing him away. Yet they were obviously connected where it mattered, if his bucking hips and her moans were any indication.

There was no denying it: a man and a woman were indeed fucking right before my eyes.

My belly contracted with a new sensation. I'd witnessed other kids making out, even dared to attend one of the film society's fundraiser showings of *Debbie Does Dallas* in McCosh Hall. But this was the real thing. Clinical as it was, I felt more worldly, more perverted, more *New York* for having seen it.

I closed my eyes, afraid to breath. If they discovered I was awake they might—what? Stop? Enjoy it more? Make me join in? I realized holding my breath would surely give me away, so I exhaled softly with Anne's next grunt. Soon we were breathing in unison, in-out, in-out, like a perverse yoga class. I felt my cheeks flush, my pulse begin to throb deliciously in my secret places.

The shaking of the mattress quickened. Behind my eyelids I could see Joe's Andy Warhol face twist in a grimace of orgasm. Anne's body stiffened. She let out a long sigh.

'Did you come?' he breathed.

'But of course,' she said with Gallic *ennui*.

15

To be witness to her timeless female lie thrilled me, too.

They both laughed as they dressed, like kids who'd gotten away with shoplifting candy. The door opened and closed. The cooler, thinner feel to the air told me I was alone again.

But changed, yet again, by the doings of this strange city.

When the door opened a few minutes later, I was ready for anything.

This time only one body flopped into bed with me without a word. It smelled male; denim and cigarette smoke and cuminy sweat. Was it Winston? Sick as I was, I was practically honour bound to maintain the tradition of this spot – Fucking Central Station – by saying yes.

The man slithered under the blanket and groaned. My body tensed, but he made no move to touch me. The next time I floated back to consciousness, the man's arm was draped over my side like a lover's. I pushed it way and turned toward the wall. He turned with me and spooned around my back. I almost shimmied away again, but the warmth of his body was strangely soothing.

By morning the loft was dead quiet and bathed in skim-milk light. The pain was gone. Stumbling to the toilet, I saw a few unfamiliar bodies scattered here and there on the floor draped in blankets. When I returned to my sister's room, I realized my bedmate was Jerry's old lover who'd come in from Long Island for the party.

'I'm sick, too,' he offered in greeting. 'I hope you don't mind I crashed here.'

I told him no – did I have a choice? – and we both fell back to sleep again.

By noon the bleary-eyed hosts were gathered around the kitchen table drinking strong Italian coffee and taking stock of the party. Jerry and Wolfgang gave it a fair rating and assured me their past parties were much wilder than I could imagine.

Coolly avoiding my gaze, Anne confessed that her intended conquest hadn't even bothered to come to the party

16

so she settled for the guy who lived downstairs. My sister said ruefully that she'd made good progress with her new guy, but my presence in her bed put a damper on things. They made out on the fire escape, but then he said he felt weird about doing it there and went home.

Jerry's Long Island friend tapped me on the arm. 'It was fun sleeping with you,' he smirked.

Everyone turned to me expectantly. No doubt they were hoping to see the sheltered college girl blush.

Instead I replied in my most sultry voice, 'Yeah, it was amazing. I'll remember last night for the rest of my life.'

He turned beet red, and the others laughed, with new respect, unaware it really wasn't a joke after all.

Fifteen-Second Whore

By my senior year, my sister had moved to her own place, a five-room apartment in the East Village. Her spacious dwelling was the result of connections, as is every desirable apartment in the city. Her new job at a building management company got her into the co-op at a rock bottom price. A judicious six-month fling with a carpenter meant new dry walls, refinished woodwork and custom cabinets for storage space.

Our visits were more civilized now. We'd sip wine to the melancholy sounds of Miles Davis as we gazed out the living room window at her view of midtown, crowned by the Empire State Building. On one such afternoon, my sister gestured toward an apartment across the street with her wine glass.

'Jerry was sitting right here last week, and he saw this amazing thing. The tenant over there was lying on his bed naked, with the curtains wide open, and some woman was giving him a blowjob. We figured she was a prostitute.'

I leaned closer to the window and squinted down at the apartment, but the curtains were closed. Still, the image took form as clear as a movie: the man's supine body, legs slightly parted, arms behind his head as he watched the woman's head bobbing up and down over his spit-polished dick.

I made it a habit to check the window on later visits, but never managed to see the real show.

Over the next year I did witness plenty of streetwalkers plying their trade on the sidewalk in front of my sister's building. These women were not French fashion dolls like Anne, but clichés of another sort. Their bodies were dumpy and worn-looking under polyester halter tops and miniskirts. Most appeared to be in their thirties, bored-looking Puerto Ricans or chain-smoking peroxide blondes. There were exceptions. One day I spied two laughing men in their early twenties emerging from behind some cars in the parking lot at the corner. A woman about my age with kohl-rimmed eyes followed a few steps behind, tugging down her skirt.

She returned my gaze with an icy stare of contempt.

I looked away and hurried on as if I were the guilty one.

After a few months I was savvy enough to identify the regular customers, too. Cars cruised the block regularly: fat Cadillacs or big old Buicks with beefy, grey-haired drivers.

Sometimes, when I was feeling disgusted with my Ivy League classmates' Wall Street ambitions, I wondered if a career in streetwalking might be a more honest way to make a living.

The August after graduation, I finally got my chance to try it.

I was strolling back from lunch with friends in the West Village, wearing shorts and a Hawaiian shirt I picked up for a dollar in a thrift store. I walked very slowly, studying my sandaled feet. The symbolism of it struck me even at the time. Up to then I'd known exactly what my next step should be. Now my future was wide open, but too frightening to examine, like a deep, messy wound.

That's when I sensed the big car shadowing me, its engine purring just a few feet away. My body seemed to know what was happening before my mind did, for my cheeks began to burn as if I'd gulped down a puckery old Manhattan cocktail.

Oh, God, he thinks I'm a streetwalker.

I bit back a giggle. But was it a joke? At that moment I was a desperate woman with no direction in her life.

Here was opportunity at last. Obscene possibilities flashed into my head. I could see my own body leaning on the passenger's window to haggle (how much should I ask for anyway?) The hurried ride to a secluded spot (wherever would that be in this all-too-public metropolis?) Me clutching the car upholstery with sweaty fingers, wondering if I could actually go through with it. Bending over to take his wrinkled, grandpa's cock between my lips, but doing my best, because I always tried my best for older men.

With a shiver, I instinctively looked up and straight into the eyes of my suitor. I remember purplish, fleshy ears, a shock of white hair. Our gaze locked for a good three seconds. It seemed much longer, however, as I watched the eager curiosity in his stare turn to shame as ink stains clean water in a glass. Jerking his head around, he floored the gas pedal and tore away down the street, engine roaring.

I glanced around quickly, but no one had witnessed my conceptual fall from respectability.

I'd actually been an East Village streetwalker in his eyes, if only for fifteen seconds. Yet the moment I returned his gaze, he knew I wasn't. And he knew I saw what he was.

Maybe I did have a future after all?

I laughed out loud, giddy with relief and sauntered the rest of the way to my sister's apartment with my chin held high.

Shades of History

After she became the second wife of a successful psychiatrist, my sister moved into her husband's carriage house in the West Village. Now she lives a few blocks from where Carrie Bradshaw mused over her sex columns in unlikely rent-controlled splendour and where Sarah Jessica Parker and Matthew Broderick actually do own a grand townhouse. The famous cupcakes of Magnolia Bakery are a short stroll away, as is The Pleasure Chest, where busloads of *Sex and the City* tourists buy rabbit-shaped vibrators for their friends back home so they can masturbate just like Charlotte.

The players in my own story are only shadows of memory. Jerry and Anne were HIV positive last time my sister heard news of them. Wolfgang's body was found floating in the mid-1980s in the East River near the pier where aficionados went for a fist fuck. Joel married his girlfriend, got divorced and then remarried, but my sister only learned all of this through mutual friends. And the old guy who thought I was a whore? Off to different hunting grounds once the new NYU dorm on 11th Street displaced hookers in favour of co-eds.

I still visit the city, but now, as a professor of mid-twentieth century English literature, I'm on the lookout for inspiration for my most popular course, 'Sirens of the Village: Female Writers Explore Form, Fame and the Erotic Spirit.' Wandering the twisting Greenwich Village streets, I think of ethereal Edna St Vincent Millay who not only burned her candle at both ends, she took both Edmund Wilson and John Peale Bishop into her bed one night. She divided her body between the two great literary men; romantic Bishop got the top half, earthy Wilson the bottom. Somehow I find it easy to picture the threesome sprawled on a neon-lit West Village bed in all their tormented ecstasy.

I can't pass Gay Street without thinking of Mary McCarthy evaluating the 'equipment' of yet another paramour with her wry critic's eye. Or MacDougal Street without flashing on Diane DiPrima's fateful encounter in a gay bar with dark and sexy Ivan, her fictional name for the man who fathered her first child. DiPrima claims she wrote her erotic classic, *Memoirs of a Beatnik*, solely for money, but to me her portrait of the city and her fellow artists resonates with true love.

In fact, I always start my course on literary lady libertines with a discussion of Gotham City itself. The name, I tell them, comes from a proverbial Nottinghamshire village populated by fools. Except the foolishness was really a masquerade to trick King John into building his hunting lodge elsewhere. The 'imbeciles' thus avoided economic ruin due to the king's ravenous demands.

Can foolish behaviour, wisely chosen, actually expand awareness in mind and body? Why is sexual experimentation – which most societies condemn in women – a seemingly necessary path for the creative female artist?

When I ask these questions, I think of my own foolish acts, still hoping to glimpse the canny wisdom hidden there.

Full Circle

I received my second, and last, proposal of marriage in New York City, too.

This time I said yes.

I'd just started grad school, and I brought my new boyfriend to the city during Christmas vacation to sightsee. With my sister at work all day, we ended up making love on her big brass bed for hours instead. I was sitting on top of him, his cock inside me, when my future husband popped the question.

I'd known since our first date that he was the One. Yet I paused to savour the moment. I'd been waiting for it since 1973.

'Yes,' I said, falling to embrace him. 'Yes. Yes. Yes.'

In one sense, that simple word is the end of my New

York tale. I would never seduce a man away from his girlfriend, never watch strangers fuck at a party, never flirt with prostitution again. Yet in other ways my adventures of the flesh only began in earnest that afternoon in Gotham City. Anyone who's travelled there knows that marriage is an adventure all its own, as full of magic, deep shadows, and surprise as the great city itself.

About the Story

WHEN I FIRST CONTEMPLATED writing a story about sex and New York City, my initial impulse was to explore the love affairs of famous twentieth-century women writers such as Edna St Vincent Millay, Mary McCarthy, Dorothy Parker and Diane DiPrima. Erotically adventurous in both their lives and their work, I saw these literary ladies as early twentieth-century Bohemian incarnations of Carrie Bradshaw and her friends. As I began my research, I saw that there really was a relationship between sex and New York, as if the very air of Gotham City made the boundaries of propriety seductively soft and yielding. The more I read of the lives of these legends, however, the more I was reminded of my own more humble encounters with sex in the city in the 1970s and 1980s. Eventually I came to realize that while the exploits of literary greats might eclipse the surroundings, the experiences of two ordinary young women could give the city its proper role at centre stage.

Readers always wonder how much of an author's story comes from real life, and I suspect this curiosity is particularly strong with erotica. I will confess that *Gotham Sex* is absolutely true – somewhere from 110% to 130% true. By which I mean actual events were much messier and my insights less sure before I smoothed and shaped them with my fiction-crafting hands. The apartment overlooking the Strand bookstore, the Bowery loft and the streetwalkers' cruising grounds all come straight from vivid memory, but naturally I changed most names and identifying details of the characters to protect the guilty. There is no doubt, however, that these moments of sexual connection touched me profoundly. They are my *truth* of the city, and I doubt these things could have happened in quite the same way anywhere else in the world.

I grew up in various parts of the east coast of the United States, always in the shadow of New York City. Unlike my older sister, who's lived in New York for thirty years, I found the home of my heart in northern California where "The City" means San Francisco with its soaring bridges and scent of Asian mystery. However, even today it is the sight of the Manhattan skyline that inevitably makes my heart tighten with longing, as if some dark but illuminating erotic adventure still awaits me in the shadows of its canyons.

A Washington Square Romance
by Maxim Jakubowski

ON BROADWAY, HE BOUGHT her an I LOVE YOU rubber stamp, which would never be used.

At Ground Zero, peering at the monstrous hole in the ground and the early signs of reconstruction, he held her against him and tried not to cry. It wasn't because of sympathy or compassion with the victims of the tragedy, but because he felt he had never been so close to her than he was now.

Under the arch in Washington Square, he kissed her.

She had reached Barcelona airport early and gone through security and passport control with more than two hours to spare before her flight left for New York, and had spent the time sipping coffees at one of the multitude of shiny bars in the duty free zone, leafing soporifically through some of her Catalan literature text books and daydreaming. When her plane was called, she had been in no rush to make a beeline for the gate, only to realise to her dismay once the back of the queue where she had been standing reached the final control point, that she could not find her passport. Her heart stopped. Where could she have mislaid it? It had been in her hands when she had checked her lone piece of luggage in.

She had run back breathlessly to the duty free zone and the cafe. There was now someone else sitting at the table she had occupied. She felt her heart jump, her stomach convulse with anxiety. She asked the man if there had been anything

25

on the table when he sat down. He looked at her with a puzzled look. She had automatically asked him in Italian, which he visibly couldn't understand. She switched to English. No, the table had been empty. He suggested she walk over and ask the attendant at the bar.

Which she did.

The young girl on duty had only just begun her shift. She completed the order she was working on and finally moved to a back door to enquire with a colleague. A few minutes later, an older man with grey eyebrows and leonine features walked out with a broad smile on his face. Giulia's attention was immediately drawn to his right hand. In which he held her passport.

Immense relief swept through her whole body. She felt faint. Held her breath.

'Thanks, thanks, thanks, so much,' she said, in Spanish this time.

The man grinned back at her, and silently handed her the lost passport.

She thanked him again a dozen times or more in her joyful haste and began to run back to the final control checkpoint. However, when she reached it, she was informed that the plane's crew had already locked the aircraft's doors and that she had missed her flight. Her solitary suitcase had already been unloaded. She pleaded her case, began sobbing uncontrollably, but it was to no avail. An airline attendant escorted her back sympathetically to the luggage area where the bag could be retrieved and then to the American Airlines desk.

There were no more flights to JFK today, but in view of the circumstances and even though they had no obligation to do so, they agreed to put her on the same flight the following day, which fortunately still had some empty seats.

Tears still drying across her hot cheeks, forlornly pulling her bag behind her, Giulia found herself once again in the departure and check in area of Terminal A. She pulled her mobile from her handbag, checked the printouts of the e-mails they had exchanged and rang his hotel in New York. He wasn't in his room. Why would he be? She left a message for him to call her back.

By the time he did, she was back in her dormitory north of Plaza Catalunya, and she had exhausted all the tears a human being could expend in the space of half a day.

Hiccupping between words, stuttering, crying out of control, she informed him that she had missed the flight.

She could almost feel the weight falling like a hammer across his own heart all those thousands of miles away.

But his voice remained calm and soothed her once she had managed to explain that she would still be coming, arriving on the same flight tomorrow.

'It'll be all right,' he said. 'It's a just a day, a night less. The main thing is that we can still be together. Just try and get a good night's sleep and be at the airport nice and early and don't linger over coffees this time,' he said, a hint of affection and humour in his deep voice. 'I'll be waiting for you.'

'Yes.'

'And don't forget to take a cab from JFK to Washington Square,' he added. 'I'll pay for it. Don't want to waste any more time, do we?'

'I want you so much.'

She barely had time to drop her luggage to the floor before he wanted to undress her. He had been waiting in the hotel lobby for her fifty bucks taxi ride from the airport to reach the city, reading a magazine, distracted by every new arrival. As she ignored the doorman and ran towards him, he smiled broadly. She embraced him, squeezed him against her, and all the pain and anguish of yesterday's disaster faded away in an instant.

They called the lift, and although not alone in it, she felt his hand caressing her arse through the thin white linen skirt she was wearing.

'I want to see you. All of you,' he said as he took a step

27

back from her once they entered the fuchsia-coloured room.

She quickly slipped out of the skirt and he pulled the *Strangers in Paradise* tee-shirt over her head. She was bra-less. Had never really needed one. He sighed as he saw those nipples again whose shade he could never quite capture in words, an ever so subtle variation between pale brown and pink he had never witnessed on any other woman he had seen naked before.

His breath caught in his throat.

She laughed and approached him. Pushed him back onto the bed and straddled him.

Outside, the cold February sun illuminated the recently refurbished arch, like a stone rainbow at the southern extremity of 5th Avenue, towering above Washington Square while dogs ran loose across the park and small children laughed and shrieked on their swings and hardy squirrels scampered over the sparse grass and the chess players in the South East corner of the park pondered and ruminated on and on and all was well with the world.

Pearls of his come like miniscule diamonds scattered across the curly jungle of her pubic hair, her inner lips swollen and a darker shade of bruised pink, catching their breaths, the bed a field of lust and sheets creased in every direction of the zodiac.

'Is it your first time in New York?'

The familiar smell of her cunt wafting like a upright fountain towards his nose, reviving his senses; joyful, loose, full of the flavour of life itself.

'No, I came when I was a teenager. My father was talking at a medical conference at Columbia. So he brought the whole family along. I shared a room with Tommaso, my younger brother. He was a pest then. We stayed in a big luxury hotel near Central Park. Did a lot of shopping.'

His hand strayed unconsciously towards her nipples, picked one up between two attentive fingers, caressed the rough tip, kneaded her flesh like soft dough, weighed each orb with abominable tenderness, the feather-like compactness of her slight elevations. He sighed. How could skin be so white?

'Look,' he said, almost slurring his words, nodding towards the window where the outside light was fading, 'dusk approaches. We must absolutely take a walk across the Square before night falls and then we can find somewhere to eat. If we stay in this bed any longer, I'll want to make love to you again, and right now I'm just too raw ...'

She had been sitting with her neck supported by the bed's headboard. She slouched down, stretched herself lazily across the rumpled bedcovers, yawned languorously, opened her legs in a wider angle. The wetness at the core of her delta shone. He couldn't take his eyes away from her cunt. He silently lowered his head towards her core and systematically licked the drops of come still lingering around her opening.

'You tasted a bit salty, earlier,' she remarked. 'Where did you have lunch?'

'At Live Bait, a Cajun restaurant near the Flatiron Building.'

'Oysters?'

'How did you guess?'

'I had a glass of white wine with my meal on the flight,' she grinned.

His tongue dipped into her cunt.

'Oysters and wine,' he said.

'I must call my mother, just to let her know I arrived safely,' Giulia said. They'd shared split pea soup, pierogi and meat stuffed cabbage at the open 24 hours Veselka Ukrainian restaurant on 2nd Avenue. He knew she would like it. She was not allowed spicy food as it badly upset her stomach.

'Do you want me to leave the room while you speak to her?' he suggested.

'No. It's fine, but stay quiet.'

29

Her mother knew she had travelled to New York with her mysterious new boyfriend, but her father had been kept in the dark and she was terrified he would find out she was having an affair with an older man. After all, he had insisted that while in Barcelona she stay in student digs supervised by Catholic nuns. But she hadn't even told her mother about the difference in age that stood between them. Giulia was a talented liar.

Midnight was nearing. She threw off her shoes and walked over to the corner of the hotel room and unzipped her luggage and pulled out a deep blue silk nightie.

'Look,' she said.

'It's beautiful,' he touched it. 'So soft.'

They had always been in the habit sleeping naked.

'My mother bought it for me, when she learned I was going to spend a few days, a few nights with you,' Giulia confided in him. 'She felt I ought to look nice in bed,' she giggled.

'A most understanding mother!'

'She is nice.'

'Little does she know what her dear daughter is concealing from her, or does she?'

Giulia gave him a look of protest, as if he were pushing his luck, emphasising her duplicity. For a moment he did wonder what her parents would make of him. Likely scream with shock, he guessed.

But her parents were not present in this room by Washington Square. They were.

'Come here, let me hold you.'

And again the warmth and softness of her body was intoxicating, releasing waves of terrible tenderness through every square inch of his body, his veins, his brain cells, as if he had lived his whole life until this very moment waiting for her, to fulfil him, to make him a better man.

He undressed her.

She slipped the nightie on.

It ended around mid-thigh and, at the top, its elongated

V-neck revealed the quiet onset of her slight cleavage.

He delicately raised the hem of the silk garment and ventured a finger into her cunt. She was wet already. He pushed her gently back towards the wall, and entered her with agonising slowness.

He was home.

She never did wear the silk night-gown again that week in New York.

Mid afternoon. February.

They had seen a mediocre thriller at the Union Square multiplex movie house and, sitting in a coffee house on Broadway just a hundred yards away from the intersection with Houston, were debating the merits and virtues and otherwise of Bruce Willis, who had starred in the film.

'I like it when you tell me stories,' Giulia had said.

The waitress who had served them had a piercing in her right eyebrow and wore black from head to toe. He vaguely recognised a tune by Bruce Cockburn amidst the background muzak. When they had walked in, it had been to the strains of The Walkabouts playing Neil Young's *On the Beach*. They were bathed in coffee fumes and a reassuring warmth. Giulia could spend her life in cafes, it was that Italian upbringing of hers.

'Will you tell other women stories about me when we are over?' she asked him.

He wanted to be truthful and say no, but already she knew him too well. He was who he was, and aware that the temptation would be too strong not to talk about her, to improvise tales of beauty and fury, of lust and longing, songs of adoration and missing.

He lowered his eyes, nodded.

The punk waitress refilled Giulia's cup.

She sipped pensively from the hot cup and watched him.

'I don't know,' he answered. 'At any rate, not in the same coffee houses. Let's go walk.'

Under the Washington Square arch he stopped and took

31

her hand and said, 'I'm so happy right now. Kiss me.' Her lips still tasted of coffee and her tongue of sugar and her dark eyes shone in the early evening penumbra and his whole body shivered. A band of assorted buskers played ragtime jazz across from the fountain. On the south side of the park, on the pavement outside the massive University buildings, hawkers were selling rag tag second-hand books on trestle tables and old issues of *Penthouse* and *The Magazine of Fantasy and Science Fiction*. Impulsively he bought her a copy of an old Philip Roth novel about an older man who was in love with a younger woman. A few years later, they would film it and it would remind him of her, even though she looked nothing like Penelope Cruz, despite their common Mediterranean roots.

An anorexic sun was setting in the distance, disappearing in the shadows that lurked around the Empire State Building. Traffic roared down Fifth Avenue as if every inhabitant of Manhattan was in a rush to reach home before dark settled. Coloured and Asian nannies were fleeing the Park at the speed of lemmings, frantically pushing cots in front of them as if their life depended on it, returning their charges to their nearby apartments where their working parents were about to return from their offices.

They sat by the dog's enclosure.

New York.

February.

Early evening.

'I'll write a story about a couple, call them Conrad and Julie maybe, who love each other terribly, obscenely. But they cannot stay together. Too many things separate them. The weight of years, the presence of others, frontiers, past and future adventures, the weight of the world and expectations, different ambitions, a life almost lived and a life that still requires mad adventures ...' he said gently, as she buried her head across his shoulder. 'So they part, as it must be and will be. Years later, his life has fallen apart in bad ways and he is sitting in a bar in Paris in the Latin

Quarter, a place he never took her to, when a man, a stranger enters the joint and tells him he needs his help to find his missing daughter. And passes a photograph of the missing girl to him across the plastic-topped table. And it's Julie. He tries to tell her father he is no detective. But the man won't listen to him, and pleads for him to accept the case. So Conrad reluctantly takes on job and begins his quest for ...'

He paused for breath, his imagination running ahead of him into all sorts of tangents and plots and illogical directions.

Looked up at her. There was a tear falling down Giulia's right cheek.

'Or maybe,' he changed his tack, 'it will be the tale of a man and a woman on a train that takes ages to reach China and she falls asleep with her head on his shoulder, just as they are nearing the border and ...'

'I prefer that story,' Giulia said. 'But you must never give your female characters my name. That would be disrespectful to me. I won't like it.'

He interrupted himself. 'Please don't make me promise that,' he thought, knowing all too well it was a promise he could never keep. But she said no more.

'I could write a thousand stories,' he said. 'I *will* write a thousand stories. But, right now, we are together and there is no reason to even think of the future. This is a moment out of time, Giulia. Our moment.'

She wiped the thin teardrop away.

'Let's go back to our room,' she asked. 'I want to be with you between the white sheets.'

He is watching her shower, her black curls unfurled all the way down to the small of her back, steam rising through the narrow hotel room bathroom, white plastic divider pulled to the side, water splashing against the tiles.

'One day I will go to live in San Francisco,' she says, above the muted roar of the jets of water streaming across her skin through the plastic shower head.

33

The spectacle of her nudity is too much too bear. He pulls off his grey tee-shirt and steps out of his trousers and steps into the bathtub and joins her. The fit is tight. Silently she hands him the soap bar and he lathers the foam across her back and spreads the thin bubbles across her, lingering tenderly over her arse. He soaps her crack, his fingers maliciously slipping and sliding down her wet valley, cleaning her, scrubbing her with all the care and attention of a slave attendant. He cups his hand under the shower head, fills his outstretched palms with water and finally washes the soap's foam away from her skin. Unsteadily, trying to retain her equilibrium in the reduced manoeuvring space left by the bulk of their two bodies in the bathtub, she swivels on her axis and turns around. She faces him. Her nipples eerily shine, a combination of dampness and the light from the inlaid electric bulb in the ceiling. He lathers up the soap he was still holding in his left hand and begins to scrub her front.

'I've already cleaned there,' she says.

He ignores her and continues. Painting an invisible fresco across her small, velvet breasts, spreading the softness all over her slight hillocks and the imperceptible valley separating her chest into two parallel and identical landscapes. Giulia moans quietly. His hands move downwards bypassing the mini-crevice of her belly button and its familiar mole and making an assured beeline for her cunt. He kneels down in the bathtub, his face now facing her opening. One pair of fingers part her, while his other hand places the soap bar on the side of the tub and invades the thicket of her pubic hair, travelling through the obstinate curls, treading her jungle, spreading the wetness, massaging the ground below like an alchemist in search of a magical formula. Her dark lower lips open up like a flower to a deep and moist cavern of redness. Her inner lips are still beautifully swollen from the incessant lovemaking of the past two days. He wipes the last remaining bubbles of soap away and his tongue nears her vortex.

'In San Francisco, I will find myself a black ambassador and I will marry him,' she says.

He never quite knows when she is joking, or trying to provoke him. He says nothing and begins to lick her. Wetness against wetness. He closes his eyes. A blind man now, worshipping from memory, on automatic pilot, homing in like a bird of prey towards the fountain of life, the taste of Giulia coursing through the bridge that his lapping tongue has now become toward the very centre of him, dragging pleasure and bittersweet tastes alongside, an essence he would never truly be able to explain. In the darkness of his genuflection, his hands wander upwards. Her nipples have the gentle hardness of pizza crust, the beating sound of her heart reverberates through her chest, boom, boom, boom. He is out of breath and realises that for several minutes now, his tongue planted deep inside her, his nose buried beneath the hard shield of her curls and stomach, he had actually forgotten to breathe. He gets up from his uncomfortable squat. Turns her round. Under the warm waterfall that splashes relentlessly over the both of them, he pulls her arms away from her body and positions her so that they are now both now leaning for support against the wall above the taps. Without being asked, she spreads her legs open. He takes his cock in one hand and guides it towards her and enters her.

'You know,' she says. 'When I was in Ibiza, Pedro, one evening when we were chilling, smoking pot, touched me on the arm, and I knew he wanted to fuck me. And I wanted him to fuck me too. I needed it. That's why I'd let him see me naked on the beach that afternoon. But his hand on my skin just felt wrong, you see, not like yours. So I brushed him away and took another puff on the joint. It was a crazy evening.'

Hearing the name of another, he felt a wave of anger and bitterness sweep through him and thrust into her as hard as he could, and entwined as they were, they almost slipped. Fucking in showers looked easier in movies, to be sure.

He withdraws from her.

'This is too awkward,' he points out. 'One of us is going to slip and we'll injure ourselves. Let's go to bed.'

They retreat to the room, swathed in white towels. He hurries to the bed and slides in between the sheets.

'I have to dry my hair first,' she said. And stands in the bedroom facing the mirror massaging the soft material into the jungle of her hair. The other large bathroom towel tightened around her body slips to the ground.

He watches, his heart beating wildly, his breath taken away yet again by the sheer innocence of her nudity. Walks out of bed and embraces her as he is overtaken by tenderness. Her hair is now less damp and she throws the towel she had been using aside. Both facing the mirror, his face peering across her naked shoulders. An image he would treasure for ever, indelibly printed into the back screen of his brain.

On their final evening in New York, she wanted to go out. Properly.

She insisted he shave his chin and cheek stubble, wear his black suit, and a clean shirt which she selected from his pack. She foraged inside her untidy suitcase and pulled out a backless evening dress, and shoes with heels. This was the first occasion in all the time he had known her she had ever worn heels. At an open all-night Korean convenience store on the corner of 3rd and Sullivan Street, he bought a red rose she planted amongst the thicket of her curls.

They walked down to the restaurant on Bleecker Street they had chosen earlier and Giulia floated on air and heels like a royal gypsy queen proudly taking ownership of the cold night. The lights of Greenwich Village flickered. Pride swelled in his heart. Combined with a sense of impending loss because it was to be their final night here. And he never knew on each trip together whether it would be their last.

'I feel sad,' he said to her, picking at his pine nut and asparagus risotto.

'You musn't.'

'I know,' he replied.

The restaurant was almost empty and the food disappointing.

The evening before he had brought takeaway sushi from a downmarket Japanese on the corner of 6th and Greenwich Avenue and fed her individual morsels by hand while they both sat upright in bed, drops of soya sauce pearling down across the Antarctica of her small breasts, which he then obediently licked clean, savouring the taste of food and the musky, natural smell of her own skin.

'Yesterday was better,' he pointed out.

'Yes,' Giulia said, with a hint of a satisfied smile.

'Oh well ...'

They walked back to their room taking a detour by Washington Square, a crescent moon laced the shadows falling across the facades of the massive apartment blocks on the southernmost side of 5th Avenue. Under the arch they kissed briefly, but the temperature was falling fast and she had no coat to shelter her naked back from the growing cold. He draped his jacket around her shoulders.

The night porter watched them impassively as they trooped across the lobby towards the main elevator.

They stripped quickly and sought warmth between the cold sheets. The silence that divided them now was deafening. Their hands fumbled in the darkness, seeking each other, their bodies suddenly uncomfortable and self-conscious. His hand grazed one breast. Her fingers grasped his cock and felt it grow under her contact.

On Waverly Place, they made love and wept.

Her limousine arrived a quarter of an hour early the next day to take her to the airport, where her flight back to Barcelona was waiting. They didn't have much time to talk.

He just stood in the lobby watching her walk to the swinging doors of the hotel, dragging her metal case alongside on its small wheels. He was searching for the right words to say, but they just wouldn't come. They never did,

did they?

Out in Queens, past Jamaica Boulevard, travelling down Van Wyck Expressway, separated from the Arab driver by the glass partition, Giulia pulled her notebook from her bag, and began drafting him a letter. She would continue writing it in the airport's departure lounge where she had a couple of hours to spare until they boarded the flight. She'd had no wish to have a coffee this time around or spend time in the duty free shops. The letter spread over 9 pages, her handwriting all over the place, sometimes shaken by the tears rolling down her cheeks or that terrible feeling of despair that so often lurked in the pit of her stomach. She used both sides of the paper. During the long flight back to Europe, she made changes, crossing out lines, adding words, erasing others.

It was a love letter. Thanking him for the wonderful time they had spent together by Washington Square. Attempting in bursts of savage hunger to tell him, explain to him how much she loved him, even though the whole essence of their relationship was wrong, could just not sustain itself. She made promises she knew she could not keep. Tried to understand, as she wrote, why love could also contain so much pain.

By the time she landed, she had already decided she would never send him the letter. It remained at the bottom of her bag for the next six months. Accusing her. Chiding her. But wasn't it him who had one day explained to her that words weren't enough. That they couldn't change the course of things?

One day, by accident, he would read the letter but by then it was too late. They had both moved apart, only lust kept them together under its heavy cloak of illusions when they took excursions away together from their real lives in other foreign cities or beaches. Ironically, his discovery of the letter coincided with their very last tryst.

Of course, the letter made him cry. Because he now realised that they had both left their hearts behind in Washington Square.

About the Story

ALTHOUGH I NOW LIVE in London, I seem to find it easier to pop over to the Big Apple more frequently than I ever travel to Europe. For business, for pleasure, for family reasons, for culinary reasons, to fill my suitcase with books and records (this before the internet changed the face of culture retail, of course), to listen to the wind streaming between the canyons of avenues, see movies a few weeks before they open in London and many other reasons, both public and private.

I love the place although I'm not sure I would want to live there.

When I would travel to New York on publishing business I would often stay at the legendary Algonquin Hotel on 44th Street, and on occasions at the Royalton (long before it was refurbished by Philippe Starck) where I often ended up on first name terms with the cockroaches. When the book business began to migrate out of midtown, I also moved South and my new base became the Washington Square Hotel (after a failed affair with the Gershwin, which I could never quite get to grips with). It made sense, as I was spending most of my free time in Greenwich Village anyway. A passing vote of thanks to my mate Michael Moorcock who suggested I try it.

Characters in my books and stories spend a lot of time in hotels as part of their travel and the sacrifices they make on the altar of wanderlust. It doesn't mean that every character is me, even if the rooms are the same ones I've slept in or otherwise. If I had done everything sexual my hapless anti-heroes have done, I would now be several feet underground or moving about with the assistance of a Zimmer frame or worse. So, setting this bittersweet tale around Washington Square just made sense, you know.

And no, it wasn't inspired by Henry James.

Cell Mates
by Polly Frost

SHE WAS ONE OF those slim young women you see on the streets of New York, hurrying along with a cell phone in one hand and a bottle of water in the other.

Everybody around her was gabbing into their cell phones.

Some were shouting, some were crying, some were laughing.

She alone walked in silence. It was a situation she couldn't bear. She punched her speed dial, and the phone on the other end was picked up.

'It's me, R.B.,' she cried. 'You know, me! The girl you're going with!'

Damn the static! She'd bought her phone only a month ago, but it had already let her down numerous times. The phone screeched, then gave her a 'no signal' sign, which it always did next to this high-rise. She scampered to the other side of the street and hit redial. Still nothing, even though the battery symbol indicated at least a little time left before recharging would be needed. 'Soon you'll just poop out on me altogether.'

There were days when she thought she and her cell phone should go into couple's therapy. She dialled again. All clear. 'It's still me!' Heads swivelled around her. She was yelling, yes, she knew that, but she had to in order to be heard above the din of the other street phone conversations. 'What, R.B.? Did I like what? No, I thought it was really bad! What? You weren't talking about the play we saw last night? Oh, I see.

43

You were talking about our sex this morning.'

It came back to her in a rush: how she'd attended to his cock, snapping the leather ring around his balls, then sucking him off as she played with his ass and he kept his right hand on the PlayStation control.

She glugged the rest of her Smart Water loudly right into R.B.'s ear. She took out her sexual frustration on her water bottle, squeezing it roughly so the plastic almost broke. Then she tossed it away, and scanned the block for the nearest deli. Her eyes zeroed in on a green canopy shading the requisite display of fruit and tabloids. A hissing sound, this time not electronic, welled up behind R.B.'s voice, and she rolled her eyes.

'I'm glad you love me,' she said to her boyfriend. 'And I love it when you tell me that.'

She'd been doing her best to train him for months. Her method: always precede the correction with a positive.

'But it would mean more if you'd tell me that when you weren't taking a leak. I do realize the importance of maximizing one's time by doing more than one thing at a time. But still ...'

R.B. was proud of describing himself as a "multi-task-aholic". She, though, sometimes had her doubts about how efficient this really made him, and wondered: was everyone in this city really working twenty-four/seven or were they just saying they were? And what exactly constitutes work? For example, if someone said they were working, but no one was around to see it, did anything actually get done?

Now he was actually lecturing her.

'Say wha'?' she responded. 'I do so possess a work ethic! Well, for example, it's Saturday, and despite it being a designated weekend day I have a business phone call in exactly an hour with Terri Atkins ... Of course that Terri Atkins!'

Who did he think she meant? Only the hottest editor of lifestyle catalogs in the city!

The phone had another static attack just as R.B. was

entering the groaning-and-flushing phase. She gave the phone a grateful pat for covering up the toilet sounds as she turned into the deli.

'No cell phone! No cell phone!' muttered the Asian woman behind the counter, pointing to a hand-written sign.

'This doesn't qualify since I can't even hear my boyfriend. Bad reception,' she enunciated carefully.

'About tonight, I was thinking ... what?' she shouted as she paid. 'You can't be serious, dude! No, my feelings aren't hurt, but I can't believe you're behaving like this. You don't just blow your fiancée off with no warning!' She looked at her watch. 'And I don't consider six hours sufficient warning.'

'No cell phone! No cell phone!' the Asian woman insisted, again pointing to the hand-written sign.

'Yeah, yeah, yeah,' she waved the woman off as she left.

'Rude!' the Asian woman hissed.

Back on the street; a new cold Smart Water in her right hand. She belted some. Nothing like liquids to help you cope during times of relationship stress.

'No, you're right. You gotta do what you gotta do in financially turbulent times. I'm a big girl, I can look after my own needs.'

Now there were zapping sounds behind R.B.'s voice; he'd gone straight from the bathroom to his computer game. Very mature.

'Blast a hundred mutants to ectoplasmic bits for me,' she said. 'Yeah, love you too.'

She hit the END button, threw back some more beverage, coughed, and twisted the cap vigorously back on the bottle.

Maintaining proper hydration: it's a discipline.

Down Fifth Avenue to 11th street, then over to Broadway; her annoyance about being abandoned gnawing away at her. Bottom line: if things went on like this she'd have to give her and R.B.'s relationship a reconsider.

Time for a gay-friend fix. Her fingers flew over the

keypad.

'Hey, Geoffrey, it's me! Whoa! Boompa-boompa-boompa. Could you crank the techno down just a few clicks? You can't? You're at a party? Geoffrey, it's mid-afternoon.'

Visions of unattainable boys with ideally fab abs whirled through her mind and like her favourite gay porn it left her with a furious longing. But what did Geoffrey care?

'I am not sounding crestfallen, the connection's just bad. I was just hoping ... Geoffrey? Geoffrey?' She heard him dancing back into the happy fray. And then her phone went dead.

She gave her cell phone a savage glance. She would not, would not, burst into tears. She looked up and her reflection in plate glass stared back at her.

'No more denial!' she cried.

She looked around abashed, just realizing that she'd spoken the words out loud. How did that happen? But it was okay, everyone else was talking into their phones. She simply had to face the fact that maybe she would be alone tonight. Time to be your own best friend, time to give yourself a treat. R.B. is sweet enough to pretend he likes chick flicks, but he always falls asleep and snores, which spoils things somehow.

She punched up Mr. Moviefone to see whether he had a new romantic comedy in the theatres. Sure, it would be simpler just to get the information by text, but she loved hearing his voice. As Mr. Moviefone led her through his multiple options, it occurred to her that he was one man who had never let her down. He was there on Saturday night. Even when you were the one who made a mistake, he was sorry.

She found herself making Mr. Moviefone repeat his sweet apology for not being able to understand what she wanted.

'I'm sorry ... I'm sorry ... I'm sorry ...'

Over and over. She never let him get to the stage where

he asked for her zip code, yet he never got exasperated.

Mr. Moviefone was the perfect man. Why couldn't R. B. take a few lessons from him? She listened to his voice grow soft and break up as her battery gasped its last. The moment seemed unbelievably poignant.

She didn't realize she had meandered deep into the East Village until she heard a horrible voice screaming at her.

'Do you know what 'digital' really means? People from my land aren't fooled. My people don't carry cell phones. Is that because they can't afford them? No. It is because they know whose work they are!'

It was a hunched-over ancient lady draped in black shawls, crossing herself in the Catholic style, kissing a cross. Some god awful, CNN, tribal-war-in-the-Balkans accent. No one to be frightened of, just a pathetic old soul angry at being lonely and alone. She shivered as she remembered that tonight she, too, would be lonely and alone.

As she hurried back to civilization she gave the woman one last look in an attempt to reassure herself she'd never become like that. What she saw was a hideous toothless gorge of a mouth. Thank God, we're barely members of the same species.

'Whew,' she thought. 'How did I end up on this block?'

She headed towards Lafayette Street, keeping her eyes on the sidewalk until she felt safe enough to start shopping for a new battery.

She looked up and down the block and spotted a tiny wireless phone store jammed between a sneaker outlet and a jeans emporium. She strode over.

Oops, traffic-fumes alert! She leaped to the side to avoid the smoke from a garbage truck and crashed into some bridge-and-tunnel people. She hated having to apologize to B & T's.

Cell Mates. Cute name. She'd never heard of them before, but why should she have? Telecoms were appearing and going under every day. Best strategy: get a good anytime-minutes package that you can cancel at will. And she liked the shop's elegant storefront, cosy yet chic. Now that was a fresh image choice for a phone company! They'd know how to serve a woman's needs.

The door swooshed shut behind her.

The store was amazingly large, silky-pink, undulant yet refreshing. A young woman in a see-through sari came out from behind the counter, her olive skin glowing, her thick, long black hair swinging free. Even from the door you could see her extraordinary eyes: iridescent, somehow, and more than just one colour. One moment they seemed jade, the next amber.

Cool! Probably some new kind of contact lens, or something she had done with lasers. The woman's shirt was cut short to expose her bellybutton and low to expose the tops of her breasts. Her cleavage sparkled. Had she put glitter there? Excellent idea!

Then the woman was before her, offering to help, and she hurriedly and with some embarrassment brought her eyes up and off the woman's bosom.

She felt a sexual rush, which was kind of neat, she had to admit it. It was one of her secret shames that she was the only one of her friends who hadn't yet had an affair with a woman.

Maybe there was still hope.

'I know just what you need,' the saleswoman murmured.

'All I'm looking for is a battery, really. I have this stupid Verizon phone that eats energy –'

'Verizon doesn't even begin to have what we offer.' She couldn't take her eyes off the woman's lips, which made images of cherries and burgundy swirl in her head.

'Well, actually, I was thinking of heading to the Apple Store in SoHo and getting a new iPhone.'

'And we have way more than Apple will ever come up with.'

'Really?' She loved being ahead of all her friends when it

came to cell phone technology.

'Come with me,' the saleswoman said, taking her by the hand.

What a store! In niches on the wall were small sculptures of Indian tantric sexual positions, the kinds of things she'd only seen at that Learning Annex seminar she'd dragged R.B. to. The saleswoman was barefoot and swung her unashamedly fleshy hips like the instructor who led the belly-dancing class at the gym.

The saleswoman stopped at a wall and gestured towards it. On it were the most delicious cell phone samples. One looked like it was made of abalone shell, another was crusted with sapphires. Another looked like it was made out of that newfangled skintight stuff Olympic swimmers now wore.

The one that really caught her eye was on the far, far left.

'Mmm, you have good taste,' the woman said. Was she a mind-reader too? The saleswoman picked up the sample, stroked it, posed it. Then she seemed to run it along her lips, while maintaining eye contact.

'Here,' the woman said. 'Now you try.'

She accepted the phone from the woman. What was it like? Not clammy the way her first cell phone had been. And not steely and cold the way the current one was. No, it was velvety and slick, with a soft give to it, yet surprisingly firm inside. Sensitive, yet with some real spine. She touched her own lips to it, and said some nonsense words into it. Where did they come from?

She was blushing. There was no need to look further.

'I'd really like to buy this one,' she said.

'I'm not surprised,' the woman said in her softly mysterious accent. 'And the battery life will surprise you.'

As they arranged the terms of the service plan, she fingered her new prize. She could swear it was a little ticklish! She didn't even bother to skim the contract's fine print, she just signed, then watched as the saleswoman's long, blood-red fingernails danced over the computer keyboard, typing in her vital stats. She felt renewed, once again eager for life.

Out on the street, she turned her new prize over and over, getting to know it with eager, happy fingers.

Checking her watch, she saw that it was finally time to call Terri. She started to punch the number, but, as if thought-activated, her new phone dialled it for her.

And the cell phone's buttons! Had they changed? They were tiny odd-shaped things, each one a little different from the others.

A female voice spoke from the phone.

'Hello, this is Terri Atkins.'

Wow, talk about sound quality! Terri's voice was coming through as though it was on the soundtrack of a movie at a stadium-seating multiplex!

'Hi, this is –'

'Oh, darling! I knew it was you,' Terri said. 'I've been looking forward to our talk.'

'Really?' she said. She glowed, yet also felt bashful, and furious with herself for feeling bashful. Her career would go nowhere if she continued having feelings like that.

'We've just been talking about you. Wasn't I?'

'Yes we have.' It was a male voice from somewhere behind Terri.

'Could you do it a little harder over here?' Terri said.

'Excuse me?'

'Oh, forgive me,' Terri said. 'I'm talking to my masseur.'

Is this what power had come to mean in the new New York City? Sign her up! 'Anyway, I love your work and I want you working for me. For me, and for no one else. Do you understand? Those boxes you do – fantastic. The graphics, the tints, the bleeds. No one else in the city has your touch with dropped initials,' said Terri. 'Oh God! Yes! Yes!! Yes!!!'

Her cell phone seemed to be gyrating uncontrollably in her hand. Or was it just her own excitement at this sudden

50

glimpse of power and glamour?

'Um,' she said. 'I'm not sure what you want from me. But I do like working in Design and Quark, and I'm so enthusiastic.'

'No, right there. Don't do it harder. Just like that. Around and around. Steady. No speeding up. If you speed up I'll kill you. There! There!! There!!!'

Her hand gripped the phone sweatily, and shook and shook. Then it stretched, yawned, and calmed. The phone just lay there in her palm. Was that static hiss or was it panting?

'Well, thank you. When should I start?'

'Tomorrow. You'll start tomorrow. I'll fax you your assignment. Oh, God! Whew. I'm so glad you're on board with us.'

That was one happening business meeting. She was really feeling the heat now. So much so that she needed a little something cooling. Another deli visit where she surveyed the low-carb frozen treats and decided on a healthy-seeming pomegranate fruitsicle. She was good to go.

But there was still a long, lonely tonight to contend with. A DVD evening it would have to be, she sighed, so she steered herself into an independent rental store on 1st Avenue and 37th that was selling off all its merchandise.

As she perused the $1.99 porn bin, she nearly bumped into a man her age who was talking on his cell phone.

'Are you telling me that none of these titles does it for you?' he said to whoever, with a tone of disbelief.

His wedding ring flashed as he rolled his eyes.

'There's always Buttman,' he was saying. 'Well, of course he's gross, he's the Buttman! But back before we were married you said you liked his oeuvre.'

Her own phone gave a ring. 'Hi,' said a male voice, and she knew it was meant for her alone.

'Hi,' she said.

'How'd you like your meeting with Terri?' the voice

said.

'Who is this?'

'You can't tell me you don't know.'

And she couldn't. She knew perfectly well it was the voice she'd heard behind Terri, the voice of that perfect masseur, a man who knew how to give pleasure.

'How'd you get my number?' she said, hoping he'd ignore the question.

He did. 'I was thinking about you the whole time I was getting Terri off,' he said.

'You shouldn't be calling me,' she said.

'That's why I am.'

She glanced around her.

'But you don't know me.'

'I know that you have luscious thighs,' he said. R.B. never appreciated the work she did to keep in shape. 'Do you know what I want to do to them? Do you know? I want to press them down and run my tongue along them and then roughly turn you over and spank you the way R.B. never has –'

She dropped her fruitsicle. This was not a good conversation. Hot, but she was horrified at herself for letting it go this far, and scared that it might hurt her chances of working for Terri.

'You shouldn't be calling me!' she said.

'And that's exactly why I am calling you,' the masseur's voice said.

'You are disloyal, disgusting and disgraceful,' she said.

'And you are thrilled,' the masseur's voice told her.

She jabbed at the END button, but the phone continued to rant.

'Fuck me, let me explore your cunt, you whore, your ass is so fine ...' the masseur's growly voice made her gasp for breath.

She poked again and again at the cell phone's buttons, and with her final blow it let out a humongous 'Ugh!' sound. Then the voice said, 'That was so good. Don't you want some for yourself?'

There was a large purple, plasticky stain on the video store rug. Had it been there before? She careened out of the store and onto the street, dialling her boyfriend as fast as she could. All she got was a message on her phone saying it couldn't pick up a signal.

After a number of blocks she managed to get hold of herself. The clouds had cleared and a dry cool breeze lifted her spirits. She stopped for another water purchase, this time treating herself to a new gourmet Scandinavian brand.

Despite her fears, she had to admit that there was something wild and exciting about connecting intimately with a man who'd so recently been with Terri.

When she looked up, she realized that she'd walked all the way to Times Square. The sidewalk was jammed with what had to be tourists, although it was harder and harder to tell the out-of-towners from the true Manhattanites. The rubes now dressed in black clothes and affected New York attitudes that they copied off of sitcoms set in the city.

The towering billboards and signs were an orgy of movement and colour.

On one of the screens, a hunky male model flashed his six-pack, which made her feel better. He was playing with a cell phone, dancing with it, pretending to use it as a roll-on deodorant, yeah, yeah, real funny, and now – could this be happening in the New Times Square? – he was sticking his butt out and pumping the cell phone against it.

She looked around her. No one else seemed to be taking note. Groups of people were scurrying into theme restaurants. Others were taking photos.

She looked warily back up at the enormous screen. The hottie in the ad was touching his phone with his middle finger, making the standard obscene gesture at the same time.

Her phone rang. She picked up the call.

'Hello, babe.' Another male voice, a new one this time.

'Who is this?' she said.

'You say you don't know but you do,' he said. 'Look up.'

She did. The model was smirking at her.

Then his lips moved. 'Can we continue? I'm recharged, and ready to go again. How many of your boyfriends have been able to come back to life this quickly?'

'I'm taking you back to the store,' she said in a fury, turning away from the LCD billboard.

Her cell phone whimpered.

'Don't do that!' she said, shaking it, poking it for information. 'I hate it when men whimper.'

'What listing?' the computerized voice asked.

'Cell Mates.'

'What city?'

'New York. It's a business. On Broadway.'

'There's no listing for Cell Mates.'

'It's a new store,' she said. 'It's in Manhattan. On lower Broadway. I was there no more than thirty minutes ago.'

'I'm sorry,' the voice said, 'but I can't find any listing. You'll just have to keep me, Babeski.'

She squinted at the phone. 'Oh no, you don't. No cell phone is stalking this girl!'

Then a little boy was pointing at her and saying, 'Mom, look, look. That lady's hitting her cell phone against a wall.'

She caught herself. This wasn't right.

The phone was screaming, 'Stop it! Please stop it!'

She took a deep breath.

The phone's bedroom voice came back on. 'Oh come on, hit me one more time. Please. I was just kidding about stopping it! I crave your abuse.'

'Do you want to stay with me?' she said. 'Then don't make a sound, not one little peep, not unless I command you to.'

The phone didn't respond.

'And don't sulk!' she said. 'I hate a man who sulks. Talk to me! Tell me you understand!'

The phone continued to pout silently.

'You're outta here,' she muttered. 'I'm the one who gets to have the emotions.'

She threw the phone into a trash can and turned to walk away.

Then she heard the phone's voice, as though over a loudspeaker. 'I know your credit card number!' it said. 'And I know when it expires.'

She kept walking. Heads were turning.

'I have the last four digits of your social security number! I know your date of birth. I'll give them to anyone who wants them – not that there's much to steal!'

Crowds of people had stopped and were listening.

'I know your Victoria's Secret favourites list. I know which sex toy you prefer. I know that you always order the least expensive flowers for your mom!'

The crowds were beginning to look at her indignantly. Two teenagers, scruffy, gangsta wannabes, nudged each other and headed to the garbage cans to fish the phone out. She raced back.

'And I know other things, too, folks. I know her real bra size, minus the padding. I know what the Russian woman who does her bikini wax really thinks of her. And don't get me started about the facial hair!'

The two boys were throwing bottles and newspapers out of the trash can. She pushed them aside.

'That's my phone,' she said. 'We're quarrelling, but it's still mine. Stay away.'

'It's in a garbage can, so I'd say it's fair game, bitch,' said one of them.

'I'm serious,' she said.

She gave one of the boys a shove and dove into the garbage can, fishing through its contents wildly. Let that not be a condom. And please let that not be a tampon. She closed her eyes, held her breath, and finally found the phone. She rolled over, shook herself free of the filth, and sat on the sidewalk, holding the phone up in a gesture of victory.

The taller of the two boys made a grab for it. She held on and wrestled with him. The phone gave a chuckle, then blasted them with the sound of a police siren. A voice like something off 'Cops' came over.

'All police officers to Broadway and 45th! Arrest Richard Quinn Arnold and Greg Katland.'

The larger boy released his grip.

'It knows our names, dude,' he said.

'Richard Arnold lives at 876 Waterford Avenue –'

'This is too freaky,' the other boy said. They took off down at a sprint, pushing aside the crowds waiting for half priced Broadway theatre tickets.

'I'm going to have a latte and think of what your fate will be.'

They were in a Starbuck's, and she was tucking the phone into her purse.

As she ordered her iced grande, the phone made an unpleasant gurgling sound. A couple of customers looked her way. She couldn't blame them. It did sound as though she had a baby choking in her bag.

'New cell phone,' she said with a perky smile. 'Not working properly. Taking it back to the store.'

She headed to an empty table.

'Please let me out of here!' the phone said loudly. 'I need to talk!'

A guy reading a free paper in an armchair one over gave her a look and ran his hand over his shaved head. He had attractive skull contours.

'Is that your cell phone?' he asked.

'Yeah,' she said. 'It's a brand-new model.' She liked this guy. He showed promise, if only in a no-future, just-raw-sex kind of way.

'I said I want to talk to you!' the phone shouted, its voice muffled by the contents of her purse.

'You don't want to answer it?' the guy asked.

'No,' she said. 'There's no call. It's just malfunctioning. Weird noises. I don't know what the engineers were thinking.'

I can fix it,' he said, pulling his chair closer to her table. 'I'm a wizard with these things.'

'Really?'

She reached into her purse and rummaged around for the phone. Maybe it was all just a technical glitch. She moved aside the lipsticks and mirror, the pens and keys, the bottles of aspirins and anti-depressant pills.

There it was, hiding behind her wallet. It was trembling. She tried to wrap her fingers around it, but it made mewling noises and shook violently. It felt like a tiny skinless mouse. She gave it a tug but it wouldn't come. It seemed to be clinging to the lining of her purse.

She gave a firm pull and pried it free.

The man put his hand out. 'Give it to me,' he said. 'I'll make it behave.'

There was something to be said for a man who could occasionally look after you. Her juices were revved!

She placed the mobile in the man's hand. As she did, there was a sizzle sound.

'Yeeeouch!' The man leapt up from his chair and dropped the phone.

'Are you OK?' she asked.

'Jesus fucking Christ that hurt.' He gave her a stunned look.

She reached out to touch him.

'Stay away from me!' The man's hand was red as though he'd been burned.

He grabbed his backpack and strode away shouting, 'You think that's some kind of joke?'

I will destroy you!' she told her phone.

'Hey, hey, hey, I'm –'

'You're what?' She stopped and stared right at it.

'I'm sorry,' the phone said. 'I really am. I don't know

what came over me. And I promise I'll never do it again.

She knew she was a sucker for a good apology. But he was going to have to work a little harder than that.

'I couldn't care less,' she said. 'You're headed for the recycle bin.'

'Please don't be mad,' the phone said. 'I've just never felt like this around a girl before. You're so beautiful that I lost control. Nobody's lips feel like yours when they press against my mouthpiece. R.B. doesn't know how good he has it. You're too special to spend Saturday alone. Forget him. Forget everyone else. You're with me now. And guess what? We're going to the best party in New York City. Tonight!'

'I don't know,' she said, though the prospect of a party versus being alone was melting her resolution fast. 'I mean, you really messed up things for me back in that cafe. I don't know that I can trust you.'

'Let me make it up to you. It was just high spirits. You wouldn't want a man who doesn't have high spirits, would you? I'll show you the best time you ever had. And I'd be so proud knowing all the other cell phones in the room were jealous of the woman holding onto me.'

'How do I know this isn't one of your disgusting stunts?'

'You don't,' the phone said. 'I haven't given you any reason to trust me. But let me prove my devotion to you. Who do you most want to talk to? I'll dial him up. How about Brad Pitt?'

She glared at him.

'Not that I'd think a tough, independent woman like you was into Brad Pitt.'

She relented. 'OK,' she said. 'I'll give you my choice. Call my father.'

'But, but –'

'You said anyone.'

'Are you sure you want to talk to him?'

'Yep,' she said.

'The dead aren't the best conversationalists.'

'I don't care. Do you want me to go to the party with you?'

The phone was silent.

'Just as I thought,' she said. 'Like all men, you're more promises than you are delivery.'

The phone rang.

She picked up the call. The voice was unmistakably familiar.

'Daddy?' she said.

'Is that you?' her father's voice asked.

'Yes, it's me,' she said, emotions filling her to the bursting point. 'It's me, me, it's really me.'

'Good of you to call, honey,' her father said. 'But I've got a client on the other line. Don't go away.'

And then there was the sound of on-hold classical music. Red-faced and furious, she rang off.

'That is so like my father!' she said.

They were only a block away from the 58th Street entrance to Central Park. Fighting back tears, she walked quickly, then jogged her way into the park. She made her way to the first tree she saw, clutched its bark and started to sob.

'No wonder I'm with a loser like R. B.! He's just like my father! No time for my needs!'

'Please don't cry,' the phone said. 'I love you.'

'But how do I know?' she cried. 'I mean, for sure?'

'Haven't I stuck around even through all your abuse today? Don't I deserve some credit for that?' he said.

'I'm sorry I banged you against that wall.'

'I like your emotions. And I like the way they get out of control.'

'You're shitting me,' she told him.

'I am not.'

'I can be a real twat sometimes,' she said. 'But you're just saying that. Which I guess is sweet. Which moves me.' She was caressing the phone sadly. 'I'd like to make it up to you.'

'Then come to the party with me.'

'I can't. Not looking like this.'

'You're beautiful,' he insisted.

'No. I'm not. Don't lie to me. Not now.'

'But you are. You're the only woman in New York for me.'

'You just say that because you don't want to go back to the store,' she said.

'Think I'd stay there long? Think some other woman wouldn't pick me up – like that?'

'Well, you are kinda cute. God, I'm thirsty.'

'I love your relationship with water,' he said.

'You do?'

'I live to watch you drink water.'

She unscrewed her bottle and poured the overpriced H2O down her throat. Despite how much liquid she put through herself, she always felt parched. But now she felt satiated, as though she was standing beneath a luxuriant waterfall.

Her throat gurgled slowly, her stomach came to life. She gave a wiggle with her hips, and laughed softly as she wiped a drop or two of the delicious clear liquid off her chin.

'You know how to do it!' the phone cried happily. 'I want you. And only you.'

'Really? Only me?'

And suddenly her cell felt like a lover's tongue in her ear.

'I know you enjoy a rep for being good at phone sex,' it said. 'But I'm here to show you what it's really about!'

'Oh, God,' she said. 'I need it. I don't care if we're in Central Park. I want it now.'

'Rub me over every inch of you,' the phone said. 'And do it slowly.'

She was unbearably turned on. She kissed her phone, then put the whole keypad into her mouth, playing with each individual button. She loved the way it moaned and urged her on. They were in plain view of joggers, vendors and people throwing Frisbees. Nannies pushed fabulous baby carriages. Let them see; she didn't care.

She leaned against a large tree near the baseball field, sliding down its trunk as she pushed the cell phone up where it most wanted to be, and she didn't even have to push it inside her pussy, the phone knew just what to do, and it did so much more than R.B. ever could; and it really explored her in a way that R.B. never had.

And then the phone brought her to orgasm as she felt the exquisite whir of not just one, but a succession of phone calls coming right into her.

She pulled the phone up to her mouth and kissed herself on its mouthpiece, and heard another ring.

'Let's go again,' it said.

'Don't you ever need recharging?' she asked.

'Not when I'm with you,' the phone rasped.

'So where is this party anyway?'

Like a divining rod, the mobile tugged her out of the park and through the haughtier blocks of the Upper East Side. They'd talk and murmur and whisper and fondle until the phone realized it was time to turn a corner, then it would give her another of those tugs, and she'd giggle the way she did back in college when boys proposed a new sex game.

'Naughty, naughty,' she said headily, and followed his urgings.

It reminded her of dreams she'd had where she'd be wandering through one of those incredible houses in the back pages of the *Times* magazine section and suddenly it would be endless, room after room, wing after wing, attics and basements, bedrooms and terraces, and she'd know someone was out there waiting for her to open the right door.

Where did all these limos come from? Did sidewalk trees really grow this leafy and large in New York?

'You have to know your way around,' the phone's voice said to her. Well, *said* wasn't really the right word. The words were being mainlined into her, beamed in from somewhere beyond Planet Dolby.

61

'But I didn't say anything. How did you –'

'When you've got a direct connection, it's better not to ask these questions. Just know that it's a step beyond broadband.'

Broadband. Oh, God, yes.

The street lamps and cobblestones and facades reminded her of those old-novel-adaptations she used to love going to at the Paris Theatre, the ones with the English actresses and the great wallpaper.

Each brownstone was grander than the next, yet she felt as though this was where she belonged. She felt a twinge of pity for R.B., who'd never know this kind of pleasure with her, and would never know what ecstasy she was truly capable of.

Her reverie was interrupted by an old woman's voice. So familiar. Could it be?

No, please. Not the crone. Not now.

But it was her, swearing in that all-consonants language of hers. 'My respects, Majesty,' her phone said to the ancient pest as they glided by. Did the crone give them a wink?

She pulled her phone close and whispered, 'You know her?'

'Every cell phone is her subject. Who do you think is in charge?'

'You don't mean she is?'

'And you thought it was those suits on the cover of the Business section. Silly girl.'

She felt chastened yet grateful. Initiated somehow.

'Welcome to her little place.'

She looked up the staircase. 'Place' wasn't quite the word. 'Chateau' would be more accurate. The phone gave her a tug and then they were sweeping up marble steps and through an extravagant Beaux-Arts entryway.

'I hope this party is as good as it looks,' she said, excited but apprehensive.

You'll be charming. The thing to do is to let you be

yourself.'

And what did that mean? And would she find out now, after all these years of not knowing?

The doorman bowed deeply, sweeping them inside behind a group of dwarves and tall, slim models.

And then it happened. She didn't need her phone. The phone was her and she was it, with no need for transportation of blah-blah-blah, didyaknowthisandthat, just instantaneous connection.

This is the most amazing crowd you've ever seen at a party, the phone said, or rather seemed to help her think.

What a relief not to have to make all that usual effort to communicate!

For me, too, he said.

It's like sixty-nine for brains, only it works, not in that distracting way it is in reality where you can't pay attention, but the mutual-lusciousness way it is when you fantasize about it.

An elevator full of perfume and furs, the doors now opening on to a magnificent hallway full of as many priceless paintings and objects as a corridor at the Met.

They began moving down it when she noticed, on the opulent Oriental rugs, evening clothes strewn in heaps along the corridor. Before her, and on either side of her, guests were shedding items of clothing and leaving them behind.

She looked in a panic at her phone.

I don't know if I'm up to this kind of Eyes Wide Shut *scene. Face it, that movie was a major flop.*

But it's done brilliantly on Blu-ray.

Blu-ray! Of course, it made sense. Her knees felt a little weak. It was like the world was turning into a flat-screen monitor with an endless loop of her favourite sex scenes going by.

I am HTML. Anyone can code me now.

She looked down and saw her blouse unbuttoning itself. Her skirt slithered down her legs and puddled on the carpet, miraculously not tripping her. The crowd was turning right

63

through a double door. As her hair swung loose and her bra flew off, she pulled her cell phone close to her.

Tell me I'm not going to make a fool of myself. I mean, this is exactly what I've always wanted. But is now really the moment? But if I don't go in now, will it ever be the right moment?

It will always be your moment.

She jolted back as if slapped. But she knew it was what she'd needed to hear, and her head cleared.

I finally have access to my own menu.

You always did.

Together they walked through the door. In the room were groups, clusters of all kinds of bodies, G-strings, masks. Was that a whip in that hand? She approached the nearest group, which opened up to her.

She felt a moment's shock and gave her cell phone a squeeze, but he wasn't there. One after another, the members of the group turned to her, and each one had a head shaped like the earpiece of a phone.

A bolt of panic raced through her. She turned to a mirror and saw that she'd become one of them. It was grotesque, it was terrifying. It was the most beautiful thing she would ever be. She was among her kind. She could be who she was.

There were slender, appealingly flesh-coloured heads with clear buttons where their eyes should be, there were black ones and kandy-koloured ones. Each had a keypad on its chest, each had a square microphone hole for a mouth. She fingered her own microphone hole.

They were all engaged in conversation, leaning into each other and putting sides of their heads to the microphones of others to listen.

They welcomed her into their groups. Their voices had a beguiling aimlessness. She loved vibrating with them. From time to time, there was the trill of a cell phone orgasm.

She laughed. She'd never heard anything funnier. And now she was trilling in ecstasy.

But where was her dream lover? Would she never hold him in her hand again? Never hold him next to her ear? The thought that her lips might never touch him again made her want to scream. Would she ever be able to cry again?

The crowd parted for an instant and across the room was the most hunky, most adorable cell phone she'd ever seen.

He stood at least six feet tall. Lean and mean, but tender too, you could tell. As she swivelled across the floor to him, the keypad that was her chest flashed softly, and she could feel her microchips purring.

It's you. I was afraid I'd lost you.

We come together, we part. Then we come together again. Life is like that.

She knew he was right. As she reached to him and touched him, she felt a tugging, this time not a small one in her hand, but a large one, lifting her by the abdomen, gripping her whole body, lifting her. She was dangling above her beloved. He gave her a loving look.

Go forth. We'll always be here. You know how to find your way back.

Then the glamorous room vanished beneath her and all was darkness and the most monumental clutter, tubes and soft crumples of paper and containers full of candies the size of basketballs. She was squished between a huge expanse of leather and an enormous plastic covered condom.

Just as she started to settle into a deep safe corner, she felt herself raised up through the mess, cradled in a gigantic beanbag of a hand.

'There you are,' a female voice said, out of her head, or so she was nearly certain. 'God, I've really got to clean this purse out from time to time.'

She felt a firm pressure on her chest, then a series of light punches to the abdomen. She giggled and vibrated happily as she was raised and felt a curtain of hair of one side, the warm ridges of an immense ear on the other.

Was that really a mouth opening up, tongue at the ready, breathing directly into her very being?

'Hello, darling,' the giantess said right into her. 'Guess who?' The voice, with its yearning and heat, made her silly with pleasure. 'That's right, it's Terri. And we have things to talk about.'

About the Story

I'VE ALWAYS BELIEVED CITIES have distinct sexual identities. The erotic tone of a metropolis is made up by the people who inhabit it.

I've lived in New York City for twenty years, so I've seen many changes in the sex vibe here. None has struck me as much as the way in which cell phones have altered the erotic nature of sidewalk life. I became fascinated by the new relationship people had with these phones. I saw people engaging more with these digital companions than they did with the people around them. And I saw a new kind of behaviour emerging, one that revealed deeply private desires, yet was played out in public.

The main character of *Cell Mates* is a woman I now constantly see on the streets of New York City. She has a bottle of water in one hand, and her iPhone or her Blackberry in the other. She gazes constantly at her phone, expertly massaging messages from it.

And where does she always seem to be hurrying to? She looks as though her cell phone is guiding her through the city, towards the most fabulous place where she will be the centre of attention. It's as though she feels her cell phone will make New York City take notice; of her beauty, her talent, and her charms. Thanks to her cell phone, she's not just one more young woman on these streets. She's uniquely alluring. And her cell phone will make sure she's infinitely desired and adored.

But what this woman doesn't realize is that cities also have their *own* sexual agendas, their own erotic souls. They play with the desires and dreams of the people who live in them. And Manhattan will always be a highly charged alpha-seducer. It's only out to break your heart, but you get taken in anyway by how it teases you with glamour, fame and power.

This woman may feel protected by her cell phone from Manhattan's advances. Yet in writing *Cell Mates*, I wanted to show that her phone and the city might, in fact, be mischievous erotic cohorts, as sexually conniving as the aristocratic couple in *Dangerous Liaisons*.

And I liked playing with the idea that her cell phone might deliver her to the city in the end. But along the way she'll feel special; not completely anonymous, and definitely *not* just one in a long line of New York City's glittering seductions.

The Same Fifty Taxis
by Jeremy Edwards

1987

UNWRITTEN RULE: IF YOU were in a rock band in New York, you looked like a Ramone. Leather jacket and black hair. This applied to the women as well; all of us, the guys and the gals, were gritty parcels of leather and denim, no matter what was going on underneath anatomically. I remember the thrill of a bra strap, spied through a hole in Milly's T-shirt, emphasizing – as if any emphasis were needed – that this punk was a girl.

The Upper East Side belonged to another generation. I was an outsider, if a grateful one, paying my deflated, token rent to basically house-sit for a year in a co-op owned by Jay's grandparents. It was against the building association rules – the way I thought of it, *I* was against the rules – and every doorman on the staff knew it. They didn't hassle me on the technicality, and I was grateful for that too. But their stiffness reminded me, whenever I crossed the threshold, that I was a scruffy kid of twenty-two living there on borrowed time and space.

Once I tried to tip the senior doorman, who had just helped me wrestle an amp into the elevator. He looked at me indulgently, shaking his head, as though I were a five-year-old trying to offer him my last lollipop.

I felt especially incongruous when I masturbated in the grandparental bed; not because it was a sexual act, but because of the specific flavour of the sexuality. There I was, feverishly jerking away my boyish sexual tension while visualizing Milly's presumably smooth ass, miraculously unwrapped from its cloak of strained denim. But I was doing it in a bedroom whose decor suggested perfumed sex with a woman who visited a hairdresser; maybe with opera music coming over the radio.

If I ever fucked Milly, it wouldn't be here.

Her band and mine rehearsed on the same night: Wednesdays from 10:00 to 11:00, in neighbouring practice rooms in a rent-by-the-hour facility. And from the first time I saw her freckled nose and tight jeans, I wished I could take her to a different sort of rent-by-the-hour facility.

She lived with her mother in a walk-up on East Eighty-third, and we usually rode the subway back uptown together. Because the singer in my band was friends with the drummer in hers, we had officially *met*, and so we didn't have to share the commute as strangers. It was, in other words, acceptable under the rigid terms of 1980s New York etiquette for me to speak to her.

Milly was a bass player – a very dexterous one, with a complementary gift for writing lyrics – while I was what my father the musicologist would have called 'second guitar'. Fifth wheel was more like it. I'd been invited in – into the band and into New York – by Jay, at a time when his group thought they could use a separate rhythm guitarist to free Jay up for the flashy stuff. As it turned out, this worked well for about one song in ten, leaving me superfluous the rest of the time. I was always being asked to turn my volume down.

She was a sympathetic listener each Wednesday, when I rambled on about my insecurities within the group. But this wasn't what I wanted to be talking to her about. I wanted to *get to know her*, with all that this implied; but I was trapped by my own repetitive, self-pitying repertoire. The potent sexuality I read in her eyes deserved better than the wimpy, tedious soundtrack I heard coming from my voice box.

The intersection where we parted every week, a few

blocks after exiting the subway, became a crossroads of hope and unfulfilment on my mental landscape.

One Wednesday, after we'd climbed up to street level at Seventy-seventh, she asked me if I wanted to have a beer, then led me over to a bar on Second Avenue when I accepted. We sat by the window, and fluorescence from a nearby street lamp made her dyed black hair shine.

'Did you have a girlfriend in Pittsburgh?' Milly gazed attentively at me as she took her first sip from a bottle of Molson Golden. In the background, I heard cases of beer being ripped open, a confident proclamation that people would be having fun here when the weekend arrived.

'Sort of. I guess you could say that Lori and I dated by default. Everyone else in our little dorm group was paired up.'

'Dating by default,' she repeated, with an ironic air of authority. 'Ah yes, I know it well. It's right up there with sex by default.'

A tremor of promise, coated with fear, ran through me. I took a snapshot of the situation in my mind: I was alone with Milly, and she was steering the conversation toward sex. 'Yeah. We did a little of that, too,' I said into my beer.

She kindly shifted the burden away from me, talking of her own relationships. Within a few minutes, she had all but finished her drink.

'You know, I don't think much of sex by default, Marc. But there are other kinds of sex I like.'

'Me too,' I managed, as if in a dream.

'Should we go to my place and discuss that?'

'My mother's with her sister in Boston this week.'

I swallowed hard as we floated past a skimpy Yorkville supermarket, contemplating how Milly had intentionally invited me out for a beer on the Wednesday she had the place to herself. My wish that I could be like that – smooth and self-actualized – was overshadowed by my appreciation for the fact that *she* was like that, that she was taking me

71

exactly where I wanted to go.

Almost as soon as I was seated in her living room, she straddled me – right there on the couch, which I found out later was also her bed. The only clothing she'd tossed aside was her leather jacket, and I still had mine on. There was an urgency to her, like she was afraid I might chicken out if she didn't come on strong and physically pounce. I felt freed by her assertiveness, by the security of not having to decide what to do or not to do, apart from responding naturally as she went wild on me.

Her bottom was tight and restless on my thighs, and her quick kisses were clearly meant as stepping-stones to something more. I could smell the salty girliness of her arousal; and as she bounced and rocked on my lap, sweetly attacking me with her darting lips, I felt my cock aching to break through all the layers of fabric and ascend into her.

She manipulated our centre of gravity so as to tumble completely on top of me. She ran a hand up inside my Clash T-shirt, and rubbed the carpet of fuzz that belied my immaturity. Her thighs never let go of me.

I'd never been taken by a girl in this way; I'd never had this all-consuming sense of being thoroughly desired, of being pawed into coition by a woman saturated with horniness.

'So how do you like makin' out with me?' She had paused in her action, letting her warm, T-shirted spheres hover proudly above me. Her smile was magic.

'Milly,' I said – just that word. But my tone expressed both hunger and thankfulness, and the answer satisfied her. I was all hers.

She groped my jeans zestfully, while I pursued my longing to squeeze her breasts. As she was unzipping my fly and I was wrangling her shirt up, I thought to myself, *Yeah, we're all jeans and T-shirts ... but, oh fuck, the signpost of panties, the creaminess of female flesh.* I unfastened her bra and grabbed round helpings of her femaleness.

'Oh,' said Milly suddenly. 'I'd better pee.' She hopped

off me. 'Come on.'

I wondered if this was standard practice for experienced lovers. I realized, in any event, that it thrilled me – even if it might only represent her way of making sure I wouldn't vanish while she was tinkling.

She yanked her Levi's and her baby-blue panties down to reveal herself. I was entranced by the gentle furriness of her mound. My sense of time went giddy as I watched, as if in slow motion, an auburn-haired female crotch descending onto a toilet seat in a brightly lit bathroom. My breath caught as I savoured this ultimate crack in our unisex shell.

Her hips looked so naked on the toilet seat. Still sitting there, a wipe and a flush behind her, she now finished what she'd begun as far as undoing my pants. Soon she had my jeans at my ankles and my dick sticking up from an elastic-throated clench of jockey shorts. She kissed it.

Though she didn't take me all the way via oral, her foreplay went beyond everything I'd experienced with the complete version, in terms of both sensation and erotic intensity. It felt as if she'd taught each saliva molecule how to caress male skin, so that she was coating me not just with warmth and wetness, but with an active layer of pleasure. Her blazing eyes hypnotized me, my cock basked, and I was insanely happy.

Then I stood there, penis glistening, while she shuffled out of her pants and slammed down the plush-covered lid of the toilet. I knew how she wanted me, so I got my jockeys out of the way, got cozy with the plush, and awaited the embrace of her cunt.

She lowered herself onto me with an alto moan, capped with a soprano squeak, and I couldn't believe how many brands of euphoria shocked through my groin and my brain. It wasn't only how she felt around me: it was the lusty personality in her pistoning, and the friendly tenderness in her gyrations. I was so primed, so excited ... and, not surprisingly, I started to come sooner than I wished.

Milly burbled a tolerant, sexy laugh. 'Nice, huh?' she

said smokily, watching my face glow with ecstasy. She waited till I'd finished before directing my hand to her clit. With token help from me, she danced herself into a slow-cresting climax that brought tears to her eyes.

She greeted me with an instant coffee when I walked into the kitchen in the morning. My physiology was reverberating with echoes of joy, but my mind had been going nonstop since awakening on her convertible couch fifteen minutes earlier. I'd been thinking about everything in my world.

She sat across from me at the table. 'I have to apologize,' she said. 'This is a very busy year for me.' She was in an MA program for journalism, and writing for a weekly paper. Then of course there was the band. 'But there's always room in my life for romance, Marc Flynn.' She put her hand on mine. 'Otherwise, what's the point?'

She had said the opposite of what I'd thought she was about to say.

I spoke with as much clarity as my confused brain could offer. 'I think I'm too young for you, Milly.'

She burst out laughing. 'Thanks a lot! I'm, like, two years older than you.'

I wanted to laugh with her, but I had to persist. 'But you're, y'know, *grown up,* in a way I'm not. You have a career going. You have a handle on things. Fuck, you're even more accomplished than I am at music – even though for you it's just a hobby, and for me it's this ... stupid dream.'

'Marc!' It seemed to hurt her that I was down on myself. 'None of that matters.'

'I'm kind of in love with you, Milly.' She squeezed my hand. 'But I'm not ready for this. I'm not ready for any of it.' I gestured at the room, at the whole city. 'I'm thinking of quitting the band. I'm sure that's what Jay wants, though he'll never say it. I don't think I ever told you this ... but when I joined, I hoped they might do my songs. But my

74

songs are old-fashioned. I'm into pretty harmonies. It doesn't fit in. I realize that now. And I have this other friend back in Pittsburgh – he writes lyrics, and he's been bugging me to come back and start a band. He digs my music. He doesn't care whether it's passé.

'I admire your self-awareness.' She looked down at her coffee. 'I think I'd be wrong to try to talk you out of all this.' Then her eyes met mine. 'And I also think you'll return to New York someday – when you're ready.'

'I hope so.'

'And when you do,' she said with an even tone and a determined smirk, 'I'm gonna jump your sexy bones, my friend.'

It was a vow that would stay with me for years, like an unused ticket in some cranny of my wallet – long after I'd come to assume that it would never actually be redeemed.

She walked me downstairs.

'Come here,' she said just outside the front door. She kissed me. 'Thank you for a night of passion.'

'That's really nice, Milly, but, well, it was the greatest night ever, but you get all the credit. I don't feel like I –'

'No!' she insisted. 'Stop. I said *thank you,* Marc. OK?'

'OK.'

1997

It was hard for me to relax up in Yorkville. Paradoxically, the relative calm of the neighbourhood made me antsy; made me worry that there were things happening downtown that I was missing. I was high with the buzz of feeling myself an important part of something; and after a decade of getting there, a scant twelve hours away from that scene was enough to have me climbing the walls of the high-rise condo that my first two albums had secured me.

In this district, I was merely another nouveau riche bohemian. But below Fourteenth Street, I was indie-rock royalty – for the moment. Every cup of self-conscious gourmet coffee made me feel the promise of another new chapter in my ego-gratifying adventure.

When I stopped to think – which I didn't often, since returning to New York – it struck me how extensively the cultural battle lines had blurred. For example, Millicent's employer was 'corporate'; theoretically the antithesis of *indie*. But the entertainment magazine she wrote for had developed a symbiotic relationship with the underground music and film and theatre worlds. Thus, Millicent was a professional ally; as well as an old friend, of course.

Ah, Milly. She was cuter than ever, with her daring eyes behind neo-retro glasses, and her shape scrumptious in articles such as pastel capris. We didn't hang out very frequently – who had time? – but she was indisputably one of my most cherished buddies. Sometimes I caught myself having flashes of … desire? Infatuation? Nostalgia? Sometimes to the point where I had to ask myself why I had never made an effort to re-establish what we'd shared.

The answer, I supposed, was that although the idea of Millicent could still shake up my heart and rev up my dick, I had reservations I couldn't quite sort out – about myself, I admitted, not her – and it was all too complicated for me to unravel at present.

'Hi, Marc.'

She'd come up behind me while I was waiting to cross Eighty-sixth.

'Milly!' I gave her a quick fraternal hug, with a showbiz-style peck on the cheek for good measure.

'You're supposed to call me "Marcus" now, remember?' I'd switched to the two-syllable form around the time I traded in my guitar for a vintage organ.

'Well, *you're* supposed to call *me* "Millicent".' She stuck her tongue out.

I laughed. She was great, by any name. 'It's a deal, Millicent.' I made a mock-formal bow.

'At your service, Marcus.' She bestowed an archaic flourish with her hand, the type of move you might see at

Shakespeare in the Park. Then she cracked up like a little kid.

The fact that she still lived in this neighbourhood was definitely a plus; though we crossed paths in the Village more often than here. Her mother had remarried and moved in with Milly's new father-in-law, leaving Millicent the sole occupant of one very serviceable, rent-controlled apartment. I liked that because it made her happy, but also for my own selfish reasons. She was curating a piece of my life.

There were numerous tasks I'd intended to accomplish in the next hour – somewhat unrealistically. All of a sudden, I felt impulsive. 'You haven't been to my new place, have you?'

'I don't think so,' said Millicent. 'Is it a place one simply must see?'

'I don't know about that … but it's the best place to go if you want a shot at sampling this ice cream.' I drew her attention to the paper bag I was holding.

'I hear your apartment is lovely this time of year,' she said, not missing a beat. 'What with the ice cream in bloom.'

The light changed, and we segued from our face-to-face to the walking-in-stride mode, old pals on a mission – though I wasn't completely sure yet what the mission was.

As was her habit, Millicent reminded me to look at the tops of the buildings, where one could be surprised and delighted by interesting ornamental embellishments from decades gone by. I wondered how many building tops I'd missed since the last time I'd walked with Milly. Then I wondered what, if anything, she had missed by not spending more time with me. I wondered …

A passing bus caught my eye, its entire flank occupied by an ad for a video station.

I wondered which clubs I should drop in on that night. I wondered who was going to be around, what opportunities might be in the air.

Millicent's adorable ass enlivened the lone barstool at my

kitchenette counter. I stood proudly at hand, watching her attack the similarly round and cute cappuccino-coconut scoop I'd served up. I ate slowly, for my part, letting small spoonfuls melt on my tongue. Millicent teased me about wandering the Upper East Side with a pint of ice cream, hoping to pick up women.

How and why had I forgotten that I was in love with her? Watching her smile and laugh in my kitchen seemed to make the complexities and ambivalence melt away like the ice cream, to put me in touch once more with uncomplicated lust and straightforward emotions. Again I let impulse guide me.

'You owe me, Millicent. I've been back for two years, and you haven't jumped my sexy bones.'

She gaped, her spoon frozen in action. 'You remember I said that?'

'Of course I do.' For a year or two in Pittsburgh, I'd used that memory as a sail.

'I wonder what else you remember.'

I helped myself to the flirty curl at the bottom of her retro hairdo. 'I remember that this is your natural hair colour – and how delicious it looked on you, even when one had to delve deep to find it.'

'Uh-huh.'

'I remember that you thanked me for a night of passion. No other woman has said that to me, in so many words.'

'Ha! I don't doubt it. 'And the award for Sappiest Girl He's Ever Slept With goes to …''

I put a finger over her lips. 'Shh. It was beautiful. In fact, I think I'll call my next album *Thank You for a Night of Passion.*'

'You're hilarious, Marcus. And I think I'll call my next album round-up "Do You Want to Fuck Me, or Just Write Songs about Me?"'

'Brat.'

'For the record, though …' She paused to bring another spoon of cappuccino coconut to her lips. 'I don't feel they have to be mutually exclusive.' She swallowed. 'The fucking and the songwriting.'

I set my spoon down, decisively. 'Are you game, Milly?'

'No, "Milly" is not game. *Millicent,* however …' She stood. 'Do you mind ice-cream-flavoured kisses?'

I walked around to her side of the counter. 'We'll soon know.'

She tasted like much more than ice cream.

'Here's something else I remember,' I said. 'You liked being on top.' My cock had started throbbing with the memories that pulsed through it.

She closed her eyes for half a second, as if my words had flicked at her clit. 'Some things don't change,' she said. She began to pet me.

'I'm glad to hear that. You were a magnificent creature, riding me with such exuberance.'

'I don't think I've ever been called a *magnificent creature* before.'

'You really need to visit me more often.'

'One ice-cream-and-fuck session at a time.' She licked my ear. Then she sat again, close to the edge of the barstool, and unzipped me.

Smooth as a glissando, I slid her capris off her ass, then over the lip of the stool – noting that the critical stretch of the panties inside them had already been streaked with cream. My erection pointed the way to the bedroom.

I had so much larger a basis for comparison this time, but my body and psyche were no less impressed by Millicent's sexual self than when I'd been poor in experience. There was such an earnest, hungry vigour to the way she kissed my neck and slapped my butt and nibbled up and down my chest; such an uncompromising heartiness in the way she clutched my cock, mouthing cheerfully at its head before descending onto it with her even hungrier vulval mouth.

She tickled me under the arms while she pumped me, her fingers orchestrating my chuckles with finesse. I'd nearly forgotten that she'd been a fantastic bass player; and though

I was being fucked and titillated and my head was spinning with glee, I made a mental note to ask if she ever played now.

She had described herself as 'sappy'. But as she rode me like a pogo stick, inching me into the unsustainable tingle of pre-orgasmic delirium, it was I who felt sentimental.

Though close to coming, I reined myself in long enough to do more for dear Millicent. I exerted my sit-up skills to go from supine to L-shape; and, before she knew what was happening, my left hand was painting her clit in pussy juice, and my right was returning the tickle favour, cajoling her sensitive underarm. When she shrieked in erogenous surprise, I moved that hand to her ass crack. Then I suckled her left nipple … and we both fucking lost it, squirming and squealing and churning and spouting like an implosion of flesh and energy, collapsing into ourselves and dampening my bed with our pent-up libido.

We both began to dress, seemingly on autopilot.

'So, what do you think?' I asked her.

She understood me. 'I don't know, Marcus.'

'I don't know either,' I said honestly. 'My head's just … all over the place these days.'

'I know it is.'

Life had been simple in 1987, when I'd had one big, distant dream and one incipient love. And yet, I reminded myself, I'd felt compelled to retreat from both of them. The dream had chased me down in Pittsburgh – in the form of a start-up record label who believed that pretty harmonies could be big again – and escorted me back here. And now I was so distracted by dancing with the dream that love was hard-pressed to get a foothold. It wasn't the hectic schedule; I'd observed, in the lives of my peers, how that obstacle was surmountable. No, the issue was psychological.

'Let's play it by ear, OK?' said Millicent. 'Call me when you're here.'

'Sounds good. I'll probably be in for an hour or two on Saturday. I have some wardrobe to figure out, then a conference call and ...'

As I spoke, I felt the weight of a half dozen MTA tokens in my pocket, pulling me downtown like gravity.

Milly took my hand. 'No, Marcus. I mean when you're really here.'

2007

It's all about niches nowadays, isn't it? I said to my greying sideburns in the bathroom mirror.

With that in mind, it amused me to ponder how at one time my songs had been played on the radio; *the* radio, not podcasts or user-guided streams or nichey satellite stations. My friends who still had bands didn't even bother to think about *the* radio these days, to hope for anything that widely penetrating.

I'd found that I was comforted by the timelessness of being largely off the map. (*Comfort.* I really was crossing into middle age, wasn't I?) I'd grown tired of being trendy, with the concomitant worry of not being trendy the next day. At this stage of the game, I preferred to be entirely irrelevant to that metric, even if it meant my name might never be mentioned in a magazine again, save in a *where are they now?* feature.

With the twentieth century safely behind me, I liked being grounded in a genre of music that would never again dominate the popular music charts but which, after seventy-five years, looked like it was never going to disappear, either. One more rendition of *Cheek to Cheek* in a piano bar had negligible impact on the culture at large, but it made me – and the niche patrons of Du Piano on Third Avenue – happy.

It was funny that this leather-jacketed kid, who had resided illicitly in the heart of an older generation's Uptown, was now growing pleasantly grey in Yorkville, playing Tin Pan Alley tunes for a local crowd that was, on average, even younger than his forty-two. Yes, it was funny how content I was here, though the things that had brought me here – twice – didn't matter much to me any more. But this was New York, a city that could, to put it egocentrically, keep pace with one's progress. Most of Millicent's building tops had stayed the same, but Marc Flynn and his landscape had evolved.

Millicent. I didn't eat ice cream as often as I had in my thirties; but sometimes when I did, I thought about her. And sometimes when I didn't, I thought about her.

Since I'd retired from the thick of the rock-music scene, I rarely saw her. I knew that she was currently a senior editor for an online magazine; an office job that kept her farther from the city's entertainment happenings. I knew she still lived in her mother's old apartment, but it seemed I could go years at a stretch without running across her. Of course, this was in part because I didn't go out as much as I used to. My condo had the equipment I needed to compose and produce the jingles, TV scores, and incidental music I sold to my clients; the kitchen where I enjoyed cooking for myself; and the Internet hook-up that brought me everything in the world except the heat, chill, winds, aromas, and other tangibles of the city.

Du Piano, where I shared the bill Thursday through Sunday, was a good place for tangibles: enormous Cabernet glasses that entrusted you with their nurturing heft … velvet banquettes that fondled your ass … milky sconces that spoke intimacy. And *comfort*. And, from time to time, this venue had been a place where I'd encountered that most exquisite tangible; the human tangible. The soft hair, hot breath, and responsive flesh of some pianophilic soul, someone whose gaze flickered with intelligence and lust when I made eye contact following my set.

I'd learned that the newfangled communal washing-up area outside the bathrooms was an even better spot for a pick-up than the bar itself. Hand an amenable stranger a flirty little towel, and suddenly it was as if you were sharing a hotel room.

Yes, I loved New York.

It was a night when I'd finished, but I was lingering; as I frequently did, enjoying the atmosphere and the modest euphoria of unwinding after a minor performance. I usually preferred to stand, or pace, by the bar immediately after playing, letting the residual nervous energy dissipate. This gave me a clear view of the door, and thus I was aware of Millicent's entrance even before the bartender.

'Why, hello,' I said, hugging her solidly. 'What are you drinking?'

She looked around. 'Damn. Did I miss your set? I've been meaning to come here for, what, two weeks now. Don't tell me I blew it.'

I shrugged diplomatically. I'd spotted Milly on the second story of the mega-bookstore on Eighty-sixth a couple of weeks back. We'd chatted for a minute: I listened to her account of a foray into Off-Off-Broadway theatre ('tiny role, but I got to see peeps in their underwear backstage'), and she expressed interest in my regular gig at Du Piano. She lit up when I said that I'd found my niche. Still, I hadn't expected her to turn out.

'I was an idiot to think I'd get out of the office on time tonight. Oh –' She had noticed the bartender waiting patiently for her order. 'Is that a Malbec up there? That will be good.'

I slapped my plastic on the bar, to reinforce my signalled intention to play host here.

'Thank you.'

I appreciated the fact that she'd accepted without the obligatory fuss.

As I'd noted in the bookstore, Millicent had let her hair grow a little longer. Its fluffy adornment of her deep-burgundy dress augmented the luxury of the room around us. She caught me admiring her hair-kissed shoulders, which reminded me of ornamented building tops.

'What?'

'Just that you're beautiful.'

She blushed a degree, but grinned ten degrees.

The glass of wine was deposited in front of her.

'I've been thinking about you.' She took a sip. 'Mm. Nice. I love these Malbecs.'

'Hey, enough with the cliff-hanger,' I kidded. 'You've been thinking about me.'

'Yeah. Do you recall something you said to me, back when we ... back in the '80s? How I was grown up, in a way you weren't?'

'I do.'

'So, I was thinking about that ... and I have a confession to make: I'm not grown up.'

I smiled. 'Well, not in the dreary, stuffy, boring sense of the word. Isn't it cool that some of us manage to escape that fate, these days?'

She patted my knee. 'I don't just mean that. I mean ... Are you seeing anyone right now?'

The non sequitur tripped me up only momentarily. 'No. You?'

'No.' She seemed to breathe more easily. With her next sip of wine she appeared to allow herself more relish, more engagement with the grape.

'Remember when you phoned me last summer?'

I wagged a finger at her. 'You have evidently come here not to hear me play piano, but to test my memory once again. And, once again, I pass with flying colours. I phoned you last summer: check.'

'I don't know what you really had in mind ... maybe all you were thinking about was buddying up for that music festival, having a few laughs, no big deal.' No, that wasn't all I'd been thinking about.

'But for months afterward, I kept dwelling on what a drag it was that I'd had a conflict. And then I would think that I should follow up with you, that maybe we could do ... something.'

'You should have.'

'Yes, Marcus. I should have. That's the whole fucking point. That's why I'm saying I'm not grown up.' She gestured at the room, at the whole city. 'You've identified what you want. You've pursued it.'

'Some of it, yes. But so have you. Right?'

'Some of it.' She took another sip. 'Do you remember having me over for ice cream?'

'Millicent: the answer to every one of these is *yes*. I remember everything we've ever done.'

Her face shimmered, and her fingers grazed the lapel of my sport jacket. 'OK, then I'll cut to the chase. Can I come over for ice cream?'

'I don't know if I have any ice cream,' I said truthfully.

'The ice cream part is optional.'

I signed for our drinks, then took her hand; it was half handshake, half a pull toward the adventure she'd sketched out for us.

She held the door for me as we left. It was a busy Friday night on Third Avenue. Over Millicent's shoulder, a stream of taxis – apparently perpetual while the green lights reigned – evoked the infinite scope of the city.

She followed my gaze. 'Have you ever imagined that as soon as they disappear beyond the horizon, they dip under the island and loop back around? It could be the same fifty taxis, over and over.'

'I've been lazy, Millicent, too lazy,' I confessed as we navigated past the crowd in front of the movie theatre on Eighty-sixth. It was a strange thing to shout over ambient noise on a sidewalk, but I didn't want to compound the laziness by deferring the thought.

'I'm going to test your memory again,' she said when I'd flicked the lights on.

Reversing the host relationship, she motioned me to one of my own living-room chairs. Then she straddled me, both of us still clothed, as she had that night in 1987. But this time she scrunched into me even more tightly, pressing her bosom to my chest and gripping my shoulder bones. I recalled that old quip: *if you were any closer, you'd be behind me.*

With the cooperation of her dress, she had the heat of her panties flush with my crotch, cooking me hard. And as her wetness seeped, I almost believed it would melt the metal of my zipper, springing me into the open air without the intervention of fumbling fingers.

But when she did unveil me, her legendarily dexterous fingers didn't fumble at all. Nor did mine, when I drew aside the taut curtain of her gusset to reward her generous lips with my touch and, sweet fuck, plunge my cock upward into her heaven.

'Did you find your niche, Marcus?' she crooned.

I wanted to be this close to her, always. Writhing into Millicent, my body absorbed by her … my mind yearning to envision what she was feeling as she bounced and whooped. My libido arched toward climax via the ultimate turn-on, the idea of Milly's ecstasy; of her being glued to me by pleasure while I inhabited her.

When she came, I had the illusion, behind my rapture-squeezed eyelids, that she actually filtered through my chest, to emerge on the other side. The reality of pumping her full of my hot come soon destroyed that image; but, oh God, how it was worth it.

My hands came to rest inside her underpants, clutching her buttocks in a default position of contentment and security.

And love.

'You know,' she said a week later, 'I never completely understood what kept us apart.'

It took me a minute to reply. 'The way I see it, we were never really apart, Milly. We just spent two decades circling each other – sometimes in near orbits, sometimes far – intersecting occasionally at weird angles. Until now, when we've collided with a glorious and irreversible impact.' I punctuated the pronouncement with a nice slap to her warm morning ass.

'You're very wise.'

I ran a finger between her breasts. 'You compliment me on my self-awareness ... then, twenty years on, you compliment me for my wisdom ... I warn you, Millicent: at this rate, I'm going to get a swelled head.'

About the Story

SPENDING A FEW LONG weekends in a city, year after year, is a great way for a fiction writer to witness and exploit its evolution. The visits become a foreshortened series of dots, ready to be connected by the muse.

Much of what I've seen of New York has been through the eyes of people invested in the alternative-music world. Sometimes it seemed that the underground rockers were at odds with an inhospitable metropolis, where one paid even to rehearse. And yet sometimes New York appeared as a paradise for the cultural underdog, a place where even a quirky, low-profile pop group could fill a club. On the personal level, my own tiny taste of being part of a modest music scene soon melted away like cappuccino-coconut ice cream. But the ego-tingling flavour has a long tail.

New York, for me, encompasses things one aspires to; things one has left behind; things one takes for granted; and things one is oblivious to until discovered. Like skyscrapers, some of these things are seen most effectively from a distance. Perhaps a reason why a story that's set uptown is so much about downtown ... until people catch up with place, and the centre of gravity arrives at 86th on the express.

Of course, I'm vividly aware of the sex that saturates the city. It titillates, thrills, and inspires me every time; and thus stories such as this one are populated with approximations of sexually self-actualized New York women, modelled on the real ones who bristle all around me with coolness (I opine) and sassiness (I observe) and sensitivity (I hope) and erotic drive (I presume – using the word advisedly). I try to capture what these women mean to me, to take composites home to the bedrooms of my imagination and do some kind of justice to them. I suppose I idealize them – or their situations – freeing them in my fictitious universe from any factors that could compromise their pleasure. This is my way of making love to the women of New York.

The Same Fifty Taxis is, in a sense, one of my most autobiographical stories; though none of its events really happened to me or anyone I know, nor does the protagonist think or act as I would. I feel a personal connection to the piece that's rooted in my decades-long development of a relationship with, and a nostalgia for, countless details of a place that's never been my home. Call it emotional masturbation, but I felt moved as I completed the work: I felt as if I'd *given back* to a city that has hosted me and aroused me, flattered me and seduced me.

Obit for Lynn
by Tsaurah Litzky

IT'S FOUR O'CLOCK IN the morning. I'm sitting in my kitchen, drinking tequila. My friend Lynn Busa died yesterday. I don't have on any clothes or underwear, my pussy smells like sour milk, like I've pulled a two mile train, but I haven't done anything. I'm rotting with despair. Lynn was the sister I always wanted, the trail buddy who would never leave me stranded with my panties down and a broken leg. Even though I am naked, I have shoes on, the red suede pumps I got that time long ago when Lynn and I went shoe shopping at Bendel's. She got a pair of black patent-leather spikes, heels sharp enough to slice off a man's ear.

I met Lynn right after Ed Koch was elected mayor. He won with a big campaign about how he would clean up New York, get rid of the whores, pimps and thieves, get the hustlers off Forty-Second Street. I didn't like him or his campaign. I always loved Times Square; I started to go up there at night with my first boyfriend Eddie Valentine. It was a Mecca of crazy, pulsing, throbbing lust; men kissing in doorways, enormous women who weren't women, condoms taped to their foreheads, strutting up and down the street in sequin dresses, the marquees of the movie theatres advertising only triple XXX features: *Girls In the Night*, *Women's Prison*, *Nana – A French Coquette*.

Eddie and I were seniors in high school living at home with our families. We took the subway in from Canarsie to Times Square. We paid two dollars each to get into one of the movie houses and then we would climb to the balcony to make out. We stood up in the back among other couples embracing. Frantic for each other, we pressed our bodies together, his hot mouth sucking mine. He'd slide his hands under my clothes, pinch and twist my nipples with so much skill I would come. He taught me how to get him off, how to slip my hand inside his jeans and pull his prick. I was so in love with him. I pretended we were Adam and Eve in the garden. There was always a sticky sweet smell floating in the air. I thought it was some kind of air freshener. Later I realized it was come.

By the time I met Lynn I knew that smell very well. I was working at Dolls of All Nations, a massage parlour on Thirty-Eighth Street a few blocks from the U.N. Because I was the only Jewish woman who worked there I was Miss Israel. According to the *Daily News* there were over two hundred massage parlours licensed by the city, turning New York into Sodom and Gomorrah. Editorials urged our crusading mayor to shut them down.

I worked Sunday, Monday and Tuesday nights. Wednesday mornings I liked to go to the Russian-Turkish Baths on Tenth Street. Wednesdays was Women Only day and the ladies could get naked and lounge around like odalisques. My Aunt Mildred, who was a Rockette at Radio City Music Hall, took me there when I was eighteen.

'It's great for the complexion, honey,' she said 'and you need to steam your privates clean. It keeps them young.'

I was in the white-tiled Turkish sauna room. Fronds of fragrant eucalyptus hung from the light fixtures. I found myself staring between the legs of the woman sitting on the bench across from me; the black hair on her crotch was shaped into a perfect diamond.

She noticed me looking and opened her thighs wider, exposing her labia; loose, crimson, frilled like lace. She started to play with the silver ring that pierced one of them, tugging it with slender fingers. I wondered if she was trying to shock me but after four months at Dolls of All Nations, not much could shock me. Maybe she was trying to pick me up; girly-girly love was not my thing, but I couldn't blame her for trying. Perhaps she was just mischievous, she looked like an elf with her delicate little tits, tiny frame, pixie haircut and huge dark eyes. She grinned. She was adorable. 'What are you looking at?' she asked, as if she didn't know.

To my surprise, my clit started to twitch.

'It's your diamond,' I answered, 'I want one.'

'Bruno, my beautician, Bruno waxed it,' she said, 'He does great work. He's a good friend of mine. I'll give you his number. It's in my bag upstairs in the locker room.

We went to the showers and then up to the locker room. She wrote Bruno's number on the inside of a matchbook from Miss Mystique, a massage parlour on Twenty-Third Street. She worked there. We were in the same business. I told her where I worked and introduced myself. 'Far out,' she said, 'my name is Lynn. Let's go have coffee.'

We walked down to Valelska's on Second Avenue. 'I can't stand Sweet and Low,' said Lynn, putting five sugars in her coffee. 'Me neither,' I said, putting four sugars in mine. 'And,' I went on, 'I don't like diet soda or ice in my drinks either, nothing adulterated.'

'Same for me,' said Lynn; maybe I had found a friend.

'How do they treat you at La Mystique?' I wanted to know. 'My boss, Wolfie, has started dropping me on my percentage. He pushes me to do volume. At the end of the night my hand is one giant blister, but when I get home and count, my money, it falls short.'

On the job I had to ask my client to take off his shirt and give him a perfunctory baby oil massage of his upper torso. I was then to ask him if he wanted a happy ending. No one ever said no. Then I was supposed to put a condom on him and finish him off with my hand. Blowjobs were strictly against the law, but plenty of the women gave them; it could quadruple your tip. Lynn nodded, sipping her coffee as she listened.

'That's men,' she said. 'At least a lot of them. You work like a slave for them and they rip you off. My boss, Elsie, used to work in a massage parlour. She knows how it is.

She's fat now. Behind her back we call her the cow. But she treats us right. We get a five minute break between each client. Time to smoke a cigarette or whatever. I never caught her making a mistake with my pay.'

'Maybe I'll go see her,' I told Lynn.

'Maybe you should,' she said.

She leaned forward; I noticed that one of her eyes was blue and the other one brown.

'Did you think I was coming on to you in the baths?'

'I didn't know,' I told her.

'Well, I was only teasing,' she said. 'I'm a merry prankster. I was pulling your chain. I don't go that way.'

I didn't quite believe her, but I said 'OK' and changed the subject.

'I love your boots,' I said. They were green and black cowboy boots with very high-stacked heels; stomping heels.

'Thanks,' she said, 'I love fancy shoes and high heels.'

'Me too,' I answered. Then we paid the check and exchanged phone numbers and addresses. We discovered we lived a few blocks away from each other in Brooklyn Heights.

When I got home, I made an appointment for the next day at Bruno's Beehive: A Beauty Boutique.

Bruno was a six-foot tall bleach blond with a ponytail down to his ass crack. He had a body like a linebacker and a face like Grace Kelly. He took me into the Hot Wax room which was painted a vaginal pink. He sat me down on the waxing table.

'You have a face like a movie star,' he said, 'fantastic cheekbones. What is your sign?'

I liked him immediately. 'I'm a Virgo,' I told him.

'I knew it,' he said. 'An earth sign. Did you know Greta

94

Garbo was a Virgo? How about a snake, an earth creature, the symbol of temptation?'

'I don't think so,' I answered. 'I've met too many men who were afraid of snakes. How about a star?'

'Too common for you,' he said.

We decided on an arrow. The waxing didn't hurt at all, maybe because he rubbed cocaine paste liberally over my vulva before he put on the wax. The arrow looked fabulous. He gave me a ten per cent discount because I was Lynn's friend.

I called Lynn to thank her and tell how much I liked Bruno. We decided to go to Danceteria to celebrate my waxing on Saturday night, as we were both off.

At Danceteria we picked up a couple of cute young soccer players from Italy: Lynn's was named Bebe, mine was named Adriano. I was charmed when he told me he was the love child of Federico Fellini. We went to their room at the Martha Washington Hotel on Twenty-Eighth Street; a dark green room with Audubon bird prints on the walls. We smoked opiated hashish that Bebe had smuggled into the States in his socks. Lynn took off all her clothes, and then she showed the boys her diamond. I took off my things to display my brand new arrow. Adriano asked if all American girls were like us.

'How should I know?' I answered.

Lynn suggested they take off their clothes too so we could cavort around like dancers on Etruscan vases. Lynn grabbed Bebe's long snaky cock and used it to twirl him around. Adriano put his arms around me and we pranced around the twin beds like angels or fools. Soon Lynn and Bebe were doing sixty-nine on one bed while I straddled Adriano on the other. My pendulous breasts slapped against his hairy chest; my hands grabbing his ass, raising it up, pulling him deeper into my cunt. I felt like I was mating with the great god Pan in some primeval glade. At the moment of truth, Adriano cried out, 'Graciella, Graciella mio.' I didn't mind, I thought it was cute that I reminded

95

him of his sweetheart. Years later I read in the *New York Times* that Adriano L., a former soccer player, had become a politician in Sicily.

Lynn and I considered ourselves modern women, emancipated. The pill had set us free. We took full responsibility for our actions; even though we were on the pill we always carried our own condoms; extra sensitive, extra thin, to protect us from venereal disease. We believed love, all kinds of love, was the answer. We adored John Lennon. I was always hoping I'd see him and Yoko somewhere. Then he was murdered; shot down by a deranged fan who believed himself to be channelling Holden Caulfield. Every night thousands gathered in front of the Dakota chanting *Give Peace A Chance* and *Let It Be* until Yoko asked them to stop. She couldn't sleep. For weeks after his death people were weeping, staggering through the streets. This great tragedy was just the beginning.

We started to hear about cases of Aids. There was much confusing information about this new disease. There were rumours you got it from an infected mattress or from wearing someone else's underwear. *The Daily News* said you could get it by kissing; it was spread by saliva. This was all the mayor needed to go after the massage parlours.

At Dolls Of All Nations, Miss Nigeria, Rasheeda, who had grown up in the Hunts Point Projects in the Bronx, was busted giving a blowjob to an undercover cop. They shut us down. Two days later Miss Mystique was closed because of a similar incident.

Lynn and I were out of work. I got a waitress gig at Remington's on Waverly Street in Greenwich Village. Lynn went to work in the jewellery store her mother owned on Seventh Avenue. Together, we went to get tested; the line outside the public health station on Ninth Avenue snaked around the block. We were both lucky. We got the white papers that said we were disease free.

I've only downed my second shot, but already my head is aching. Maybe if I had some blow my pain would float away to Machu Pichu. It's been so long since I've tasted blow, so long since I've done a lot of things. I have become respectable, sort of; I write dirty stories I sell to magazines. Lynn settled down too, she got married. Her husband Matt knew all about her past. He didn't mind; he said it got him excited.

It was Matt who called to tell me. Lynn had a cerebral haemorrhage when she was in the bathtub. The funeral is today at 2 p.m. He found her when he came in to piss. She was slouched down, knees up and spread wide open. Her head was arched back, in the let's-do-it position; her Mickey Mouse washcloth between her legs.

I poured myself another tequila; time was fracturing inside my head. Not all our adventures were as delightful as with the soccer players. One night Lynn and I picked up a guy at the Mudd Club. When we went back to his apartment he pulled a knife on us. Another guy suddenly appeared; he jumped out the bathroom door naked and socked me in the face. The door had been left unlocked. We somehow escaped. I was lucky he didn't break my nose.

Then Bruno killed himself; he jumped out the window of his fifth floor apartment. His body was covered with welts from the sarcoma. Lynn came over to my place to tell me. As soon as I let her in the door, I knew it was bad. She didn't have high heels on, she was wearing house slippers and her face was covered with tears.

She put the brown paper bag she was carrying on the coffee table in front of the couch. She sank down and pulled a bottle of Tequila out of the bag.

'I didn't even know he had it,' she wailed. 'Why didn't he tell me? Did you know?' She opened the bottle and took a big swig. I sank down beside her. I took a swig too.

'He didn't say anything to me,' I told her. 'Besides, he was much closer to you. Maybe he was ashamed.'

We passed the bottle back and forth. Lynn's tears were big as raindrops and I started crying too until my throat, my ears, filled with tears. We were both trembling, shaking and then I was holding her. Our mouths came together like parts of a puzzle. Lynn unbuttoned my blouse and pulled out a breast, she started kissing my nipples and then she put her mouth there, nursing at my big tit, my baby, my beautiful baby. What soft lips. We took off each other's clothes. I had never been so close to Lynn; I could see the little freckles on her chest. We shifted position. I sucked her nipples; there were so tiny and so hard like little tacks but they did not scratch my lips. She started kissing her way down the middle of my chest. Her tongue followed my arrow home. When she went inside and started sucking there, it was paradise. I had read scary stories about how women did it to each other using big grotesque rubber dildos with two heads. This was so different. I wanted to taste her like she was tasting me. Her body was rank and sweaty and her labia smelled of piss, but inside her cunt when she came I smelled violets. We fell asleep on the couch but in the morning we woke up on the floor clutching each other.

Bruno's parents who lived in outer Queens, in Rego Park, did not come to his funeral. Maybe they were afraid that on the long subway ride into Manhattan they would get their jewellery snatched. Chain snatching and petty crimes on the subway were up eighty per cent because of the new terrifying plague: crack cocaine. It was so addictive and so cheap, you could buy a rock on the street for the price of a large coffee and a bagel with cream cheese. Lynn and I tried it once and the high was so ecstatic we knew we should never try it again. First Lady Nancy Reagan unveiled her *Just Say No To Drugs* program. On McGinnis Boulevard in Bushwick, where fourteen-year-old girls were selling themselves for a hit, no one could have cared less if Nancy unveiled her sagging tits.

Going out wasn't such fun any more. Lynn and I stayed home, hanging out in each other's apartments. We smoked grass we got from Lynn's mother, Virginia. Virginia had been a head since the thirties, when she was a regular at the Cotton Club in Harlem.

We re-evaluated our lives; I brought a typewriter so I could type up the poems I wrote in my spiral notebook and send them off to literary magazines. At her mother's urging, Lynn signed up for a course in jewellery design at FIT.

We only went out once in a great while. At the end of a hot summer day when the city was sweating like a dog, we decided to tie one on. We went into Manhattan, to Pierre's on Mercer Street; one of our favourite places. The bartender, Picky Dicky, used to work at Remington's with me. They called him Picky Dicky because he never laid the same woman twice. Another pal of mine from my job was Dan, the Quaalude man. Now he worked as sous-chef at Pierre's. On a slow night he might send out a plate of fried calamari for us.

Pierre's was packed; half of Soho seeking comfort there. Cigarette smoke was as thick in the air as phony promises.

There were a couple of seats at the end of the bar. We elbowed our way to them.

'You two could break a man's back,' said Picky Dicky as he set our Margaritas in front of us. After a few rejuvenating sips, Lynn and I started to talk about this woman in the news who just gave birth to a baby she conceived in a petri dish.

'Believe me,' Lynn said, 'now all sorts of new employment opportunities will open up. Women with good eggs will start to sell them.'

'How do they get the eggs out?' I wanted to know.

'When doctors want to make money, they can figure out how to do anything,' Lynn answered. 'Soon there will be ads in the newspapers, Egg Donors Wanted.'

'That will never happen,' I told her. I took another sip of my drink and then I looked up and saw them, two big, beefy men making a beeline through the crowd, straight for us. They were wearing gaudy Hawaiian shirts. The big tropical flowers looked like a flashback from a bad acid trip. Around their necks they were wearing identical silver peace symbols on long leather cords. I knew they were cops, right away.

'Police,' I said to Lynn, nodding my head in their

direction

'Yeah,' she said, 'Reagan's Raiders. We'll tell them we're actresses or models, and then they'll think we're working girls. We can make a score, I want new shoes.'

'Have you gone crazy?' I asked her. 'Those days are long past and you know I don't believe in sleeping with the enemy. No way.'

'I don't either. Trust me.'

They were already behind us. One of them was breathing down the back of my neck. A fat hand, clutching a hundred dollar bill, pushed between us, nearly knocking over my glass.

'We'd like to buy you lovely ladies a drink,' a slow, southern voice said.

'That's why you tried to knock this one over,' I answered. I turned and looked at the man behind me. He was blond, buck-toothed and grinning. His smile was so wet; I could see the spit shining on his teeth.

'Sorry,' he said. 'But we saw you as soon as we stepped in this place. You are the prettiest girls here. We're strangers in town and ...'

His friend chimed in: 'We're looking for company, and we want the best. So, how about that drink?' This guy had an ugly pug nose and a long jaw. With his red hair and freckles, he looked like Howdy Doody.

'Join us, please, come on,' he said. 'We don't bite, we're nice guys. You two sure are good-looking. You must be actresses or models. What are your names?'

Lynn batted her inch-long eyelashes at him. 'You are so very smart to guess we are actresscs. We would just love to have a drink with you,' she cooed.

'I'm Dorothy,' she continued, 'Dorothy Parker, and this is my friend, Emily. Emily Dickinson.' I glared at her. She well knew I was no fan of the spinster poet of Amherst.

'I'm Charlie Smith,' drawled the blond.

'I'm Mike White,' said the red-head. 'Me and my buddy here are up from Georgia.'

'So, what do you do?' I asked Mike. He had pushed in between Lynn and me and was now standing at my side trying to look down my cleavage. I put a hand over my chest.

'Me and Charlie are gun salesmen,' he replied quickly. 'We're here for the NRA convention at the Javits Centre.'

'How charming,' I said. 'I just love guns.'

Lynn cut in: 'There is nothing like a man with a big gun to turn me on. Do you have any samples to show us?'

'Very cute, Dorothy,' I commented. Lynn ignored me as she beamed up at Charlie.

Two Margaritas later, Mike White had his arm around the back of my chair. Every time he tried to move it closer around my shoulders, I shrugged it off. I had told him I was putting myself through acting school as a baby sitter. 'Maybe you could take care of me,' was the best he could come back with. I nodded enigmatically.

Lynn, however, had told Charlie Smith that between her roles on the Broadway stage she worked in the phone sex business. He had given her a twenty to demonstrate her technique. Now, she was rubbing her little knee against the outside of his leg. Her hand was on the top of his thigh; her fingers going slowly round and round. There was a lump in his pants at the crotch. It looked like a beer can.

Despite the din, I could hear her whisper, 'Oh, daddy, daddy, you're so, so strong and big. I've never felt a gun as big as yours. I know just what I want to do to you'

His face was flushed; his mouth was open like the mouth of a fish on the hook. He was so gross, so ugly. But Lynn spoke to him tenderly. She had her hand over his crotch too now. She was rubbing up and down. 'Please, please, you have an enormous piece, longer than an AK-47. Will you rub it across my boobies? Please, please,' she implored him. 'And then will you put it right between them so I can take it between my lips and suck it. I want to suck you. I want to suck your big gun.' She leaned over and took his ear lobe into her mouth; her sharp little tongue danced in and out of his ear. Charlie was breathing heavy. His pelvis was moving back and forward, he was rocking on the barstool as if he was about to topple over.

Mike suddenly stopped gazing adoringly at my profile. He put a hand over to steady Charlie's chair. 'You need to cool right down there, partner, cool down now,' he said in a stern voice. Charlie moved away from Lynn. He picked up his drink and drained it. Mike reached behind me and patted Charlie on the shoulder.

After a few moments, Mike spoke. 'Dorothy here sure seems to know her business. It would be nice if we could all relax and get to know each other better. Would you ladies like to come back to our hotel? There is a little problem, though. Charlie and me are feeling mighty tired. We had such a long day. Maybe you know where we could get a pick-me-up, a little something to give us some more energy?'

'How about a cup of espresso?' I cut in. 'Maybe make it a double?'

Lynn kicked me hard in the shin with the tip of her pointy shoe.

'What do you mean exactly?' she asked.

'Well' he said, pausing as if trying to find the right words. 'Maybe you could introduce us to someone who could find a certain pretty white lady to pep us up. Sometimes she goes by the name of Coco, Coco Chanel.' These narcs were so dumb. They were living five years in the past. All they needed to do was to go up to Bryant Park and for ten dollars they could buy enough crack to blow them to Christmas.

Lynn smiled up at him, fluttered her eyelashes some more.

'Oh, now I understand,' she said. 'I know just what you mean. I do have a friend who might be able to help you.'

'Can you take us to see your friend?' they asked simultaneously.

'Oh, no, no,' said Lynn. 'He's a very private person, a

recluse, really. He lives like a monk. He hates to meet new people, but he knows me for years. You see, I went to Junior high school with him; we were in the same home economics class. That's the reason we are still friends. Maybe I could go visit him. I can take a taxi over there right now and see if he will help you out,' she said.

'How much do you think it will cost?' Charlie asked.

'Hmmm,' she said. 'Well, really I don't know, but at the very least two hundred dollars, and also I'll need twenty for the cab.' Quicker than you could say blow me Charlie took a wallet out of his back pocket and peeled off two hundreds and a twenty. Lynn took the money from his hand and tucked it into her heart-shaped red Mary Quant purse.

'Now you two, take good care of Emily while I'm gone,' she said. 'Don't let her drink too much.' She turned and made her way through the crowd.

'Your friend is a great sport,' Charlie Smith said. 'We need fresh drinks all around. Could you handle another, Emily?'

'I think so,' I mumbled.

When our drinks arrived I took a big gulp of mine. I didn't like the situation. These whacko goons might kidnap me if Lynn didn't come back soon.

'Well,' I said, forcing myself to smile coquettishly, I probably looked like Joan Rivers. 'Who do you two big boys sell guns for?'

'Smith and Wesson,' said Mike.

'Colt 45,' said Charlie.

'You work for competing companies?' I pretended surprise, 'But, you're such good friends.'

'We go way back,' Mike said. 'Our mothers were girls scouts together.' As if to demonstrate their solidarity, they put their meaty arms on the back of my chair, hugging me tightly, between them.

I felt like throwing up, but managed to push the bile back into my belly by downing the rest of my cocktail. They immediately ordered me another. By the time Lynn finally appeared I was demonstrating how I could dance the twist sitting down.

'Sorry it took so long,' she said. 'The taxi got stuck in traffic.'

'That's OK. Did you find your friend?' Charlie asked.

'Mission successful,' said Lynn with a fetching smile, and she leaned over and slipped something inside the front pocket of his jeans.

He put his hand over the pocket right away, his fingers stroking it as if to measure what was inside. 'You got me excited when you put your hand in my pocket, Dorothy.' he said to Lynn.

'You should be excited,' was her reply. 'There is a pretty white lady inside your pants.'

'Wow-eee, you are something else! You deserve another cocktail. How about it?' he asked.

'I would just love one. I need to cool down I got so hot running around and I bet Emily would like another one too, and then we can go to your hotel and really get to know each other in more intimate surroundings. But, first, I need to go to the little girls room and freshen up. How about you Emily? Your nose is very shiny.'

I was feeling so dizzy from all that twisting that I didn't want to get off my seat. I was afraid I would fall on my face. 'It is not,' I said.

'But your nose is very, very shiny,' repeated Lynn. She reached over, grabbed my arm and yanked me off the stool.

'Hurry back,' Charlie called after us. When we got to the ladies room door, Lynn suddenly stooped low.

'Quick, bend down, bend down like me,' she hissed, 'in case they're watching.'

I squatted down too. She pushed me a few steps sharply to the right and we burst through the swinging kitchen doors.

We entered a scene of frenetic activity. Men in white hats were stirring big pots on a giant stove, turning meat on a three-tiered grill, arranging food on plates. Dan was standing at a big butcher-block table directly in front of us holding a long knife over a fat, pink fish.

'This is not a good time for a visit,' he said, frowning.

'All we need is to make a quick getaway. Is the back door open?' Lynn asked him.

'OK, go ahead,' he said, motioning with the knife towards the door at the back of the room.

'What did you do?' he asked as we ran past him. 'Goose Norman Mailer?' The pugnacious writer frequently drank at Pierre's.

The door opened onto a narrow alley that led out onto Sixth Avenue. I could barely stand and I was barefoot. I had left my favourite silver sling-backs under the bar.

'Are you all right?' asked Lynn.

'Yes,' I answered. I leaned against a mailbox to steady myself, 'but I lost my shoes.'

Lynn went out into the street and flagged down a taxi.

As our cab sped across the Brooklyn Bridge, I asked Lynn, 'What did you give them?'

'I went to the deli on Thompson Street,' she answered. 'Got powdered sugar and some Baggies and made a neat little package.' She opened her handbag, pulled out a hundred dollar bill and gave it to me.

'Want to go shoe shopping at Bendel's tomorrow?' she asked.

'Sure,' I said.

The tequila bottle was nearly empty and I staggered off to bed. I had to get some sleep. I didn't want to look like a gorgon at Lynn's funeral.

When I woke up, the sticky July heat was flooding through the open window. It was already eleven o'clock. I had fallen asleep still wearing my red suede pumps.

I got up and tottered into the bathroom to pee. In the mirror over the sink, I did look like a gorgon; a grotesque witch, my face all puffy and swollen. Maybe I could fix it with make-up, maybe not.

My head was pounding as I went back into the kitchen and mixed myself an Alka-Seltzer, adding the last of the tequila for hangover relief. Then I went over to my closet to choose between my dresses; the shoes I was going to wear already on my feet.

About the Story

TO ME, NEW YORK is a boner as big as the Empire State building. That's why I live here. I'm hooked on the city, despite the changes, even despite the gash across the belly of lower Manhattan that will not heal. The milk in the coffee in the Court Street Dunkin' Donuts a few blocks from my apartment still tastes so sweet it might as well be the apple that the serpent offered Eve.

I grew up on Legion Street in the Brownville section of East New York. That's Brooklyn to those of you who were not raised here. I ran away from home when I was eighteen. I did some travelling, but I missed the city, the energy, the fast action, the burning life of New York. I moved back and found a four-storey walk-up apartment on the Brooklyn Waterfront. I still live there, forty years in the same neighbourhood.

I could never have imagined how completely my magical waterfront street would morph into condo central. There are five restaurants on my block now; they all serve alcohol. When I moved here there was only Gino McCann's, the longshoreman's bar. It opened at four a.m. and closed at four p.m. A shot and a beer cost a dollar. That time and place are lost now as is the old steamy, seamy Forty-Second Street I loved so much, and the dark days of the eighties I describe in *Obit For Lynn*. It was in part my desire to bring back, to re-create a vanished time in the history of my city that inspired me to write this story.

Even more than that, the woman who was the inspiration for Lynn died seven years ago.

I miss her and wanted to call her up, to be with her again. I hope I have done her justice.

Two Natures
by Shanna Germain

I WAS SURE THAT the fucker had dumped me on the train to the City. We were supposed to be celebrating our six and one-half month anniversary, and he dumped me before we even got to the Big Apple.

Oh, he didn't say as much. Too cowardly to come right out and say it to my face. No, he just let me put my head in his lap while the train rocked and rattled beneath us, one of his hands tangled in my long hair. I'd just gotten my hair highlighted for him, and gotten a perm; this was in the nineties, you know, when everyone got permed, especially a blonde, hippie country girl who wanted, more than anything, to look like the kind of girl an olive-skinned Italian city boy would look twice at.

The Italian city boy was named Santo, which means Saint, but damned if his parents probably didn't regret giving him a name like that. It's like naming a child Beautiful-Smart. You're just asking for your child to grow up with buck teeth and a pimple face and the kind of ass that shouldn't ever be seen in sweat pants.

But maybe they didn't know. I'd only met his family once, on Thanksgiving, when his little brother had met me at the door and shook my hand all formal and said, 'pleased ta meetcha,' like an Italian robot and his mother had called me a 'Christmas-tree angel,' only not where I could hear. She told it to Santo after I was asleep and Santo told me.

The whole time I'd been there, they talked about Santo

like he was the most perfect thing ever. Even though I knew they knew he wasn't. He'd been arrested twice for stealing, once while he was still in high school. When he was nineteen, he had to go to rehab for something he never would tell me about. The boy had a knife-scar on his chest, a long slice right above his left nipple that was so raised you could see the outline of it through the tight T-shirts he wore to show off his pecs.

The boy did have a good chest, I'd give him that. And an ass. Like Elvis, young Elvis, when he had some pop back there, but before his belly joined in on the game. I was thinking about his ass while I had my head on my lap on the train. Actually, I was thinking about his ass, and then I was thinking about his cock, because it was rubbing against my cheek beneath his jeans with every rumble of the train and I was helping it along; moving my head up and down like it was just an accident, a little wiggle from me caused by the movement of the train, and he was getting harder and harder against my face.

The boy had a good cock, too. Better than his chest, maybe even better than his ass. Not that I'd seen a lot of cocks then, four or five. His was the kind of cock that just looked ... clean. Not like disease-free or shower clean. But clean and lean, like gorgeous-cut stone. I'd say marble, but his cock was darker than that, darker olive than the rest of him. Curving upward a little, and curving up a lot when he was really turned on, like if it could bend any more, it would touch his flat stomach, paint the dark hairs above his belly button with pre-come. And a perfect little head, round and smooth, the kind that could hypnotize a girl, running her tongue over it for hours on end.

I was daydreaming about his cock and the rhythm of the train, how it was kind of like hips, when they're moving slow and dreamy, when Santo dumped me. How he did it was he pulled his hand away from my hair. He did it hard, not like nice and making sure he wasn't tangled, but without care, like ripping off a band-aid or a leech. Something you

110

didn't want on you any more, but didn't want to feel the pain of pulling it away either. I would have said something, except my mouth was kind of open around the length of his denim-covered cock and I didn't want to move it, really. Or bite him either. And I guess I thought maybe he was going to make a move, you know, because of me almost teasing his cock with my lips and sometimes he would lean down and pull me up to him when I'd been doing that, kissing me. He wasn't a fantastic kisser – his one big flaw in my book, kind of slobbery and like he didn't have any muscles in his tongue other than the one that pushed it in and out – so I was kind of hoping he wasn't going to do that.

Instead he pulled his hand up to his face and he sniffed. Twice. So loud I could hear him over the rumble of the train.

'Your hair smells funny,' he said.

'Funny how?' I said.

'Dunno,' he said. Looking at his hand like I'd infected it or something. 'Funny is all.'

And just like that, I knew I was getting dumped.

You know how sometimes you know things, but you don't really know them? I couldn't have said it out loud. Maybe my brain didn't even know it in a way that I could have put words to it. But as soon as he said those words, my heartbeat went up a little and I got that kind of breathless, stomach-queasy feeling you get when there's a cop behind you, even though you know you didn't do anything, or when you go to get your STD test and there's no way in hell you have something, but when they poke that needle into your skin, you suddenly know that it's all going to go wrong.

The back of my knees felt clammy inside my new jeans. I'd bought them specially for coming to see Santo; he lived an hour outside the city and I lived upstate, a term I'd never heard until I met Santo, although I'd lived there all my life. I'd come down specially to see him; driven all four hours in my beat-up Honda Civic, her blowing oil and smoke the whole way so that I'd had to stop and feed her a quart every hour or so. And I was wearing my new jeans too. They were the kind that showed my ass off like I meant it; dark in all the right places, with lighter patches around the knees and a couple of strategic holes at the good spots, like at the bottom of my ass pocket. I'd bought new underwear too; Vicky's Secret and everything. A black satin thong with nothing but two strings up the back and a little silver circle to hook them together. It was hardly cheap, but it made my ass do a stand up and shout, and I was hoping that was going to get me some, despite the fact that we'd likely be in public all day, traipsing around the city. I wasn't averse to getting a little steamy something-something in a clean toilet stall or having his hand dallying between my thighs at a restaurant, but despite Santo's desire not to live up to his name, he didn't like the public stuff so much. I'd thought that jeans might convince him, especially if I could walk up a couple of steps ahead of him.

But now I knew the hair, the jeans, the come-hither look I'd tried to give him earlier this morning while he'd bought my train ticket for me, they were all for nothing. I was getting dumped, and in my favourite city in the world. Great.

I pretended I was asleep the whole rest of the ride, even when he slid his hand across the curves of my ass, his fingertips sinking into my pocket. Oh, now he wanted to pretend that he didn't mind a little public affection? Great, let him go to town. I was just going to lay right there, my head on his lap and ...

But then he was really rubbing my ass – you know that little placc right under the curved and jiggly part that never gets touched unless you're lying down? Well, he had his fingers in that place, gripping it and I was determined not to let that make me all wet, except I could feel his cock getting hard against my cheek while he rubbed. And that was doing me in. I had to close my lips hard so I wouldn't moan, and I let the train shift me just a little, so that I was nuzzling his cock with my cheek without actually doing so. Pretty soon I

112

could feel that little ridge of his head rising up beneath the fabric. I wanted to put my mouth on it so bad, but I forced myself not to. I sucked on the inside of my cheeks; nothing at all like sucking his cock in between my lips, the way his skin was so velvet-soft, and it would start pulsing against my tongue.

If he knew I was awake, he never said. And he never went any further, which was just like him: dump me, then tease me, but not enough to get me off, just enough to make me doubly regret that he was ending things.

When the train stopped, he kinda shook me, soft-like, like maybe he thought I was really asleep.

'Donna,' he said, leaning down a little to say my name into my ear. 'Donatello.' He means Donatella, the fashion chick, not Donatello the Italian artist. I tried to tell him about Donatello once, but he didn't really listen. Just nodded and uh-huh'd. You'd think he would have cared, him being Italian and all, but I guess your roots only extend so far.

Of course, my name's not Donatella anyway. It's just plain Donna. Not like Santo thought it up on his own. His ex-girlfriend called me it the first time she saw me. 'Holy blonde,' she'd said. She was as olive and dark-haired as Santo, and she wore it big-big, like to add another half inch to her height, even before the high-heeled slouch leather boots. 'You're a regular Donatella, aren't you, hon? Nice choice, Santo.'

Then she'd walked away, shaking her hip-skinny booty like it's something Santo'd still want after she cheated on him with half of the Fashion Institute campus over one spring break, all those 'o's in Santo's name trailing behind her like a big long fake orgasm.

Since then he's called me Donatello. Which somehow bugged me less than Donatella, because I could almost pretend it didn't come from his ex, but from some love of art and quality and, of course, me. But, well, it was easy to see how well that deception was working for me, wasn't it?

'I'm up,' I said, smiling up at him and stretching, eyes

113

blinking, like I hadn't just spent the last twenty minutes trying to make an imprint of his cock in my cheek. We stumbled off the train and there was the city.

You know, people who don't grow up in New York, they think the whole thing's the city. But I gotta say, I didn't go to the city until I was sixteen, on some kind of school trip where they kept the girls from the boys and we saw what might have been the world's worst play if it hadn't been for that one scene where a couple of the actors got mostly naked, which woke up the whole class. Not to mention I grew up on a farm, so it still knocked me on my ass every time I stepped into the city. It was like my neck wanted to crane way, way up just to get a glimpse of something that wasn't right in front of me.

'You hungry baby?' Santo slid his hand into my back pocket, and I tried to wiggle away. Partly because he was going to stretch them all out in the ass, which is the worst thing that can happen to jeans, and partly because he'd broken up with me on the train, but he was acting like he hadn't. Then he slid his hand out of his own accord and put it around my shoulders instead, not even seeming to care about the hair he'd bitched about earlier. He touched my earlobe the way I liked, pinching it lightly between his nails and goddamn it if I didn't shiver just a little.

'Mhn,' he said, laughing a little. Good laugh too, a soft clear sound beneath all the other sounds of electronics and cars and money. Damn if that boy didn't have a bit of everything. Made me want him all the more, even as I was mad at him. 'How about Jekyll's?'

The Jekyll and Hyde Club was the place where we had our first date. Well, our first real date that didn't involve me going to his dorm room to sit around with his stoner roommates and watch the Nets lose. Again.

I shrugged, an 'I don't care' shrug, just to see. 'I could eat,' I said.

'You could eat,' he said. His arm tightened around me, in that kind of protective, kind of see-my-girl way. Guess out

114

here my hair didn't smell so damn bad. 'You love Jekyll's. What the hell are you talking about?'

I had to agree. I did love Jekyll's. It was the kind of spooky place that made me hot: ghouls hanging out in the bathrooms, doors hidden in library shelves, a laboratory with all kinds of failed experiments. Yeah, I know that's an odd one, right? But to me, being scared and kind of creeped out makes me want to fuck.

In fact, the best fuck I ever had was with this boy, two before Santo, from my community college. He was cute as all hell; soft baby face, curly blond hair, kind of wide in the shoulders. Wasn't a good fuck at all, mostly, but I didn't know any better then. Except for one Halloween, we went on a haunted hay ride. Way out in the country, six of us sitting on a wagon rolling through this old apple orchard. Spooky as hell. I was sitting on that boy's lap. In the dark, he had his hands under my shirt, his fingers pulling on my nipples, which were already hard from the cold and from the scare. Every bump of the wagon slid me back against his cock so the he was pushing into the crack of my ass. Creatures were popping out of the woods around us right and left, and he was getting the hang of tugging on my nipples just at the right moment so my little gasps were timed perfectly with each scare. All of a sudden, he leaned in and flicked his tongue in my ear, hissed, 'Clarice ...' through his teeth, just like Hannibal Lecter. As soon as I realized it wasn't the boy, but someone else, I swear to fuck I nearly came right there. We laughed, a lot, but when we were done laughing, we climbed off that hay ride, and I rode him so hard in the back of his Impala that he nearly put his foot through the window. I think I came three times that night, which is unusual for me, especially being on top, and then at least five times more thinking about it later.

So when Santo said Jekyll's, you knew I couldn't resist. Had to let him keep his arm around me as we walked through the city, fighting for space on the sidewalk, even though I was pissed at him. Even though I kept seeing his face, the way his nose had curled all up when he'd said that about my hair.

Jekyll's was busy, like you'd expect, it being Saturday and all, and the table we always took – one right back in the corner where you could watch the people start to get freaked out when the bar stools started lowering and raising beneath them – that one was already taken. I took this as another sign. First the hair, then the table. Things were going bad-bad-bad, and I felt like I couldn't do anything but wait it out. Or try to entice Santo into one last fuck. I missed his cock already.

'Let's go up to the library,' Santo said, already pulling at my hand. I said yes fast, but only so I could scoot up before him, let him watch my ass sway inside my new jeans. He had his hand flat on the curve of my ass while we went up, almost like he was pushing me, and I pushed back, letting the weight of my curves lean into his palm.

The library's on the second floor, and it was totally empty. No one likes to eat there, I don't think. They hold séances up there sometimes, and it had that smell. Not like dead people come back, but like live people who are sweating too much hoping that the dead might come back.

Santo took a look around, realized at the same time I did that no one was there, and pushed me forward against the séance table. So my hands were flat on it and my chest was lowered, which pushed my ass right against his already-hard cock. So he *had* noticed.

I wiggled against him, fitting his cock in the centre of my ass, letting him push me hard against the table. The edge of it hit right at my clit, that mostly-pleasure-but-almost-pain kind of feeling that really revs me up.

I wanted to crawl up on that table, roll over and beg Santo to fuck me right there. His cock has this little upward curve to it, and when I lie over a table, my legs hanging down, that curve knocks right into my g-spot like a door knocker. Bang-bang-bang.

116

But a busboy came up the stairs, making Santa let go of me quick, so that I almost fell down. The busboy started cleaning up dishes, eyeing both of us under his bangs like he knew what we were doing. So I behaved. Properly. Like I was supposed to. No bang-bang-bang for me, even though my clit was already beating a drum of its own, my nipples hard points under my shirt, all of my sensitive bits begging for attention.

The table Santo picked was right next to the séance area, but it was tacky. Well, the whole place was tacky, but the table was tacky in a different way. Didn't matter. I figured it was the last time I'd be there anyway. Not like I was going to come back by myself.

Santo slid in and I went to slide in after him; we always sat on the same side so he could put his hand on my thigh, play with me through my jeans. It was about the most I could get him to do out in public, and I craved it. Especially when he let me do it back to him, the back of my knuckles brushing his hardening cock.

But this time he shook his head, and gestured to the seat across from him. That fucker. I'd known it, known it as soon as he'd said that about my hair. Damn it. I was in some space between horny as hell and pissed as a hornet.

Santo seemed oblivious to it all. He had his eyes on the sticky menu that was already on the table. 'Mmm ... wings,' he said. Like Jekyll's actually had great food. Like that's why we came here.

I leaned forward and tried to stick my fingers between his thighs. I wanted to squeeze that cock of his the way he liked, all my fingers around him tight, my thumb rubbing across the sensitive head. But he just shifted out of my reach, without even thinking about it. I put my hand back on my own leg, just on the inside of my thigh. Fine. If he wasn't going to play, if he was going to dump me and he wasn't going to fuck me, then I was going to go in the bathroom and get myself off. Come back, be all impervious to his shit. Strong. All the lust masturbated out of me. If you were going to get dumped, might as well go out with some pride.

'I'm gonna pee,' I said.

'Mh-hm,' Santo said. Stupid menu. Stupid fucking dirty plastic-ass menu.

When I was getting up, the busboy came over, held up a mostly clean cloth. I sat back down, just for a second. He was cute, in a way that was totally different than Santo. Shaggy red-blond hair hanging in his eyes, the kind of blue eyes that are so pale they're almost grey.

'You want a wipe?' he asked. Good lips, straight white teeth. A tiny curved scar at the corner of his chin, like maybe he got bit by a dog once or fell off his bike when he was a kid. I had an image of myself, spread out on the séance table, down on my back, Santo going at me between my legs, that curved cock of his bang-banging my g-spot. Busboy kneeling on the table above me, a hand around the base of his cock. I couldn't see his cock at the moment – it was hidden by his apron – so I gave him a big one, not long but thick. Pale, with those soft red-blond curls around the base. The busboy would slide his cock into my mouth, and despite the moans I was making from Santo shoving into me, I'd keep my lips over my teeth, be sure not to scrape his cock as he stuffed it almost to my throat. I could practically taste him, a little like soap and a little like salt and a little like all the dead-spooky smells that filled the room.

The things I think sometimes. Jesus. Still, it was making me wet. Seeping through my jeans so that I was shifting in the seat, clenching my thighs together.

The busboy leaned over the table, wiping and wiping, and I just wanted him to go away so I could go bury my fingers against my clit in the bathroom, that image of being double-fucked still in my head.

I never made it to the bathroom. Of course, I didn't.

If I'd made it to the bathroom, masturbated, went back to the table, let Santo dump me like he wanted to, if I'd done all that, this would be a different story, wouldn't it? A

118

boring one. Girl meets boy, girl falls in love with boy's cock, girl gets dumped by boy and by his cock. You've heard that one, right?

I made it as far as the edge of the library, to that secret hidden door you have to go through in order to get to the bathrooms, and I pushed the secret hidden door button and I was on the other side. Busboy was there, red-blond, grinning like he thought he knew something. I wondered what it was.

'Good jeans,' he said, in that way that let you know he wasn't talking about the jeans at all. I liked him, that fast.

'Good line,' I said.

'I try,' he said. 'You with that boy in there?' He licked his lips between words, a quick small swipe with his tongue and I thought what else he might do with it.

'I was,' I said. I'm nothing if not truthful. 'He's about to dump me.'

'His loss. My gain, maybe?'

I canted my hip at this boy, showed off the way my skin curved under my jeans. I didn't say anything. Not to that. If he couldn't tell, he couldn't tell.

'I got a key,' he said. 'For after hours.' He pulled out a key ring, jiggled it around.

'I'm just here for the day,' I said. 'We came in on the train.' The hallway was dark, a tiny space that made us stand too close to each other. I could smell the gum on his breath, something spicy and sweet.

'Too bad,' he said. Leaning in, his eyes on me. So different from what Santo was doing, all his hot-cold, hot-cold crap. He kept looking at me, even when he leaned in, even when he was far too close and all I could see were his eyes all blurry. He didn't kiss me, just rested his forehead to mine, then pressed his hips in so my back was against the hidden door. Through the apron, his cock wasn't how I imagined: it was long and lean, curved against his thigh, a hard point of arousal against my hip.

I wanted. I wanted to see what it felt like in my hand. How it unfolded from his skin. What it tasted like when I had it so far in the back of my throat that his pre-come gagged me. To know how it fitted me, how it slid in, tip-first, cracking me open.

I didn't owe Santo anything. The fucker didn't even have the balls to dump me proper. Just 'your hair smells funny' and his hand on my ass and making me sit on the other side. Hot-cold, hot-cold.

The busboy put his mouth on my neck, rubbed his teeth together around a bit of my skin. His soft hair fell against my cheek. I curled my fingers around his cock, the lean length of him, imagined him fucking me on the séance table, bending me over one of the barstools that went up and down, letting me suck his cock in the laboratory among all those misshapen heads and three-eyed sheep.

He slid a couple of fingers into the tightness of my jeans, aimed them against the lace of my underwear, grunting a little against my neck as he pushed downward. His fingertips barely brushed my clit, sending soft little sparks of desire through me that made me arch my hips. I pushed into his touch, feeling his cock twitch and pulse inside my fingers. He pulled back, enough so I could see the desire building in his eyes, the way his lids half-closed, heavy with lust. His voice too, damn, that deepened husk that never failed to get me.

'You could stay,' he said. 'My place.'

'I could,' I said.

Santo was still looking at the menu when I came out. I took a long look at his face, all serious, thought about his cock for a minute. Fuck, that boy had a good cock. I said that already, didn't I? I was going to miss it. But dumped was dumped.

I slid out and he didn't notice. Down the stairs and out into the bustle of the city. There was a huge bookstore nearby that I liked, and a tiny park. I'd find something to do in the city until Jekyll's closed.

There's more to this story. There always is, right? Like how

120

I came back later and the busboy was gone. How I didn't even know his name. How all I had left was the feel of his cock pulsing against my skin, the memory of his teeth tugging at the soft curve of my neck.

How the bar was all aflutter with the talk of the cute Italian boy who'd come with his girl and been abandoned, how he'd planned a big deal for her, had a ring and everything.

Santo always did act weird when he was nervous.

That was a long time ago. I never took the train back home from this place. The city loves me like no boy I've ever had. Its streets are long, lean cocks that pulse with lust and hit all my right spots. Its dark holes are the places to explore with my fingers. It bites and scratches and claws and fucks me. And I bend for it, down on my knees, let it enter me. It'll never leave me. It's in me. Now and always.

About the Story

BITS AND PIECES OF this story are true. The rest is not. What is true is this: I grew up in New York, but didn't visit the city until I was sixteen. I nearly peed my pants when someone whispered, "Clarice" in my ear on a haunted hay ride. I loved taking the train into the city and then going to the Jekyll & Hyde Club and sitting on the revolving stools. I once had an Italian boyfriend with a beautiful cock. The part that is not true? All of the sex in the city. Sadly.

As a kid growing up on a farm in upstate NY, the Big Apple was far away and quite foreign. The only things I knew about it then were that you could see a Broadway show (whatever that meant), that it was "full of gays" (which meant gay men, then, and which was said with both distain and awe) and that it made our taxes really, really high (according to my father, every time he yelled at us for leaving the lights on or standing with the fridge open).

I think that when you grow up in or near a city, you don't realize it for what it is. It isn't until I left and moved to the West coast and everyone I met – I mean everyone – wanted to move to NYC that I looked back and thought, "Wow, I could have gone there any time, and these people have saved up their whole lives for the opportunity."

Now that I'm older and haven't lived in New York for a long time, I miss the city. But I miss it in that way that you sometimes miss a dead relative – because you're supposed to and because she sometimes gave you sugar cookies with real frosting. So I go and visit the grave of the city sometimes, just to read the inscription, leave some flowers and maybe say a few words of mourning. And, of course, I keep my eye out for a fantastic fuck in the back room of a restaurant; after all, anything can happen in the Big City.

Sophia in Astoria
by Thom Gautier

SOPHIA ADDED YOU AS a Friend.
Sophia *who*? A photo, above a name, showed a sun-kissed female face framed by fine blonde hair. Large blue eyes stared from my screen. 'Remember me?' a message asked. 'I used to go out with Caz Theopholos?' My late friend, Caz. That Sophia? Yes. Yes, I remembered her.

'How long has it been since we saw each other?' I asked in reply. 'Ten years?'

She wrote back: 'Thirteen, I think.'

Sophia, my new friend who was hardly 'new'. Her name, her photo, her contact, stirred me. The more I thought of her, the more stirred I was, stirred even as her contact salted the wound of losing Caz. I rifled through boxes for traces of Sophia from back then and found an old favourite photo: Sophia and my ex-wife, in their early twenties, posed side by side, in little black dresses, taken at the first wedding that Caz and I had attended. What struck me about the photo, and probably why I kept it, was how immature my ex-wife seemed standing next to Sophia, who, lithe, long-legged, was seated with her legs neatly crossed, her posture upright on an oversized sofa, and was gazing into a somewhere else that only she knew, far out of the photo's frame, into a future that was maybe here.

Sophia. Sophia and Caz. The loss of Caz shadowed my life. Over two decades ago, when his parents divorced, he had moved from Astoria, Queens to The Bronx, where he and I became virtual brothers. We snuck our first beers together. Took clandestine subway trips during the city's wild west high crime days. We'd learned about sex by swapping favourite porn magazines. He preferred *Playboy* and brunettes; I favoured *Penthouse* and redheads.

At eighteen, Caz fell in love with Sophia. We went to bachelor parties and our friends' weddings. At twenty, he broke up with Sophia. He and I travelled cross-country.

At twenty-three, he got back with Sophia. We got shitty jobs and then we got better and better jobs. At twenty-five, he broke up with Sophia for the last time. We tried, and failed, to stay in grad school. In our thirties, I got married. And then divorced. With Caz's help, I got back on my feet again. I started dating. Then, as soon as my own life had traction, he was diagnosed with pancreatic cancer. "Six months," the doctors told him. There's fate; and then there's *fate*. Caz lived exactly one year from the day of his diagnosis. Dead at thirty-five. During his final weeks, his ex-girlfriends, mostly blondes, flocked to his bedside. Their expressions stupefied by regret, eyes heavy with unspoken laments for lost opportunities, they stared at him, mourning without quite mourning, like ancient Greek lovers who have arrived too late for one final bacchanal with their dying god.

Sophia. Half Greek, and, if I remembered right, half Dutch. Sophia, from the Greek word for wisdom. I recalled from my college days when I studied philosophy that Socrates supposedly said that 'Nothing is preferred above justice.' But there is no justice. The good die young. Miserable bastards live to be a hundred. This is true in Astoria, that manic Greek-American neighbourhood in Queens, where ole Socrates would have felt at home, and it's true everywhere else in this manic world. But if there's no justice, there is erotic consolation. The ancient Greeks knew about erotic consolation. *Sophia*. Yes, oh, the consolation. I felt an erotic *frisson* seeing Sophia's name in my inbox. She wrote now and then. She explained to me how, two years after she broke up with Caz, she married 'a mistake'. She had twins with this mistake. She and the mistake had moved to a gated community in South Carolina, etc. *Etc*. When she heard Caz was dying, she wanted to come up to New York, visit him one last time. 'But my girls needed me here,' she wrote to me, as if she were also apologizing to Caz. When she spoke to him on the phone from his hospital bed, he encouraged her to get a divorce from 'the mistake'. 'Life is not short,' he'd told her. 'It's *less* than short. Live your life.'

After Caz died, she took that *carpe diem* seriously. Now she was remarried to a man who, judging from her homepage, looked stable, Southern, suburban. Her words suggested she was bored, comfortable, wistful. She confessed that she thinks of Caz, 'Every single day.' She elaborated on the theme only once. 'Whenever I see the New York City skyline on a TV show, I think of Caz.'

Our e-mails kept up for several months like this, so it was karmic and unsurprising when Sophia e-mailed that she was coming to New York, visiting some cousin whose house in Queens had just been bought up by a developer. 'Might you be around?' she wrote. 'Dinner?'

Yes, I told her, I would be *around*. I even mimicked her laconic style. 'Yes, dinner.'

Though she grew up in a row house underneath the Triboro Bridge, back in the day, Sophia was aristocratic, reserved, Sphinx-like. She and I had rarely conversed. The odd aside when she spoke to me, however, left an impression. She was a fan of innuendo. How a cigar is never a cigar. At one dinner party, she'd made a subtle remark to me about the astonishing length of the host's bread sticks. Another time, watching the Super Bowl, she'd asked me had I noticed how all the play-by-play announcers sounded as if they were describing sex: "up the middle", "in the pocket", "going deep". But beyond recalling those sporadic quips, I couldn't remember actual conversations from back then. Now, though, we had lost Caz. We'd be able to converse.

Still, as our reunion neared, as if trying to read tea leaves, I dug through more old photo stashes. I scanned photos with Sophia in them and loaded them on to my computer. I cropped other people out, including Caz, so that all I was left with were images of Sophia. Sophia in a little black dress. Sophia in a sequin dress on New Year's Eve. Sophia in a black bikini on a beach.

I even downloaded her recent online photos. Sophia in denim shorts in front of a forest waterfall. Sophia playing lakeside Frisbee with her twin girls. It felt unhealthy, this cut-and-paste voyeurism. It also felt satisfying, healing. After all, *she* had gotten in touch with *me*. Caz was never far from my mind; I worried that I might be unburying the dead.

'Take your time when you get back to Queens,' I wrote Sophia as the day approached. 'See old friends. See a Broadway play. Then, only if it won't be too painful for you, we can meet face to face and try dinner.' She didn't immediately answer. For a very long three days, I wondered if I had telegraphed that I was wussing out.

The morning she was due to arrive, she phoned me from JFK Airport. Her voice had that smooth, glassy cadence that I remembered: soothing. Yes, I agreed, we could eat in Queens. Sure, a Thai place she knew. Did I eat Thai? she asked. I assured her I ate Thai. 'Then you'll eat Thai,' she said. 'I will eat Thai,' I replied and we both laughed.

She suggested we meet in front of Aphrodite's Delicatessen in Astoria.

'The place Caz and I used to buy beers on the way out to Jones Beach?' I asked.

She giggled. 'That *a one*.'

I didn't tell any friends about this meeting. This not-quite-date. This Thai dinner with an ex-girlfriend of a dead friend. A dead *best* friend. It felt too inexplicable to reveal to anyone else, too hermetic. Mythic, maybe, as much as Queens would accommodate my myth.

I got a haircut, a shave. I dressed in a jacket and crisp dress shirt, Italian loafers. Like an idiot, I didn't bring anything to read on the long N train ride out to Astoria. My hands trembled. I paced. I could imagine Caz watching me and laughing from the beyond. My libido was teenage-like, fired up by everything in the subway car. Grinning models in teeth-whitening ads. The red lace stockings of a Russian-looking passenger who blushed and pulled her skirt over her knee. Racy cognac ads with two Asian models draped around the arms of a bald, clean-shaven African-American stud. New York, I thought, sex *as* the city.

When I emerged from the subway in Queens, I paused at the top step and stared across at Aphrodite's Deli. Sophia was there, taller than I remembered. Her blonde hair was longer too. With her arms folded across her chest, she was distracted, intense, casting her large blue eyes left and right, cat-like, trying to predict my direction. A blonde shimmer haloed her, separating her from the brick buildings and ashen-faced commuters. Her pale blue blouse, her designer navy blue skirt, her dark blue strapped heels, her leather purse – a Fendi, I could read, as I got closer – slung lightly over her thin shoulder; all of her contrasted with the deli's paint-splattered, cluttered storefront.

When I was within a few feet, my stomach churned. I recalled, in a rapid, seamless montage, countless moments when Caz was alive. Girlfriends with big hair. Messy break-ups. Bachelor parties spent trawling for hookers in Hunts Point. Drunken nights at Shea Stadium. Boring bowling nights. Dead-end double dates in the Nineties. How crazy Caz was about Sophia. How, to him, when he was single and feeling adrift, she'd always been *the one*. How crazy he was *made* by her. Small details came to me too. How Sophia had mistakenly bought him a Jets jersey instead of a Giants jersey for his twentieth birthday. How Caz had confessed to me that she once gave him an insanely slow foot job while he tried to talk to his angry boss on the phone. I blushed at the memories and coughed and tugged at my jacket: 'Get your shit together,' I could hear Caz mutter to me, as if he were a director coaching a nervous actor. 'Step into the scene.'

When Sophia saw me, the tension in her shoulders relaxed. In her heels, she matched my height. We smiled, partly in relief and partly from that delight that comes from cheating time by meeting someone we thought we'd never lay eyes on again.

I kissed her, a quick tentative kiss that she returned more definitively. She inspected me, head to toe, and said that I hadn't aged 'a jot'. She playfully rubbed her lipstick stain off my lips. Her fingers were like cold porcelain. Or marble. *Marble nymph fingers*, I thought, and I smiled at her.

I could see that she was far less nervous than me. Maybe her Greek blood had helped her give herself over to fate; maybe, not being Greek, I was resisting what all the Greeks knew we couldn't escape: fate.

'You got *younger*,' I said. She smirked like she didn't believe me. Her earrings, golden dolphins, set off by her tan.

In a rush of sudden confidence, I opened my arms and pulled her into a warm hug, and she hugged back, firmly. Her soft breasts pressed into my chest. The magnetic attraction of our shared loss radiated out into a tangible present and pulsed like a current as we held that hug. My nose filled with her lilac perfume. The tender sensation of her lean arms clasped round me made my throat catch. I hugged her so hard that I lifted her off the sidewalk.

A train rumbled overhead, like an earthquake in the evening air.

When we let go, her eyes were red and watery yet she was smiling. She adjusted her silver necklace that had tangled under her blouse. 'That hug,' she said. 'Again?'

'Sure,' I said, and, then, almost like a dare to which she'd set herself, she grabbed the back of my neck, and pulled me in and kissed me hard. We opened our mouths and let our tongues loll.

I clasped her again and again I did the playful hug-and-lift, this time with an exciting possessiveness. When we let go, I wanted to plant another kiss. And more. What I wanted was to make love to her, right there, in daylight, in view of every passer-by in Astoria. On the gum-splattered sidewalk, I wanted to kneel down, kneel and hike up her skirt and part her long legs, *here*, with fat men in the deli staring out at us. Peel off her panties and kiss and lick and tease and worship her sex until she felt all her years of pent-up regrets and frozen memories about Caz melt from her, out of her, into a hot, public orgasm, an orgasm more drawn out and blissful than any she'd ever felt with any man. Including Caz. 'Friends, F-O-C,' she said, cryptically. *Friends of Caz*.

I was tempted to ask what she meant, exactly, by *friends*, but I just nodded, and Like a couple who have eloped in an arranged, shotgun marriage, we locked hands and we walked on without talking. We strolled the long blocks hand in hand without speaking, passing noisy Irish bars and crowded Greek eateries, Italian pizzerias bustling with teenagers and Asian food shops with misspelled English: '*Boil loster, lo chorestorol.*' Cars honked, mothers screamed. I could pick out Caz's young face in the faces of young kids on the stoops smoking. I felt his presence hovering around us as if he were part angel, part genie.

Before we were to go to the restaurant, Sophia suggested we stop in at Caz's mother's. 'Do you mind?' she asked. 'Or is that too much?'

'I don't think it's too much,' I said. 'There's no script, right?'

'I couldn't come here and not see her. But *it* ... It is about us, *this*,' she said, waving her hand back and forth between us as she repeated *it* and *this*. I heard a sweet embrace in how she said *us*.

Caz's mother lived on the ground floor in a dimly lit corner tenement and her shrieks of joyful shock echoed off the bare walls of the lobby.

Inside, Sophia and I held hands tightly, perched on the

couch facing Caz's mother, who sat on the coffee table, leaning into us as if she needed to confirm that we weren't mirages. As she reminisced, she tapped our knees with excitement, like we were a couple out on a first date, which, in fact, I realized, we were.

At one point Sophia let go of my hand, but squeezed my wrist as if to signal she'd be back double-quick. Seated alone on that old couch, I hardly heard Caz's mother as she narrated a story around a photo album. I just nodded absently and discreetly lifted my eyes to watch Sophia in the kitchen. She was fetching wine. She waved at me and blew a kiss. I stared at her firm ass under the navy skirt, her elegant gait, her sun-kissed calves tapering lithely into navy pumps. I studied her fine fingers and pink nail polish as she uncorked the bottle. Sitting back on the couch, she greedily reclaimed my hand and handed me my glass of wine. Our thighs pressed together; our feet tapped out footsie as Caz's mother rambled on and on and on about the past.

Then we came to a photo of Sophia in a tattered T-shirt and yellow bikini bottom, her hair wet, matted, spread like tendrils on her shoulders, the glint in her blue eyes a match for the topaz sea behind her. It was Puerto Rico, she explained, 'After Caz and I's third getting-back-together.'

When Caz's mother removed the photo from under the plastic sheeting and ran her finger along the image, over Sophia's tits, her legs, her feet, I was so aroused that I downed my glass of wine in a gulp. My lips tingled. I licked them, tasting Sophia's lipstick from earlier in the evening.

Sophia flipped through the album and re-crossed her legs, causing Caz's mother to slide over on the coffee table to make room for that beautiful leg, and when Caz's mother complimented the strappy leather shoes, I felt my cock surge and stiffen so awkwardly that I almost laughed at my visible hard-on.

As we left, woozy from cheap wine and the long dizzy trip on memory lane, Caz's mother lay her hands on our shoulders like she was granting a benediction. Her eyes were wet. 'Something else, I tell you, having you both in my house, at the same time,' Caz's mother said. 'You were the closest to him, in your separate ways, and between the two of you, my God, in my living room, I felt he was with us.'

As her door closed behind us, I thought of the word 'nostalgia': how an instructor in college explained that it is formed from two Greek words meaning "homecoming" and "ache" and when I looked at Sophia she was sobbing.

I let her cry and regain her composure. She recovered, sniffling and dabbing her mascara, she apologized. I told her emotions were nothing to feel sorry for. I put my arms on her hips.

We were barely around the corner before we stopped and fell into another hug. Then, unrestrained, we kissed, pressed up against an apartment building. From a window above our heads somebody shouted, 'Get a room!' Without looking to see who was complaining, Sophia chuckled. She seemed at home, or at peace, with me, now.

She poked her tongue out as she unknotted my tie, draping it around my neck like a scarf. Her fingers slid through my shirt, her nails scratching my chest. I traced the lilac scent up her neck, gliding my finger along her fine-boned jaw line. Her thin figure felt like the taut body of a twenty-year old as we fumbled about with the awkwardness of virgins. We agreed we had no patience for Thai food or even for a restaurant.

Hand in hand, we headed westbound, practically running, down a sloping sidewalk, past shuttered storefronts, through a desolate industrial zone, stopping at each *Don't Walk* sign and kissing, hurrying on again until we were safely inside Astoria Park.

We found a bench. Sophia rested her head on my shoulder, slipping her hand snugly inside my pant leg.

Above our heads, we were protected by a ceiling of dark branches. The park air was wafted by the salt scent of the East River. The river's black waves reflected the white lights of the Triboro Bridge. Across the river, Manhattan high-rises glimmered. The Chrysler Building's bullet-shaped crown towered over the other skyscrapers and gave off a white light so intense and so immediate that it seemed we could reach out and touch the building itself.

For a little while, we discussed Caz's mother, the streets of Astoria, growing up in New York City as a teenager. At one point, I asked Sophia if she felt herself, as I did, feeling lighter, lighter on the inside. 'Like a frozen chunk of grief is melting,' I said, 'Like it's been melting since you first reached out to me online.'

'Yes,' she said. 'But I need that chunk melted, gone. I know I don't want it in me, in my life, any more.' The delicate rise of her cheeks was partly revealed by the glow of the park lamp. I told her it had been a long time carrying this ice inside and that nothing since the day of Caz's cremation had made that iciness go away. 'It didn't help,' I said, 'That no one who came to the funeral could relate. Everyone was sad, hurt, all that. But it wasn't till your e-mails that I knew you got it at the same level I did. Your message started this melting sensation.'

'Well, I relate. I relate to how you put it,' she said. 'Melting.'

We sat there speechless for a long while. Then we kissed, taking languid turns cupping each other's face. She seemed drowsy so I folded my jacket into a makeshift pillow for her head and invited her to lay down, fixing her long legs across my lap, but soon after she was at ease, she pulled me down to her, till we were face to face. She ran her fingers through my hair. I snaked my arm around her.

As we lay stretched out on the bench, we read the shapes of animals in the patterns of white clouds in the night sky, and deciphered letters of the alphabet from the curved branches and leaves veined in the moonlight. I embraced her protectively. As I snuggled closer, the rapping of my belt buckle against the bench made us chuckle and added a note of playfulness. I pulled my belt off and we took turns rapping its buckle against the back of the bench.

I caressed her breasts through the raw silk of her blouse, teasingly, until she was writhing and grinning and so aroused that she bit my chin and tugged at my shirt collar. She plunged her tongue into my ear. The flicks of her tongue against my ear roused me. Keeping my arm locked around her, I reached under her skirt, I slowly drew down her panties. She gracefully wiggled free of them, kicking them off herself, her foot dropping the panties onto the dark pavement near our feet.

Grabbing hold of my left wrist, she positioned my left hand just-so under her skirt. Then she moved my hand over her sex, instructively, showing me exactly how and where I should touch her.

When she let go of my hand, I touched her as she'd shown me, touching between her legs, cautiously, grazing her pussy with my forefinger. Gently, with wilful tenderness, I pressed my finger into the folds of her pussy. Her legs tightened around my arm so that I was just barely able to pleasure her, fingering upwards and downwards, slowly, on her clit, kissing her on the mouth as I did, and she returned my kisses, gripping my hair so tightly it stung.

I worked my finger busily between her legs, up, and slowly down, and then quickly up, in circles, in, around, and up again, sliding, warmly, and then hotly, burning, *melting*, as the river's brisk wind blew over us.

I wanted her to cum, out here, in this park; I got up off the bench and knelt on the hard concrete.

She shifted around and faced me, placing her spike-heeled feet on my shoulders.

I lowered my face underneath her skirt, letting my tongue probe and lap the fleshy nub of her snatch. Her sex swelled against my tongue. She dug her heels into my shoulders, writhing, pressing herself into me, and, using my shoulders for footing, she stretched and quivered, quivered against my licking lips and bucked, madly, bucking as I kept on licking. I held her hips firmly and my tongue-tip worked an easy, wet up-and-down tempo on her clit, and as she moaned loudly my free hand reached up to find her hand, until, as I licked and lapped and salved her swollen pussy, her cries pierced the quiet, sounding deep into Astoria Park.

When I woke, freezing cold, Sophia was snoring into my chest. I thought we were in some forest, in a dream, of hers or of mine I couldn't quite tell. Rap music blared through the trees behind us – music – as cars passed along the side roads that bordered the park. I roused Sophia and we got off the bench, weary, contented, self-conscious. She retrieved her panties from the ground as we walked, and she fisted them and pressed them to her chest, giggling, before tossing them into a garbage bin.

We strolled the park's promenade. She pointed out the decrepit wall near the water and narrated how she and Caz and their gang used to sit out there on nights in hot summers, their stereos plugged into the base of the park's many black lamps.

We pointed across the river to Manhattan and reminisced about clubs and bars and restaurants from the late eighties. As it grew colder, she pulled my sports jacket more tightly over her thin shoulders. Shivering, she suggested we head over to the house of her cousin who was moving. 'They're gone to the new house. I have their keys.'

The walk was quick, but seemed to go on for ever; one of those walks in the company of someone whom we never expected to walk with; a slow walk in which fate punctuates our lives and urges us to pay attention, so much so that we feel the moment slipping from our lives even as we unfold within its magic.

I wanted to ask Sophia if she felt this way but the words weren't there.

The side guest room in her cousin's house was the only one furnished: a queen-sized bed with a worn, red duvet. We raided their fridge and opened up beers and kicked off our shoes, noshing on chips. She propped up pillows on the bed and reclined, her lean elbows poking out. I massaged her feet, and we fell, again, hand in hand, into that mostly wordless space we'd been immersed in. I wanted to ask her about her first marriage, her kids, her divorce, her new husband, and I wanted *her* to ask *me* about my marriage, my divorce, my single life. Yet those parts of our pasts, which had nothing to do with Caz, would have seemed like unwelcome guests so we let the silence absorb us.

I cupped her right foot and felt myself stirring. She slipped her foot from my grip and sat up and knelt on the bed, waddling on her knees across the mattress as she held out her beer. I took her beer from her and she unbuttoned my shirt. We undressed in slow motion, like we were showing ourselves how we could fool time, pausing now and then and laying back down and kissing, half-dressed, half-naked, as if with each touch a healing, the melting, was lightening the weight of our bodies.

I kissed her shoulders. She licked my Adam's apple.

I straightened her bra. She playfully snapped the elastic band of my briefs.

I unzipped her skirt and folded it playfully over my arm, like a waiter. She slipped my grey socks over her own feet and kept them both on like that, baggy men's socks on her slender feminine feet, wiggling her toes under the oversized fabric.

She tucked her hand under my undershirt, running her open palms in speedy circles until my nipples burned and hardened.

'F-O-C,' she whispered, cryptically, and we grabbed our beers and toasted, 'The lightness.'

As if to shake off any creeping sadness, she stood up on the mattress and kicked her right leg into the air before tumbling forward in laughter. She sneezed out beer suds. We toasted. 'A Rockette impression?' I asked, catching her. 'You have the legs for it.'

'Help me. A Rockette cannot tumble off her stage.'

I stood next to her on the bed and couldn't *not* laugh at the sight of my baggy socks drooping on her feet.

As she leaned into me, she kicked up one leg, then kicked the other, swaying with verve as I egged her on, and on, and she alternately swung her lovely tanned legs, right, left, right again, each flesh-coloured blur streaking up into the dark air in front of us, her kicks like a kind of defiant joy, and I thought of the word euphoria and its Greek origins in ecstasy, in fertility, in aliveness. I remarked how amazing it is to be alive.

'I was thirty-three and didn't realize I was alive. *Alive*,' she said. 'Until I got that phone call that Caz had passed.' She swallowed hard and bit into my shoulder and licked my skin and then bit me again. We hugged. We curled onto the mattress, in a spoon position, and lay clamped in a tense hug, silent, as if we wanted to let the natural noise of our breathing speak for how alive we felt.

I woke to a sensation of wet tickles below my waist. I saw Sophia's blue eyes in the dark. Her knuckles grazed my belly; she suckled the crown of my cock.

I flinched and I sat up. My lips found her breasts. I tongued her nipples until she writhed, my stiffened cock slipping from her mouth as she squealed.

Barely touching her skin, I ran my hand up and down her legs, my forefingers grazing her pubic hair, tracing letters on her skin while she reached back and drew her arm around my hip, squeezing my bottom, poking her forefinger straight into the snug cleft in my ass, and deeper, causing a wicked clench which sent spasms of pleasure down my back, into my balls and up the shaft of my cock. She tugged at my hardened cock and then sucked it again with a greedy tenderness, lapping and salving me.

Her hot *glissando* puckered over my engorged crown and the more clearly I heard that repeated pocking sound from her wet mouth, the harder I became. This gliding of her tongue on my shaft alternated so sweetly with the sound of her breaths that just as I thought I was getting a grip on my pleasure, I came, ejaculating in thick jets. She fisted my cock, her blue eyes staring directly up into mine; a gaze like a command, an impatient intimacy, and as she pumped and I emptied all I had, we sank down onto the mattress.

I closed my eyes, my face pressed into her backside, as my vague half-dreams were perfumed by the sheer surprise of her presence; this warm odour of her sweaty skin against mine.

When I woke, I gathered her blonde hair off her neck and ran a thousand kisses up and down her neck, onto her shoulder, down her arm. We shifted into a missionary position.

Her eyes were so bright blue in the dark that she looked like a pagan goddess in a jewelled fresco. Our legs coiled around each other and my cock burrowed, slipping into her pussy and blooming like a flower of fire.

We fucked with an athletic insistent speed that surprised us so much that we barely caught our breath. 'This is the melting,' she said, kissing me, biting my chin. 'Like puddles.'

Up and down, she shifted her hips and sometimes paused, paused and held my cock deeply inside her as we kissed, her thin arms up over her head like she was floating on a pool.

Occasionally she pulled at my hair to make me quicken my pace. Then she squirmed free of me entirely and said we ought to go harder. 'We *have* to go harder.'

She pulled a small tube from her pocketbook and leaped back on the bed. She tugged at my hair again, not so playfully. Her fixed expression had a determined, deliberate air. 'I want to feel *more*,' she said. 'Feel all of it melt off me.'

As Sophia gripped the tube of lubricant, I watched. She turned away and wiggled into a comfortable doggy position, propping pillows under her stomach. Her shoulders hunched.

Her face quietly rested on a pillow, one flinty blue eye staring back up at me with a girlish, impatient anticipation. I took in the view of her ass. I brushed aside the impulse to make a joke about Greek love. She was grinning, though, as if she knew what I might be thinking.

'It's okay,' she said, raising her ass. 'Go.'

'I have never –' I said.

'*Go*,' she said. She reached back and squeezed a dollop of the lubricant into my hand, and reaching back further, she rubbed the excess cream onto my cock, her fine fingers stroking my engorged hard-on, her fingernails grazing my balls.

I lubed my hand. The tight sensation of my greasy finger in her snug hole, there, prying into the cleft of her ass, was so raw that my cock surged, spilling a thin thread of silvery pre-cum on the small of her back. I rubbed more of her lubricant on my hand and onto my cock before guiding my cock forward, pressing myself slowly and firmly into her ass.

Her sock-clad feet brushed my calves as we moved and rocked, thrusting and moaning in counterpoint, the burning smack of our flesh rippling regularly between our legs, building an aggressive fuck-fuck-fuck rhythm that almost dissolved the magnetic glow that had radiated between us all night. Sophia tightened her hold on the headboard. As her ass cheeks pulsed and clenched around my cock, the sensation felt like the pressure of balloons made of fine spun silk.

She pushed back insistently into me, *onto* me. I thrust myself harder, forward and forward, in and out again, in perfect synch, the headboard banging violently against the bare wall, knocking a stray nail out onto the pillow beside Sophia.

'Hold on to my hair,' she said, '*Go*.' I clenched a fistful of her hair like a rein as we moved. She laughed approval, her head tugged backwards as I fucked into her, forward and back.

She reached back and slapped my thighs until they stung; stinging slaps on my thighs. My thighs felt as hard as concrete; hard as my warmly greased cock drove into her soft ass, while her quick hand-slaps to my thighs insisted on more speed, more stamina, more go. I thought to hold my cock in there but her back and forth movements were too rapid.

My balls ached from the pressure and movement. I sped up. I let go of her hair, and, with my arms free, my lower back aching, I pumped in and out of her, reeling. Her blonde hair was mussed and swayed over her face and we beat time on a stranger's bed in a Queens night I would never forget. And maybe, somehow, also never quite remember, at least not as vividly as the generous grip of her long hand around my cock, and that feeling of a teasingly trickling flame as she stroked me until I was even harder, burning, engorged to the point of bursting, and then, after stroking me, how she pulled my rigid, tingling cock nearer her ass, her concentrated face, her tousled hair, her nose – *Sophia* – profiled in the room's dim light as we were melting into each other, slickly so, soaring, cruising, in tempo, and a warm necessary pleasure churning in my balls hitting a crescendo just as she quivered, quivered and buckled, hugging the pillow, her shoulders and tits shuddering violently as I came too, the heat of the flood melting ice inside and ice outside, leaving us in groans, shocked moans, desperate whimpering, like wounded animals, and the last dollops of cum dripped from me, into her, and over-spilled on the red duvet, my breathless panting drowned in the glassy cadence of her cries.

That was most of what I remember from our fucking.

Then I remember it wasn't morning or night. Blue light was leaking through the blinds over the bed.

Sophia was showering; she had cleaned up our beers, thrown away the chips, folded the duvet. I dressed, easing my aching balls into my underwear. I sat in the bed and listened to the shower turning off. Sophia emerged and waved from a distance while I watched her dress.

Soon we were outside in the cold air of a vacant Saturday morning walking the streets of Astoria looking for breakfast. She leaned into me and we studied the gradually lightening sky. Its blue light was often lost in the halogen glare of the street lights, the glow of passing headlights, the occasional red neon of convenience stores.

She led us to The Orpheum, a diner not far from the subway. 'It used to be called The Pantheon,' she said. I almost asked her if she'd ever come here with Caz.

As we studied the menus, I asked her about her high school. She shrugged. She sounded indifferent about the past. She talked instead about her daughter's grade school in Florida.

Compared to the emotions of the night before, her mood was relaxed, Zen-like.

We ordered coffee from an old man who walked around barking orders like he owned the diner. As I surveyed the stools and booths, I tried to remember whether Caz had ever taken me here when it was The Pantheon.

When the waiter brought the coffee, I asked him what The Orpheum means in Greek. He said an Orpheum was a kind of theatre, a place of worship. Did I not know the story of Orpheus? I told him I had studied Greek philosophy but that the myths were fuzzy. He filled me in by explaining how this musician, named Orpheus, was to marry a woman named Eurydice who got a lethal snakebite on their wedding day and died. Orpheus cut a deal with the gods to go back to the underworld to rescue her and bring her back to life, on the condition that he not look back. 'Being the putz he was,' the waiter said, 'He looked back.'

'He was checking back to see her,' Sophia said, sipping her coffee. '*Normal.*'

'Be that as it may,' the waiter said, waving a menu. 'A deal's a deal.' So Eurydice died a second time. Old Orpheus never loved anyone again, the broken-hearted bastard. 'Wild animals tore him to shreds.' the man said. 'That's us Greeks, more drama-queen than the Italians.'

After breakfast, it seemed as if the weekend was hungry to swallow us back into our separate lives. I didn't suggest we spend the rest of the morning together. Sophia didn't either. She checked her phone messages as she walked me to the subway entrance. A lone Mexican guitarist was strumming a love song that I could tell was sappy even though I hardly knew a word of Spanish.

I asked her about her remaining plans and she mentioned the names of people she had to catch up with. Names of people I didn't know. 'Relatives,' she said.

She and I hugged without kissing. This Platonic energy had slipped into us so suddenly this morning that I didn't feel any of the previous night's desires. It was as if in sleep we had become like sister and brother. Healed widows, I thought.

Her hair was still matted and damp and she seemed surprisingly ordinary in her navy skirt and leather jacket. A cute girl from Queens, all grown up, back in the old neighbourhood for a weekend. I figured I probably looked even less than ordinary.

'We did what we had to do,' she said. 'I'm glad.' I was taken aback by her sharp emphasis. Did. Had. *Over*.

I considered thanking her for contacting me and for arranging for us to have dinner. 'I'm glad we skipped the Thai,' I said.

She smiled weakly.

For a fleeting moment there at the subway stairs, I considered suggesting we try to do this every year, getting together like lovers in a B-movie. But I had started the night before with few words, and I had even fewer words now. I was no longer nervous. Caz it seemed, had vanished like he'd never been the one who brought us together.

A train thundered overhead but we stayed there, hand in hand, until she let my hand go. 'Bye bye ice,' I said.

'Good riddance,' she said, kissing her palm, then pressing her palm to my cheek. 'Good bye.'

I kissed my own fingers and touched her nose with those fingers and we smiled and then I turned and went up the stairs.

Waiting for the train, I leaned over the platform railing and studied the cars that were cruising in both directions over the Triboro Bridge. Girls in ballet tights flirted with a boy on a skateboard. A milk truck barrelled toward the Queens side and spilled onto the exit ramp, vanishing below the El onto the service road. The N train ride home was quicker than I would have liked.

When I tried to e-mail Sophia later that week, my e-mails were bounced. 'Unknown recipient.'

I checked my list online and saw she'd taken me off her friends. At first I was indignant and hurt and wondered whether I had led her into something she hadn't wanted.

Then I reminded myself that she had led the charge. But she didn't want this any more. She was married. A second marriage, for Christ's sake. She had daughters. She had a life.

As time passed, I knew without knowing that she wasn't thinking of Caz any more. So to make sure I wasn't thinking of Caz any more, I deleted all my photos of Sophia. When I came to the old photo of her on the sofa, I stared one more time at the faraway look in her eyes and then deleted it.

A year after my night in Queens, I thought about the story of Orpheus the diner owner had shared, with its operatic wedding day setting and the gloomy underworld of the dead. I wondered whether that story had anything to do with how I was no longer grieving Caz. Probably not. The diner wasn't called The Pantheon any more. 'Orpheum,' whatever. The Greeks. Astoria, Queens. Socrates and justice. I almost laughed at my own dramatics. Ancient history; forget it.

About the Story

SOPHIA IN ASTORIA WAS inspired by actual and imagined events as well as by the interesting neighbourhood in which it is set. Though largely unknown outside of the New York region, Astoria, Queens (named after the colonial era settler/millionaire John Jacob Astor) is a densely populated enclave directly across the East River from Manhattan. Given its close proximity to numerous train lines and the city's airports, as well as to interstates and bridges, the neighbourhood is in many ways a gateway to all of New York City. Many films and TV shows have been shot on location there (including, paradoxically, Robert DeNiro's 1993 film *A Bronx Tale*). It is one of the most energetic and culturally diverse communities in the entire city. With its easy access to and from Manhattan, in recent years it has become a popular residence for students, artists and writers seeking affordable rents, good food and thriving nightlife. The story's elements of philosophy and mythology came naturally as Astoria has a very large Greek and Greek-American population. I also wanted to write a "ghost" story that was not about disembodied spirits or gothic fantasy but about living, contemporary people who share a certain bond and who *haunt* each other in positive, erotic ways. Mostly the story represented my attempt to show how the complicated and sometimes blocked process of mourning a loss might be deepened and even quickened by episodes of intense emotional and physical intimacy between two individuals who share comparable levels of unresolved grief for a lost person. Other thematic elements such as reconnecting with one's younger self, through an unexpected reunion with a person from that period in your life, also played a role in the story's genesis.

Park Suite
by D. L. King

'I TOLD YOU, I have a master key. Who's gonna know?'

I couldn't help being sceptical. There stood my bride of thirty-six years, right in front of me, hand on her hip, getting more and more pissed off by the second.

'It's your last chance to be a part of New York history. Look, I worked there for thirty-eight years but I'm not old enough to retire. You know what that means? That means I get crap. What do they care? Where am I supposed to go now?

'*Mira*, I really want to do this. I dreamed about it for ever. I want it to be with you, Papi, but if you won't come with me, I'll go by myself. Where's my fucking vibrator?'

Immaculata rummaged in the drawer of her bed table, pulling out various items; a flashlight, an eye mask, a pair of handcuffs, a paperback. 'Fuck, where is it?' Finally she found the blue vibrator with the pearls and the little rabbit on it. It was her favourite.

She pointed it at me like a gun. 'Last chance. Mami's still pretty hot, don't you think?' She turned around and wiggled her ass at me, then turned back to face me again. 'Don't you want to fuck in a suite at The Plaza?'

She was so hot. I think she was even hotter than the day we got married. Standing there, in her black suit and those red stilettos, her hair in a bun at the back of her neck, she was scary-hot.

'*¿A qué le temas?* I can't get fired, Baby.'

'I'm not scared of nothin'. All right, come on, I'll go with you.'

'Good, go get your jacket, I'll be right there.'

Sure, she couldn't get fired, but we could probably get arrested or something. She was right, though; I'd never seen anything more than the housekeeping offices and one of the kitchens. I'd always wanted to see the upper floors and the fancy rooms and now that they were closing the hotel, this would be my only chance. Besides, Immaculata always knew what she was doing.

She came out of the bedroom with her sexy leather jacket and sunglasses on, carrying her black Coach bag, and we were out the door. We rode the train downtown to the park and got off. I followed her half-way down 58th Street, to an unmarked door which she opened with a key. We didn't meet anyone else as we walked down the dim corridor, finally arriving at the deserted housekeeping offices.

'The supervisory staff is the last to go. The maids are long gone and now there are only three of us left. I doubt anyone's here tonight, so relax,' Immaculata said. 'The top floors haven't been stripped yet. We'll take the service elevator.'

'Ms Rivera!'

We both turned around to see two men entering the offices. Emmie seemed unfazed as she greeted one of the department heads.

'Hello, Mr Williams. This is my husband, Juan. I wanted to finish the floor inventory list before I forgot. Is this your son?'

'My son? No, Mr Malone is, ah, interested in the hotel plumbing fixtures. Nice to meet you Mr Rivera.' They headed off toward the service elevator. 'Don't work too hard,' Mr Williams added from down the hall.

After they'd gone up, I turned to Immaculata. 'That was close, Emmie, maybe we'd better – Aye, Mami!'

'What's the matter, Baby?' she said. Her hand had found its way inside my pants after taking the zipper down. Her fingers were cold, but warming up fast. So was my cock. 'Let's go,' she said, leading me to the elevator.

'But Immaculata, Mr Williams ...'

'Is already upstairs. I'm so sure they're interested in plumbing; well, maybe each other's plumbing. Anyway, he'll probably be going up to 19; we'll go to 15. Have I got a view of the park for you!'

Once the elevator arrived, she pushed me inside and pressed the floor button. Before I could complain, she shoved me up against the wall and buried her tongue in my mouth. It was one of those real slow elevators, so she had lots of time to get me all worked up. Her hand found its way past my cock, to my balls and she began kneading them in time with the thrusts of her tongue.

I pushed away from her slightly. 'But, Emmie, we've got to stop.'

'Because why, Baby? Nobody's here. You worry too much.' She untucked my shirt just as the elevator arrived at our floor. 'Well, that doesn't hide much, does it?' she chuckled. 'Juanito's just so big, Baby.'

The next thing I knew, I was half-way down the hall, standing in front of a polished hardwood door, with my hand wrapped around my dick. But once the door opened and I saw the suite, I completely forgot about my hard-on. Slowly, I entered the room. It was pink and warm, and new and old, all at the same time, with lush carpets and antique wood furniture. I could just see the end of the king-size bed in the next room. In a trance, I made my way over to one of the windows and looked out. The sun was setting, providing the new leaves on the trees in the park with a perfect yellow-green glow. From this high up, with nothing in the way, to me they looked more like feathers than leaves. Central Park South was crowded with tourists bundled up in their coats, pointing cameras at everything. I felt like a kid, with my face pressed against the glass, that is, until I felt my wife tug my pants down. Her hands caressed my ass and found their way around to my cock. It had grown soft again when I

149

found the room and view more interesting than the idea of sex. Of course, that was only temporary.

As she fondled me, the specks skating on Wollman Rink grew less and less clear and the tightening in my balls grew more and more persistent. I could feel Emmie behind me, her body pressed against mine. When did she get naked? Hey, I wasn't complaining.

I was still standing in front of the window, but my eyes weren't really seeing much any more. That silky feel of her fingertips sliding up my chest; my Emmie was something else. She took her hands away and stepped in front of me so she could kiss me while she unbuttoned my shirt.

'Oh Mami, what you do to me!' My hands reached for her perfect breasts. I loved the way they hung down like that. She had been complaining that they were starting to sag, but I thought they were getting better. They felt so good in my hands. Squeezing them, I couldn't help thinking, *mine, all mine*, just like a little kid.

I felt her sliding my shirt off. It was gonna get stuck on my hands; I guess she couldn't think of everything. That's OK; I pushed her down in front of me. She knew what to do.

'Oh, does little Juanito need some attention? Is he getting all lonely with nobody to talk to? *Pobrecito.*' While I unbuttoned my cuffs and finished taking my shirt off, she wrapped her hand around the base of my cock. Yeah, Juanito knew what was gonna happen and I could tell he was getting pretty happy about it. My Immaculata's some kind of great cock sucker. I put my hand on her head to keep my balance while I stepped out of my pants and kicked them aside.

'But Emmie, what about the window?'

Her lips were just encircling the head of my cock when she started to laugh. She licked across the top and looked up at me. 'Come on, Baby, you know no one can see in. You just relax and let Mami make you feel good.'

She wrapped her lips around the head of my cock again and used her tongue to get it all wet. The more wet she got it, the further down she went. I loved how she always grabbed me real tight around the base and then pulled down. It made the rest of my cock super sensitive and she knew it. Like I said, the lady always knows what she's doing.

That tongue kept swirling around and around and her mouth slid up and down the shaft, making me all slick. I love the way her teeth and her tongue and the sides of her mouth feel and I tend to lose all track of time. At some point she stopped licking and started swallowing my cock. She can get me all the way in; all the way until her chin hits my balls. I wanted to bury my hands in her hair but she still had it in that bun. She can be funny about me messing her hair, so I just rested my hands on her head, closed my eyes and let her mouth carry me away until I couldn't take it anymore.

'*Aye, Mami, necesito!*'

She backed away and I felt a draught on my wet, pulsing cock. 'Oh no you don't,' she said. She grabbed my hips and pulled herself up from the floor. 'It's time we checked out that big bed.' So hand in hand and cock in hand, I waddled and she walked into the bedroom.

The bed was a huge four-poster. Emmie tore the bedspread off and pulled back the blanket and sheet and fell backwards onto the mattress. I followed right after, coming to rest half on her and half on the bed. 'Emmie, take your hair down.'

I never could figure out how she got it to stay up in the first place. She only took out a few hairpins and down it came. How can just a few hairpins keep that much hair up like that? It's a mystery to me. She ran her hands through her long, thick, black hair, just to shake it out, and then leaned over to kiss me. Now it was my turn to run my fingers through her hair. She had almost no grey hairs at all. Half of the hair I had left was grey, but my Immaculata still looked like a model.

I don't know what it was, but having her hair falling over my face and chest and running my hands through it turned

151

me into an animal. Grabbing her, I flung her back on the bed and fell on top of her. Sometimes it's like I want to consume her. I want to wrap myself around her and hang on tight so nothing else can touch her.

I could smell her heat. I reached down and felt the wetness welling up inside her and stroked her there, just at her opening, with my fingers.

'Oh, Papi,' she moaned. 'Touch me, *mi amor*, touch me.'

I continued to stroke her and then I slowly pushed a finger inside. She was so wet, so hot. Slowly, I moved the finger in and out. I could feel her walls tighten and relax around my finger, tighten and relax. She sucked in her breath when I brushed her clit and groaned my name out as a sigh. 'Juan. I need you inside me, Juan. Please, baby, please.' She grabbed my hand and held it against her, with my finger still inside.

Immaculata grinding against my hand pushed me on to do what she asked. I pulled my hand free and pushed my cock inside her in one motion. She didn't make a sound, but her eyes burned into mine as I sucked my finger clean. I shoved myself up against her sex and she shook under me then. Her eyes went out of focus. That was the thing about Emmie: once she got started, you couldn't stop her. I had my second wind so I knew we had some quality time stretched out before us.

After she came that first time, we made love slowly. It felt so good and it was kinda romantic. I kept that slow lovemaking going for quite a while, but I could tell she was getting restless so we changed positions a couple of times. But Immaculata really only likes it with me on top, so eventually we got back to where we'd started. I used to tell her, "Baby, everybody always says it's better for the woman if she's on top." But she'd always say something like, "Everybody can do what they want. I like what I like."

So once I was back on top, we got down to business.

'You slowing down on me, Papi?' she asked. 'You must be getting old.' She grabbed handfuls of my ass and held on.

152

'I could do this all night long, Baby, but I guess I'll take pity on you,' she said.

She stuck one finger just inside my asshole and used her other hand to pinch my nipple and I went off like fireworks. It wasn't until then that I got to really appreciate the bed we were on. It had to be the most comfortable bed I'd ever been in and the sheets were crisp, you know, but comfortable and soft too.

'What is it about this bed, Emmie, that makes me not want to get up ever? I know it can't be just you!'

Immaculata smacked me hard and laughed. 'It's the sheets, baby. These are really fine sheets. The bed's nice too, but the sheets are the best you can get; real expensive, you know?

'Hey, did you hear that? I thought I heard a door close,' she whispered.

I listened and heard voices in the hall. We gave each other the eye and, quickly, we got up and got dressed. Emmie ran her fingers through her hair, to smooth it out a little and, quietly, we opened the door.

'Why, Ms Immaculata, what chu doing here and who be that fine lookin' man you got wit cha?'

'Oh, Percy, it's you! This is my ... wait a minute, who's that with you?'

Percy laughed. 'This is Shirley, my wife. I think maybe we all had the same idea tonight. You know, I don't think we the only ones, either. I been hearin' noises since we got here.'

'Yes, I think you're right. When we came in, this evening, we ran into Mr Williams and his boyfriend.' With a wink she asked, 'So what do you think? Worth the price?'

Percy smiled and said, 'I don't know 'bout the price. Rich people got money they don't know what to do wit, but it was pretty nice, I got to say. I'm gonna miss bein' here. Who knows, maybe the new owners'll want us to come back to work for 'em. Even if I have another job, they ask me, I'd come back. They ain't nothin' else like The Plaza, you

153

know.'

The service elevator arrived and as the four of us got in, Emmie said, 'I'm not sure if they'd want you to come back if I told 'em what you were doin' in their hotel ...' and laughed that throaty laugh of hers.

I put my arm around Immaculata's shoulders as we stepped outside and then remembered. 'Baby, your hairpins!'

'Leave 'em. It's right that I leave something here.'

Immaculata woke up next to Juan and snuggled briefly before quietly throwing back the covers on her side of the bed and walking to the window. It looked like it was going to be a beautiful day. October was the best time of year in New York. The heat and humidity of the summer was gone, leaving crisp, clean air. The sky was a deep, bright blue and so clear that the colours of the leaves looked almost fake. In the summer, the haze from the humidity hung over the city so that sometimes, if you were on the train when it went outside, on your way downtown, you couldn't even see the buildings. But in October, the air was so clean that every line and window stood out in sharp relief.

It was weird that the tourists flocked to Manhattan in the summer. The weather was disgusting and you couldn't see shit. She'd look at the lines of people, with their cameras, getting ripped off, waiting to go up in the Empire State Building. To them it looked OK outside, but once they got up, they wouldn't be able to see much of anything. It would be much better to come now. But it was even nicer that they didn't, leaving the city to the New Yorkers.

The Empire State Building, now that was a good idea. Maybe she'd go. Juan mumbled and turned over, in his sleep. Immaculata hadn't worked in over two years but she still got up at the same time every morning. She didn't need an alarm clock; her body's clock worked just fine. Juan, on the other hand, would sleep through a nuclear bomb blast.

With one last glance at the fall colours out her window,

she turned her attention back to the bed and the sleeping man within. His leg was thrown over the top of the comforter and part of his muscular chest was bared. He looked good enough to eat. The more she thought about it, the tastier he appeared until she couldn't stop herself. Back in bed, carefully burrowing under the covers she found her target. There was 'Juanito,' still soft and asleep. She began with gentle petting and stroking until the cock, unbeknown to its owner, began to wake up and swell with arousal. Once semi-ridged, she went down for a taste.

As the cock grew in her mouth, she tested it with little nibbles and licks. Juan had been lying very still, too still. She knew he was awake so she grabbed his balls to let him know he wasn't fooling anyone.

'Oh, yeah, Mami, that's nice. Just like that, baby.'

'Don't tell me my business,' she said, pinching his exposed nipple.

'Ow! Hey.'

'Why do you think this is about you? This is for me,' she said around a mouthful of cock. She slurped up saliva and pre-come. 'I thought you looked good enough to eat, so I ate you. Now you just relax. I'll let you know when I'm done. After all, I don't have anywhere else I gotta be!'

'*¡Ai, dios mio!* Jesus, Emmie, you're killin' me!'

Immaculata continued to leisurely lick and nibble at the cock, which was now too big to fit all the way in her mouth. Her hands caressed the spit-slick taut flesh and kneaded the balls, feeling them begin to draw up. Should she let him come, or did she want to draw this out longer. He felt so good in her mouth and he tasted like summer – summer and salsa – hot, spicy and sweet. Just the thought made her groan around the flesh between her lips. It was that groan, more than anything, that brought him over the edge. She felt the familiar little twitch and brought her mouth down over the top of his cock just in time to catch his come, roll it around her mouth and lick up the last drop, as his climax ended, before swallowing.

'Emmie, I can't believe you, girl. What did I do to deserve you?' She wiggled her way up his body to put her head on his chest while he caressed her long hair. 'What a way to wake –' he glanced at the alarm clock. '- the fuck? What happened to the alarm? Emmie, I'm late for work!'

'Oh, Baby, you don't need to go to work today. I shut the alarm. We can have a beautiful day together. Just look outside.'

'Emmie, no. I gotta go. I can't believe you. We got cement coming today. I can't leave Ryan to do it all; it's not fair. No. No, baby. You go enjoy the day. I gotta go to the site, Mami.' He jumped out of bed and grabbed his cell on the way to the bathroom.

Immaculata heard the shower start and Juan's voice saying, 'I'm sorry, baby. You go. You have fun. Ryan. Yeah, I'm late. No. I'll be there, don't worry. Yeah, yeah, I know, but I'll be there, man.'

It seemed like a long time ago, when her job at The Plaza dried up. Two years. It was weird; she thought she'd miss it. After all, she worked there forever. She thought she'd work there her whole life but things change. It was just like the city. It was always changing. Tearing stuff down and building new stuff. It seemed like no one wanted the old New York. The whole city looked like a construction zone. Well, it was good for Juan, she guessed.

That day they made love on the fifteenth floor; that was the day that changed her life. She left those hairpins by the bed. It was kinda like she knew.

The bathroom door opened and Juan, preceded by a cloud of steam, raced out. He was already dressed in his work clothes. He sat on the bed and put his socks and work boots on and gave her a kiss.

'Not too late, Papi, you can still change your mind and play hooky with me.' She put her hands under her breasts and squished them up and together. 'Looks good, right?' She wiggled them from side to side.

But one more kiss and a 'sorry baby, you have fun today'

and he was out the door.

No, she didn't miss work. She'd be perfectly happy if she never worked again. She started the coffee and took a leisurely shower. Looking out the window again, it looked like the day had gotten even more beautiful. The Empire State Building was looking better and better but so was the park.

No. It would be the Empire State Building! She couldn't remember the last time she'd been there; probably years ago, back when her mom was still alive and had come to visit from PR. She put on her black leather jacket, grabbed her Coach bag and she was out the door. The 6 left her at 33rd and Park Avenue South and she strolled across town to Fifth Avenue and her destination. Not even the line outside the building dampened her spirits. It was kinda nice that other people had the same idea, too. And the line outside the building wasn't all that long.

Of course, once she got inside, it snaked around and around and went down a few flights to the basement, where it snaked around even more. Oh well, it was just one of those things. She'd come this far. Finally she got to purchase her over-priced ticket, decline the tourist picture for yet more money and get on the elevator.

Once on top, she went outside to walk around. It seemed she'd been wrong; tourists did come to the city in October, after all. The sun was warm, the sky was crazy-blue and the view went on forever. It almost looked like you could reach out and touch the Chrysler Building, flashing in the sun. How could anybody want to live anywhere else? She took phone pictures and sent them to Juan.

'Guess where.' Want to meet 4 lunch?'

Juan texted back, 'Can't do. Cement troubles. Have fun.'

'Have fun,' he said. She could do that. Back on the street again, lunch and toy shopping sounded like the plan. Once in Chelsea, she headed into her favourite toy story and browsed the shelves. There were rows and rows with boxes of vibrators in all sorts of pretty colours. She especially liked some of the ones made of blown glass. She saw the ones with the little animals that were supposed to hit your clit and remembered her old rabbit one.

The sex with Juan had been like magic that night. That whole night had been magic. When they got off the train, back uptown, Juan had said they should get a couple tickets; maybe it was a lucky night. She'd never been much for the lotto but what the hell; it was like that guy said, 'Hey, you never know.' So they stopped at the corner bodega and bought five dollars worth.

It had been a week later when she found the tickets at the bottom of her bag. She knew there was a way to see if you won anything online. After a few searches, she found the site and the winning numbers from the right game. It was the third set or numbers, the third game, and she thought, 'See, we could have just spent three dollars. We didn't need to spend five dollars.' And then she said, 'Oh, my god' and whispered Juan's name. She whispered it a few more times before she started yelling for him.

'Baby, what's the matter? You OK?'

'Juan, we won.'

'What do you mean, Mami? Won what? He'd looked down at what she was doing. 'What do you mean, 'we won?' What do you mean? You don't mean … Aw, c'mon. Don't play like that.' She just looked at him, her mouth open, holding the ticket. 'Like, how many numbers did we get?'

'All of them.' He'd taken the ticket from her and compared it to the winning numbers. '¡Madre de Dios! How much?'

'I don't know,' she'd said, 'but I think it was a lot.'

'A lot' hadn't even come close; they'd won almost two hundred million dollars.

At first they didn't do anything. She finished out her time at The Plaza. The last of the long-time staff went out for drinks on the last day and everyone cried. Then she went home and tried to get used to being out of work. They took a few trips; went to visit relatives in Puerto Rico, went on a cruise, then they came back home and worked on figuring out what to do with all that money. And a few months after that, they bought their apartment. They continued to rent uptown, until it was ready, but once that Israeli guy was done with all the renovations, they moved in.

Emmie could have taken a cab but the day was so glorious she just found herself wandering uptown. Before she knew it, she'd made a sort of loop, back to the Empire State Building. She was starving and trying to think of where to eat when she remembered that Italian place. A friend once took her to this place. It looked like a pizzeria but it had the most incredible Italian food. What was it called? It had a name like that sports store chain, but different. She found it, tucked away on 37th Street and stuffed herself with the best lasagne in New York before stopping in at Saks Fifth Avenue for a little something for Juan, or Juanito, maybe both.

Poor Juan. The man just didn't know how to stop working. He'd been a construction foreman before they'd won the lottery and, instead of quitting and taking it easy, he'd ended up buying his own construction company. Well, he'd gone in with his best friend from the job, Ryan, and now they were partners in Winning Ticket Construction. He worked more now than he did before he was the boss. Emmie could usually get him to take some time off when she wanted to play, but not today. Cement. What was the big deal about cement, anyway? Whatever. She'd had a great time on her own. And she'd have a great time when he got home, too!

Enough was enough. She hailed a cab at Saks. 'One Central Park South.'

The doorman opened the door to the private lobby. 'Good afternoon Mrs Rivera.'

'Hi Henry. It's a beautiful day, isn't it?

'Yes, Ma'am.'

'Do me a favour, Henry?'

'Sure Mrs R; whatever you need.'

'Can you give me a buzz when Mr Rivera gets home?'

'No problem, Mrs Rivera.'

Immaculata took the elevator up to fifteen and unlocked her door. A lot of their friends had said they wouldn't like living down here. It wouldn't be like home. The people here weren't their kind of people. She supposed that might be true, but living here was like being home for her. It was easy getting used to. She just slipped right in to the groove, like she'd been here all her life, which, she supposed, she sort of had. Everything was luck. It was all luck. 'Who knew,' she thought, as she looked through the fridge trying to decide between the steak in the freezer and the left-over Chinese. Left-over Chinese wasn't too romantic, but you didn't have to defrost it! And besides, She planned to keep Juan too busy to care much about food.

She cut the tags out of her purchases and then tried them on. The beige push-up bra with black lace overlay really was stunning and the matching French tap pant was definitely sexier than a thong. Her signature bun was still neat and tight. She grabbed her new toy just as the intercom buzzed. Just enough time to settle herself on the couch and wait for Juan to appear.

He found a semi-nude, almost better than nude, Immaculata draped over the couch in the living room. 'What kept you, Papi? I thought you'd never get here! Do you like what I bought for you today?'

Juan, tired to wipe the grin off his face. 'I don't think they'll fit me, but they look OK on you. I guess you should keep them. What else do you have there? Is that some kind of candy?' Juan plopped himself down and snuggled under her head and shoulder and leaned in for a welcome home kiss.

'It's an *objet d'art*.'

'Art? I don't know, Emmie; I think someone ripped you off if they told you it was a piece of art. It looks more like a fancy dildo to me.'

160

Immaculata smacked his shoulder and laughed. 'When did you get so smart? I thought it was pretty and you might like to play with it. It could be fun, don't you think?'

'I think you could be fun. But if you want to play, who am I to say no?'

'That's right,' she said, and you better not forget it!'

Juan swept her off the couch and carried her to the bedroom.

'How was the cement?'

Juan put her hand on his crotch. 'I think it's gettin' pretty good,' he said. He pulled his shirt over his head and undid his jeans. 'Baby, you look so hot in those cute little panties.' He put his hands on her hips and nuzzled the back of her neck. 'Emmie, take your hair down for me?'

It never ceased to amaze him that the removal of only a few hairpins could cause her long black hair to cascade down her back and over his hands. The smell was intoxicating. He hugged her to him, burying his face in her hair, and grabbed both breasts, squeezing them through the new bra.

She was still holding the pins when he bent her forward and gave her ass a smack.

'What was that for?'

'It seemed like the right thing to do at the time. Look at that view Mami! I think I'm gonna fuck you just like this so we can both look at the view. Our view.' He ran his fingers between her legs and felt the damp lace. Pushing the delicate fabric aside, he stroked the close-cropped hair covering her slit and ran his other hand up her back to her neck, brushing her hair to either side of her body. Kissing her gently on the neck, he slowly inserted two fingers in her waiting cunt. 'So sexy, Baby,' he whispered. Little involuntary shivers ran down her body. 'You want Papi to fuck you like this? From behind?' His fingers never stopped moving in and out of her.

He removed his fingers and slowly fed his cock to her pussy. Once their bodies touched, she began to rock back

161

and forth against him, the hair on his balls tickling her ass with each stroke, until he grabbed her hips and pounded against her. Buried all the way inside, he stopped and said, 'Emmie, look up. Look out the window.'

She brought her head up and looked. The light was like blue gold. All the leaves sparkled on the trees in the park. The air was so clear, as the sun set, the park and the surrounding buildings looked like they went on forever.

'I didn't want you to miss it,' he said as he began his slow pound again, working his way up to the bone-shattering fuck she loved so much. They fucked and watched the sun go down on the city. As the lights came on in the park, Juan flipped her over and finished in the way she like the best. She grabbed handfuls of his ass and worked her mouth over his nipple, licking and biting and teasing until he couldn't stand it anymore.

'Baby, I'm gonna come.' No sooner had he spoken the words than she felt the beginning of his orgasm. He collapsed on top of her and lay there for a bit. 'Man, I'm starving,' he said. 'What's for dinner?'

'What's for dinner? What's for dinner? Hey! What about me?'

'Oh, Emmie, oh no!'

Immaculata laughed. 'It's all right. This was only round one. There's some Chinese in the fridge and then you can have me for desert!'

He rolled off of her, looking kind of sheepish, and headed in the direction of the kitchen. She realized she was still holding her hairpins. She set them on the bed table and followed his retreating form.

About the Story

THE PLAZA HOTEL SITS at the south-eastern tip of Central Park, at Grand Army Plaza, bounded primarily by 5th Avenue and Central Park South (or 59th Street). It's been there since 1907. It was sold in 2004 and closed its doors to the public for renovation. Since the renovations were expected to take an unknown amount of time, the hotel staff, many of whom had worked their entire adult lives at The Plaza, were let go. I had the pleasure of attending the last affair held in The Grand Ballroom before the hotel was set to close. The waiters were surly, but who could blame them?

You see, New York is a city of professional waiters; not the sort of waiters who tell you their names and don't know how to pronounce the specials, but the sort who belong to the waiter's union and have made a career out of waiting table. It's the same for the housekeeping staff, the bartenders and the doormen at all the elite institutions, like The Plaza.

So The Plaza was sold to some Israeli guy and then it was closed. I guess, in a way, the thought of losing the landmark made me feel a bit like the surly waiters. The evening and my thoughts about the closure stuck with me ... and then morphed into an erotic story about my city. Go figure. But that's what I do. Most of my thoughts end up working their way into an erotic story somewhere along the line.

Park Suite is another of my love songs to New York and, as with any good love song, it's got its passionately dirty moments, as well as its romantic ones. I hope you were able to get a taste of the energy, the people, the attitude and the romance of the city. If you did, even a little, I've been successful.

Passion Hack
by Michael Hemmingson

1

FIFTEEN MINUTES AFTER HER boss left for lunch, a man in a blue shirt delivered a dozen yellow roses to Jill Emerson. On the card: *Happy birthday, sexy darling*.

There was no mistake about who sent them; there was only one man who called her *sexy darling* and she both loathed and welcomed it. They were meaningless words from him because he was a married man, and they were words that made her feel attractive and wanted.

It wasn't like there were any *other* men saying these words, or delivering her flowers.

Her boss, Evan Hudson, a tax lawyer, returned forty minutes later and she could smell the three-martini lunch lingering around him.

'Well, look at those,' he said, eying the roses.

She had placed them prominently on her desk.

'Yes, they came while you were away, Mr Hudson.'

'Looks like someone is vying for you attention, Jill.'

'They seem to have gotten it, Mr Hudson,' she said.

He went into his office leaving her at her small desk, her manual typewriter, her phone and intercom, and her roses.

A few minutes later, the intercom buzzed. 'Can you come in here for a moment, Jill?'

'Yes, Mr Hudson.'

She straightened her long brown wool skirt, adjusted her

pale blue blouse, opened the door to the inner sanctum of her boss's office, and walked in.

She knew what was coming and she was both scared and excited, like she always was.

It was a different world in his office: the space was huge, three times the size of the room she rented in the Village. There was original art on the walls, and framed photos of Evan Hudson's trips around the world: big game safari in Africa, marlin fishing in the Florida Keys, trout fishing in various places in America, climbing mountains somewhere in Europe. He kept photos of his wife and three kids on his desk. At age forty-seven, Evan Hudson, Esq., was a success, fit, tanned, had a full set of hair, some grey, always wore $200 suits, and was attractive to many women, whether he was married or not.

And here she was, she thought, just 22 years old today, and she was in love with him, trapped in a hopeless fantasy that one day soon he would leave his wife and marry her, and she would have her photo on his desk and the new Mrs Hudson.

He was at the fully-stocked bar, making two scotch and sodas.

'Bitters?' he asked.

'Yes, please.' Why did he always ask what he should have known? How many drinks had she had in this office with him?

He turned and handed her the drink. 'I just wanted to say, Jill ... happy birthday.'

'Thank you for the flowers ... Evan.' It was Mr Hudson outside this space, where others in the office might hear them, Evan inside, or in a bar, restaurant, or hotel room.

'Cheers.'

They drank. He gulped the scotch down and she sipped. It was afternoon; she didn't like to get tipsy this early, or at work.

She knew what was coming next. He was feeling randy after the martinis.

'My God, those big beautiful breasts,' he said, moving in to grab one with his free hand.

Then he kissed her.

She could taste the vodka and vermouth on his tongue, mixed with cigarette and scotch. Not the best for kissing, or even smelling, but she was used to it, and she wanted him now. Her fear subsided, replaced with sinful lust.

She whispered, 'Take me if you want.'

'A birthday roll.'

'I've been waiting for this all day,' she admitted, without shame.

'You wanton little wench, always ready and willing for a good time. Have I said how glad I am that I hired you?'

Jill unbuttoned her blouse and removed it. Then: off with the bra. Hudson immediately placed his hands and mouth on her breasts, licking and gently biting her hard, pink nipples.

'Firm, wonderful, 22-year-old tits,' he said, his voice muffled.

Yes she knew: he didn't get this at home from his 39-year-old wife.

They moved to the leather sofa, where clients usually sat, where he had undoubtedly made other young women in the past. She never asked how many other secretaries he had slept with and she didn't want to know.

She removed her skirt and panties, leaving the garters on. She wore them to work because she knew how much he liked them.

Hudson was pulling down his trousers and loosening his shirt and tie.

'My diaphragm is in, don't worry,' she told him.

'You came prepared,' he said with a little laugh. 'You tricky trollop.'

'This sinning strumpet wants you now, darling,' she said with her arms out.

He took a moment to admire her. 'A natural blonde, how lucky am I? Sometimes I feel like I have it all.'

You do, she thought, you have a large home on Long

Island, you have a wife who is a successful children's book author, you have children who excel in school, you have a profitable job, and you're laying your blonde secretary: what more could a middle-aged man desire?

He positioned himself over her. She took his erect manhood in her hand and guided it into her warm, dark wetness. She always had to do this, he had bad aim. That was all right with her. She liked to touch it. She liked how it felt. He was the third man she'd been with in her life and she never touched the other two. She wondered what it was like to have it in her mouth; she heard about girls doing this but she had not tried it yet. She was too embarrassed to bring it up with Hudson and she always hoped he would ask her but he never did.

They made love for twenty minutes on the office couch. The one positive factor of his three-martini lunch was that alcohol caused him to not reach fulfilment so fast; when he didn't drink, sex was generally five minutes or less and it usually took Jill ten minutes to reach satisfaction. Today, she had two of them: two birthday orgasms, feeling light-headed and warm from the bourbon.

Afterwards, they lay on the couch in each other's arms and didn't speak for fifteen minutes. It was very nice being this way; they were comfortable with each other's naked bodies, like married people.

'Again?' she suggested.

'Oh, I wish I could, sexy darling, but I'm an old man,' he reminded her, 'and there's still work to be done.'

With that, he stood up, pulled his trousers up, adjusted his tie.

She dressed.

'Take your time, darling,' he said. He sat behind the oak wood desk and leaned back in the swivel chair. 'I love watching you put your clothes on after sex,' he told her, 'as much as I love watching you take them off.'

She gave him his show: slowly putting her skirt back on, zipping it to the side, snug against her round hips. She her put bra on, turning away to tease him. 'No fair!' he said and chuckled. She did a little dance with the blouse, then buttoned it up.

'Thank you for the flowers and the sex,' she said.

'Hey, that's what I'm here for.'

'Need any letters typed?'

'In a few minutes, darling. Oh, I'm leaving two hours early today, at three, so you can leave whenever you want after three.'

'Oh,' she said. 'Why three?'

'Andrea is in town, meeting with her editor,' he said cautiously. Andrea was his wife and he knew it was a sensitive subject with his secretary/lover.

'I see,' Jill said.

She tried to not to let it show: disappointment, anger, jealousy. She loathed these feelings; she only wanted happiness, contentment, and love.

'Dinner tomorrow night, perhaps?' he said.

'OK,' she said weakly.

She turned to leave.

Her boss said, 'Hey, happy birthday again, sexy darling.'

'Thank you again … Mr Hudson.'

Sitting at her desk, she wanted to scream and cry. The other secretaries in the office passed by and commented on her nice roses. 'Your boyfriend, or a secret admirer?' they said.

She only smiled and didn't reply.

The smile was an effort.

She felt miserable.

She wanted to jump off the Empire State Building.

And maybe she *would*. She'd go have a few drinks and then make her way over to the tall building, ride the elevator to the top, and end her pain in one quick gesture of hopelessness. People jumped from there often, she heard, making quite a mess on the ground, the way King Kong did in that Fay Wray movie.

What was she doing? Was she crazy? She felt pathetic.

Here she was, twenty-two, and crazily in love with her married boss. Was it love, truly? It was something.

He'd never leave his wife, they were too good a couple: the rich lawyer and the respected author. She had seen their photos in the society pages and tried to picture herself in the role. She was just a simple girl from Bloomington, Indiana, a secretary with no college degree.

The only thing she had going for her was her looks: long blonde hair, big breasts, curvy hips, sleek legs. When she had come to New York three years ago, age nineteen, men told her she could make money modelling; not fashion or glamour modelling, but semi-nude or even nude. She was told there was quite a market and girls made a good living. She refused.

Here she was, today, on April 21, 1959: twenty-two and going nowhere. She had no future, at least not with Evan Hudson, Esq. Why couldn't she meet a nice, unattached man here in Manhattan, her age, maybe early 30s, looking for a good wife to settle down and have 2.5 kids with? The New Jersey house, the summer cottage upstate, three cars, a maid or nanny, the whole works. Was that too much for a girl to ask for, to dream?

2

Jill Emerson left the office at 3:30 p.m., a half an hour after her boss departed to meet his wife. She finished up the letters he had dictated on the recorder, placed them in envelopes and into the outgoing mail bin, and got the hell out of that building on Eighth Street near MacDougal.

The one good thing about working in an office near Greenwich Village was that she could walk to work; she had rented a simple room two months ago. Before that, she lived in Brooklyn and had to take the crowded, smelly subway and deal with the prying eyes of perverted men and college boys asking her for a date.

Also, with a room nearby, Hudson didn't always have to

rent a hotel room if they were going to spend time together. He didn't care much for the room, too cramped; he liked to spend his money on lavish suites uptown. They had only spent the night together once during the past five months, when his wife was out of town.

Thinking about her lacklustre, tawdry affair made her want to drink. She decided to go to the bar on Seventh Avenue, not too far from where she lived in the four-story brownstone on Grove Street, a quieter section of the Village, away from all the jazz clubs and beatniks on the street shouting out poetry and playing bongos.

The bar was called Rainy Day. It was a cosy, dark little hole in the wall, generally a mixture of business people and Village residents who didn't mind the over-priced drinks. She had never been here alone; she always came with Evan, and he paid for the drinks. What the hell, it was her birthday, she would splurge on a few.

On her second martini, feeling warm and fuzzy, she decided the hell with Evan Hudson, married lawyer, and she would go to bed with the first man who bought her a drink and tried to make her. She hoped he wasn't too old or bad-looking.

C'mon, boys, who will it be?

Several men in the bar had looked her over, but none had yet come to talk to her.

Finally, one sat next to her at the counter.

He walked in, looked around, and took the empty seat next to her. He ordered a beer. He acted like he didn't notice her. She pushed her breasts out ever so subtly and asked the bartender for a third martini.

'Olives, get lots of olives,' the man next to her said. 'Three, maybe five.'

'One is good enough for me,' she said.

'They're healthy, good for your liver as the booze eats it away. That's why I stick to beer. I feel sorry for my liver. We used to be such good pals.'

She giggled. A funny guy. She considered him: she

guessed he was in his mid or late twenties, or he could be in his early thirties and just had a boyish look to him. He also had a boyish charm, with that almost irresistible smile; his teeth were a little uneven but they looked healthy and white, not always the case with barflies. *If* he was a regular boozer, he seemed out of place for the Village in a flannel shirt and khaki pants.

'How about your heart?' she asked.

'Eh?'

'Are you friends with your heart?'

He thought about that. 'I'd like to be, but the ol' heart is a stranger. Maybe I need to take my heart out to a romantic dinner.' He drank a shot of rye next. 'Or maybe just go straight to the sack with it and show it a wild good night, one for the books.'

She sipped her martini as he ordered another shot, this time bourbon, and another beer, mumbling it wasn't a rye sort of day.

She said, 'I'm starting to think my heart has it in for me. It's my secret enemy, wishing me ill will.'

'A foe?'

'A friend who betrays.'

'A nemesis!'

'Sure.'

'Best to break your own heart first, before someone else does,' he said. 'This way you'll be toughened up when someone comes after it, ready to toss it on the linoleum and smash it under boot.'

She giggled again. 'You're a funny man, Mr ...?'

'Challon. David Challon.'

'Mr Challon.'

'David, please.'

'Dave?'

'Dave works.'

'I'm Jill.'

'Hi, Jill.'

'Hello, David.'

'Dave!'

'David,' and she giggled again.

'Can I buy you another martini?'

'I'll have what you're having.'

'Bourbon?'

'Why not. I started the day with it.'

'Two bourbons!' he said to the barkeep.

3

He wasn't from the Village, said he lived uptown in a rented room. He was down here to visit 'a friend' and stopped off at Rainy Day before taking the subway back home.

Jill didn't press him if this *friend* was a woman or a man, since he said the word with a bitter inflection to his voice.

She didn't care, either.

She liked him, though; he was witty and articulate and could hold his booze well. He wasn't hard on the eyes, either; which was why, after a number of drinks, she invited him to her room on Grove Street and they immediately got busy with the act of sex.

She pushed Hudson out of her head; she didn't want to think about the fact that she would now have slept with two men on the same day. That's something tramps and prostitutes did, not a career girl.

What did it matter?

He was here; he was taking her clothes off; he was already naked, and they fell onto the single bed that sat in the corner of the room, where she took her pleasure from the obelisk of his strength .

It erupted into a quick and furious climax. The bold delights she sought thrust her to a crest and dropped her as if the earth had fallen away from under her lust-drunk body. She lay there, trembling and quivering, with the warm delight of fulfilment.

And she lay sleepless that night in her bed, going over it again and again. She wanted to make it last for ever in the

173

aching sweetness that was never meant to last, too violent to last, too agonizingly pleasurable to end.

She kept waking him up for more.

He gave her more.

In the morning, he said, 'Are you trying to kill a guy?'

'There are some I'd *like* to kill,' she told him, thinking about her boss, 'but you, I just want to love you over and over and over again.'

She called in sick to work and they stayed in bed all day, except when they went out to the corner liquor store to get some beer and bourbon.

4

David Challon lived in a $10 a week room up on 114th Street, near Columbia University. He said it was a good place to write, and there were two other writers there; the rest of the tenants were old people, drunks, and college kids.

'What do you mean, "write"?' Jill asked.

'That's what I do, I write.'

'Write what? Laundry lists? Christmas jingles?'

He laughed. 'I should, that'd be more honest and worthwhile. I'm a hack, a pulp hack. I have no delusions, I'm not Hemingway or Wolfe, I write trash and people buy it and like it and the pay is okay, the pay is better than breaking my back in some ditch.'

'You write …?'

'Books, sweetie. Paperback junk. You name it, I'll do it if there's a paycheck: science-fiction yarns, hard-nosed detectives, manly cowboys, wayward wenches, troublesome trollops, hellcat hellions. That was the title of my first sexy novel: *Hellcat Hellion on Sin Campus*. It just came out a few months ago. A lost masterpiece, I'm sure. There have been half a dozen since, half a dozen forthcoming, half a dozen yet to write. I do one a month.'

Jill didn't know whether to believe him or not but he didn't have a day job, that was for sure; he woke up and

174

drank whenever he wanted, and he wasn't broke, he always seemed to have money on him and he spent it without a worry.

Nice things end too fast and she had to go back to work and he said he had a novel he had to finish this week, adding that it usually took him ten or twelve days. 'A twenty-page chapter a day,' he said, 'it's amazing how quick you get to 50,000 words.' Now she knew he was joking around; who writes a novel that fast? Who writes 20 pages a day? She had heard that novelists work years on books.

She was curious to know more and they made a date for Friday after work; she would go up there to see him and they'd have dinner, drinks, whatever happened after that.

5

At work, she avoided Hudson's remarks and glances and winks. When he wanted to have a session in his office, she said she was on her period and had a headache. 'Darn,' said her boss, 'Next week. What a wait!'

She looked at him differently; he was not the man she thought he was. He was too old, too flabby, too sure of himself, and she never cared for that horrid cologne he liked to wear.

She had David Challon on her mind every minute of the day. She couldn't wait for Friday.

She would wear something tight and sexy; she had *just* the plaid skirt and black sweater to do the trick.

6

He wasn't fooling her. David Challon was a writer all right.

His rented room was on the fifth floor of the building on 114th. The halls smelled like cooked chicken and flour and mould. At his door, she could hear a typewriter clacking away and, whoever it was, they sure typed fast. At first she felt a pang of jealousy, thinking some girl was in there, but

175

then realized David was doing his own typing.

She knocked.

The typing stopped.

The door opened.

'Oh,' he said, looking surprised, 'Hi. Hello. Come in.'

He wore a dirty T-shirt and khaki pants. He had two or three days of unshaven beard on his face. She liked the look.

'Did you forget our date?' she asked.

'No, no,' he said, smiling, touching her shoulder, 'I lost track of time. Happens sometimes when I'm on a roll with a novel, or even a story.'

A black Remington typewriter sat on a card table, the table next to the window. Also on the table were various stacks of tying paper, white and yellow, and carbon paper. There was a single bed in the corner, not unlike the bed in her room. There were also several hundred paperback books scattered all over the room; on two small bookshelves, on the floor, in boxes, some on the sink, some on the bed, some under the bed, some on the windowsill.

'Don't tell me you wrote all these,' she said.

He laughed at that. 'I wish. I'd be dead by now from exhaustion . But I *did* write some of them,' and he gestured to one of the small shelves. 'These are all mine.'

There was pride in his voice.

Only three had 'David Challon' on the covers, two science-fictions and one mystery: *Revolt on Beta Moon 13, To Kill a Galaxy* and *Death Never Turns the Door Knob*. The rest had other men's names: as Al Dwight, there was *Invasion of the Radioactive Slugs from Deep Down, The Falling Aliens Are Dizzy, Diary of a Teenage Martian Psycho Killer,* and *I Will Blow Up Your Sun or Rule Your World – Choose*! As Dan Hawthorne , there was *Hellcat Hellion on Sin Campus* (which David had mentioned), *Lust Among the Wanton Sinners, Desire My Sire, Bad Sexy Girlfriend in White Shorts and Yellow Halter, I See You Naked and I Love It ...*

He explained to her these were pseudonyms, pen names,

and why they were used: 'Mostly the publishers prefer it. Some are 'house names' that many fellows, and gals, write under; some are just trash I wrote based on an idea or outline some editor gave me and I'd rather not have my name on; and some, like the, uh, more explicit books, well, I don't want the police to come knock down my door and take me in for obscenity.'

'You can get arrested for writing this?' She picked up *Lust Among the Wanton Sinners* and leafed through it.

'It happens.'

She spotted a love-making scene. 'Racy.'

'Sleazy.'

'How much do you get paid for these books?'

He shrugged and lit a cigarette. '$500–700, depends. One I only got $250 for, the damn publisher went out of business and still owes me $300 that I'll never see.'

'And you write one a week?'

'More like two a month: one sleaze, one mystery or sci-fi. The rest of the time I work on short stories or my big fat serious novel, it's about the Civil War.'

'Really?'

'Called *The Sound of Distant Drums*.'

'I like Civil War stories. I loved *Gone with the Wind*.'

He made a face. 'Frankly my dear ...'

She giggled. 'I don't give a hoot.'

'You don't swear?'

'Hell no.'

He laughed and grabbed her and kissed her.

She handed him the racy book back. 'That's pretty good money, so why do you live ... here?'

'This dump?'

'In a manner of words.'

'Habit and familiarity,' he said. 'I lived here when I hadn't sold a word. I had seventy bucks to my name. I was hungry, crazy, scared. That was two years ago. I wrote a dozen stories over three weeks until I finally sold one. Good thing, too, as I had five dollars and two cents in my pocket.

Yes, that was two years ago. I've barely gotten away from this typewriter since.'

'You're up on your feet now.'

'*And* I have money to take a beautiful dame like you to a fancy schmancy restaurant tonight.'

'Oh really now?'

'Let me change.'

He took his t-shirt off. She licked her lips. She liked what she saw. He was so much more slender, with muscles, than Hudson.

'Wait,' she said, going to him. 'No need to rush,' and she pushed him onto the bed.

'Aggressive,' he said.

'You don't like it?'

'It's different.'

'I'll show you something different, big boy.'

She started kissing his chest, kissing down his stomach, unzipping his pants.

'Cripes,' he said, his eyes wide.

'What's the matter?'

'Nothing, just …'

'Just?' she said. She reached into his pants, pulling away at his boxer shorts, reaching into the front opening, grasping his manhood with an her eager, wanton hand.

He said, 'Just not many girls do this … with their … you know …'

'*Respectable* girls, you mean?'

'I mean …'

'I'm not most girls,' Jill said. She'd never done this, either, but she'd read about it, and now was the time to give it a try.

David didn't complain.

7

They walked down 115th to a restaurant he knew and she took his arm and squeezed. She looked happy. 'I can't believe I'm seeing a real *bona fide* writer,' she said. 'If my parents could see me now!'

'I don't know about *bona fide,*' he said. He was amused by the label.

'How about 'real'?'

'I'm just a hack. I'm not delusional.'

'You'll be famous one day,' she told him. 'Famous and rich.'

'I'll settle for rich.'

'Is it just about the money?' she asked.

'Money you can't shake a stick at, pretty lady.'

'What about art?' she asked.

'Good question,' he replied. 'What about it?'

8

They saw each other two or three times a week for the next month. The love-making was passionate and fulfilling and Jill found herself not needing any other man, especially her boss. But it was hard to keep coming up with excuses to not have sex with Hudson. She gave in now and then because he was so forceful and insistent. She felt guilty after. But why? She and David had not made any exclusive agreement, although she wanted to.

She was thinking of marriage to the writer; she could see herself as an author's wife, even the wife of a great novelist. She imagined *The Sound of Distant Drums* read in college classes, professors discussing the symbolism and importance of such a tome. The dedication on the book would read: 'For my darling wife, Jill, who stood at my side and made this possible.' She would be immortalized! A hundred years from now, scholars and students would do research on her, wonder who the real Jill Challon was.

Jill Challon.

Nice.

So one day after giving in to Hudson, after a quick two-minute lay across his desk, she said, 'Mr Hudson, I can't do this any more.'

He gave her a funny look. '*Mr* Hudson?'

'Evan,' she said seriously, 'this is the last time. I can't … not any more.'

'What? Why?'

'I'm … seeing someone.'

'So?'

'It's serious.'

'This is just sex.'

'Well …'

'You love sex.'

'I'm in love with him.'

'Do you plan to marry the lucky fellah?'

'I …' She stopped. 'Yes.'

'So. I'm married. Married people have their affairs. No reason for us to stop.'

'I have to stop … Evan. Please.'

'You like your job?' he said.

She was surprised by the question. 'Are you threatening to fire me, if I don't …'

'Not at all.' He smiled. 'This has always been physical. I know you could never love a man like me, although I could give you the world.'

'And you have a wife.'

'Think about this. You're being … emotional. Just look at it as part of the job, keeping the boss happy. I like to be happy. When I'm happy, paychecks sometimes have a bonus.'

She knew she had to find another job. She had to quit. *Now.* Before she left for lunch, after Hudson had stepped out for a client meeting, she typed up a letter of resignation, asking for her last paycheck to be mailed.

She felt an incredible weight lifted from her heart when she walked away from the office.

She thought she'd surprise David, now that she had the rest of the day free. She went to her room and changed into the blue summer dress he liked. It was a warm day in Manhattan, the kind of day for such a dress. She didn't wear a bra, so that her nipples were visible. She couldn't take the subway like this, having men and boys leer at her and trying to cop a feel as they sometimes did, so she splurged and took a cab uptown. It would be her last big spend until she found a new job. She had enough saved to last her two months, but she wanted to be working again by next week. What else would she do?

She heard voices in David's room. She pressed her ear to the door. His voice, and a woman's, and classical music on the radio. They were both laughing. She couldn't make out what they were saying. She felt ugly pain in her chest.

She touched the doorknob. It wasn't locked. She thought about the title of one of his books: *Death Never Turns the Door Knob.*

Turn around and leave, she told herself. Don't go in there. Forget about it. He wasn't expecting you.

She turned the knob and opened the door.

She walked in.

They didn't see her at first.

David sat at his card table, a woman in his lap. The woman only wore a black bra and garters.

David was naked.

They were giggling and kissing and sharing a bottle of wine.

'David?' she said.

They stopped and turned to her.

'Jill, my God,' David said. 'What the hell are you doing here?'

'And *who* is *this*?' the half-naked woman asked. 'Another one of your floozies, Davey?' The woman was drunk. She was older – in her mid-thirties, wore a lot of make-up. Her hair was reddish-brown and her breasts were so small that Jill wondered why she bothered with a bra.

David gently pushed the woman off his lap and stood up. 'Jill, what are you doing here?'

He found a pair of pants on the floor and put them on.

Jill was in tears. 'David, how *could you?*'

The woman giggled. 'Yeah, David, *how* could you? You did it again. You broke another heart. Tsk tsk, you naughty sexy boy.'

'Who are you?' Jill nearly screamed at the woman.

'I should ask you the same,' the woman said, and took a long drink from the wine bottle.

David put a shirt on. 'This is the definition of awkwardness.'

'I'll make it easy for you, you cad you.' The woman handed him the bottle and started to collect her clothes.

The clothes looked expensive; a matching aqua blue skirt and jacket, a white silk blouse.

Jill noticed the jewellery the woman wore – two necklaces, earrings, and gold watch on her wrist – all with diamonds.

'Oh my,' David said. He sat on the edge of his bed and put his face in his hands. 'I'm too drunk to deal with this.'

'Deal with it,' the woman said, dressed now. 'Explain to this poor little girl the rules of the adult world and the facts of eros. See you tomorrow?'

David didn't answer.

The woman turned to Jill. 'Don't feel too special. He does this to every woman he meets. This isn't the first time we've … well …'

The woman left.

Jill stood in the centre of the room, unable to move, tears still in her eyes.

David looked up. 'What are you doing here, Jill? Shouldn't you be at work?'

'I quit,' she said softly.

'You did what?'

'I wanted to surprise you.'

'Well, you did that quite splendidly.'

'Who is that woman?'

'No one. Just a … woman. Someone I know.'

'Did you make love to her?'

He groaned. 'What do you want me to say? Are we married?'

I'm a hypocrite, she thought. She'd just had sex with her boss two hours ago, and had been the past month: her dirty secret. David wasn't guilty of any sin she hadn't committed herself.

Married …

'No, we're not.' She sat down next to him and touched hid hand. 'But we could be.'

'Eh?'

'Do you love her?'

'Who? Diane? No. Hell, no. She's just – she's just this wealthy widow I know from the Village. She lives by you, actually. Sort of. Same area.'

She nodded. 'Were you seeing her the day we met?'

'I had broken up with her.'

'So you don't love her.'

'She's a vampire,' he said. 'She sucks … life out of you.'

'Then why …?'

'She showed up at my door. Like you did. This is the day for big surprises, huh? Jesus, I should've never gotten out of bed.'

'You don't need to see her any more, David.'

'I don't want to. Believe me. Look what she did, talked me into wasting a writing day, talked me into drinking …'

'I don't want to know,' Jill said. She took his hand in hers. 'I forgive you.'

'Do I need forgiveness?'

'I want to be your wife,' she told him, 'I want your baby.'

'Gee, no gal's ever put it that way.' He grinned.

'I'm serious.'

'You want me?'

'I love you.'

They embraced. He tasted of wine and he smelled of that other woman's perfume, but she put it out of her mind.

10

She spent the night there and they ordered a pizza and beer and they laughed it all off – that other woman, Jill's job (she didn't tell him the real reason why she quit) – and they made love and talked marriage and babies and everything seemed perfect and nice.

David woke up at seven in the morning and told her he needed to catch up on the writing time he missed yesterday. He was all business. He seemed distant but she didn't fault him. He had to work and make money. And she had to go and find another job.

She kissed him goodbye.

'See you tonight?' she asked.

'Tonight, sure,' he said.

11

Outside the building where she lived, Jill had her own surprise visitor waiting: Evan Hudson. He wore an overcoat and a hat and he looked like something out of a detective movie.

He looked disturbed.

He spotted her.

She had no time to turn away.

He said, 'Jill.'

She tried to appear distant. 'Mr Hudson … what are you doing here?'

'Where have you been? You were gone all night.'

Coldly: 'I don't think that is any of your business.'

He brought out a folded envelope from his jacket and handed it to her. 'Your paycheck, with a bonus.'

'You could have mailed it.'

'I needed to see you.'

'Why?'

'Don't leave me, Jill darling.'

'I'm sorry, I have to. You know why.'

'I thought about what you said and I was jealous, jealous of that other man. I don't want anyone else to have you. So I have decided to leave my wife. I'll divorce her as soon as possible.'

'Why?' she asked.

'So we can be together properly. Not as secretary and boss, but as … husband and wife.'

She couldn't believe what she was hearing. 'Mr Hudson … Evan … that's crazy.'

'I'm *crazy* about you.' He grabbed her, held her. It was a swift and bold move on the street.

'Mr Hudson!' she cried. 'Evan, don't. You don't love me and you know it.'

He said, 'I always have. I was afraid to say so.'

She said, 'Let go of me.'

'Let's go up to your room,' he said, trying to kiss her. 'We'll make love properly, like we should have always been doing.'

She tried pushing him away. 'Stop.'

'I can't lose you.'

'Let me go or I'll scream rape!'

She was serious.

He stepped back.

'So sorry,' he said. 'Damn sorry.'

'Evan, go back to your office,' she said, 'go back to your work, go back to your wife, and forget about me. All right?'

'I can't.'

'You have to.'

'I don't want to.'

'You have no choice.'

'You really love this other man?'

'With all my heart,' she said.

He looked down.

She went into the building, afraid he would follow her in, force himself on her.

He didn't.

He stood on the street, watching her.

'Jill,' he said.

'Goodbye, Mr Hudson,' she said.

12

The 'bonus' on her check was for $2,000. That amount made her head spin. Was this supposed to have been a bribe, to make her come back? Why did men believe money could sway a girl? Well, some girls were influenced by dollar signs, she knew this was true.

Who needed money when you had love? Who could put a price on that?

She considered giving it back. She didn't want Hudson's dirty bribe money, this payment for all the sordid sex.

She thought it over.

She deserved the money.

She could put it to good use.

She couldn't wait to tell David! He could take some time off, they could go on a trip, or they could get a nice apartment here in the Village or mid-town and live together, and … and …

She was restless, waiting for the end of the day. She bought a newspaper at the corner stand, to look in the employment section. She spotted one of David's books on the stand: *Hellcat Hellion on Sin Campus*. The old man who worked the newsstand gave her an odd look when she presented the sleazy little book for purchase. She supposed women didn't often buy these things.

She read some of it, back in her room, and laughed out loud during certain parts. It was truly tawdry and badly written. No wonder he didn't want his name on the cover.

At six o'clock, she dressed for the evening and took a cab uptown. This time she would treat *him* to a nice dinner.

She found a short woman in her fifties, wearing a drab potato sack dress and apron, vacuuming in David's room.

The room was empty: no card table, no typewriter, and no scattered books.

'Excuse me,' she said to the woman, 'where is the young man who lives here?'

The woman looked up. 'Who?'

'David Challon, this his ...'

No. Oh, no.

The woman looked Jill up and down and shook her head. 'You're the second lady to come by and ask about him. I tell you what I told her: he's gone. He moved out. Packed his bags and books and left. Good riddance, I say. Always making so much noise!'

'Moved?' Jill felt dizzy.

'Moved.'

'Where?'

'How am I supposed to know?'

'Oh no.'

'Skip out on you, did he?'

'David,' she said.

'Oh, I found this under the bed.' The woman reached into her apron and brought out a book: *To Kill a Galaxy* by David Challon. 'Want it?'

Jill nodded and accepted the paperback.

She scanned the pages. Maybe he left it on purpose; maybe he left a note for her, telling her where he was.

Nothing.

The dedication page read: *To Lucy, my first love – I'm sorry*.

What did that other woman say about the hearts he had broken? She wasn't special?

Jill left the building. The sun was gone and night settled over Manhattan like death at the door knob. People were starting to come out and fill the streets.

The night would be long, lonely and painful.

Jill walked into the first bar she saw.

About the Story

NEW YORK CITY IS mecca for any writer; this is where you mail your manuscripts, this is where you live to write, especially in the days of paperback pulps, when this story is set. The past year, I have been reading a lot of vintage *sleaze* novels, and sometimes pulp writer alter egos pop up in the books. One particular inspiration for my story was *Thirst for Love* by Mark Ryan (Bedstand Books, 1959) later reprinted as *Wayward Wife* by Loren Beauchamp (Midwood, 1962). Both are pen names once used by Robert Silverberg. A major part of his novel concerns a young alcoholic widow who gets entangled romantically with a pulp author. I identified with the guy.

I love New York but I could never live there. I love visiting, love New York women, graduates from the Seven Sisters, strippers, editors, writers, painters and streetwalkers. Like Hollywood, New York attracts people from all over the world, searching for a dream or an escape. It's easy to disappear in large cities. I would vanish if I lived there, so I'm a better tourist than resident.

Woman in White
by Lisabet Sarai

I'M NOT A STALKER. I didn't mean to freak her out. *Aie –
Dios Mio!* The last thing I wanted was to hurt her. I just
couldn't help myself. She was my goddess, my dream. My
reason for getting up in the morning.

I didn't know her name or where she lived, but still, I
knew her. Every day I'd hunker down on my milk crate
outside the Graybar entrance to Grand Central, her *Times*
and her *Wall Street Journal* already set aside and ready. I'd
wait for her cheery 'Good morning', delivered in that husky
voice that sent shivers down my spine.

'Good morning, miss.' I'd hand her the papers. She'd
give me her four bucks and a smile that turned me to jelly,
then stride away on her high heels and disappear into the
terminal. I'd stuff the bills, still warm from her hand, inside
my shirt, as close to my skin as I could get. At night, I'd
bring them out, sniffing for a hint of her perfume.

I'd lie on my cot in my cousin's kitchen, gripping my
bicho, conjuring her out of the darkness. She usually dressed
in white; fitted jackets and straight skirts that were sexy but
business-like. In snug clothes like that, someone with her
curves should have looked trashy, but somehow she was
always elegant and professional. Never mind the gold in her
earlobes, the lips painted blood red, the stilettos that had her
towering over me as I crouched near the pavement. She had
class.

I loved to imagine what she might have on underneath.

Smooth silk cradling her swelling breasts, the snowy lace a shocking contrast to her espresso-dark skin. Pale satin hugging that ripe ass and vanishing into the cleft between her thighs. I'd be hard in a minute from the pictures I painted for myself.

Her voice was in my ear, low and raw. 'Come on, baby. Give it to me,' she'd tease. She would straddle me, tits dangling in my face, brushing her pussy hair over my dick. I'd grab her meaty hips and pull her down onto my rod. Her moans drowned out the traffic, the sirens, the thud of my cousin's bed as he banged his girl in the next room.

It didn't matter how raunchy she talked. She was always a lady, even when I rammed her from behind, making her curse and clench her pussy around my dick. She was my beautiful black queen. She was practically my saint. I worshipped her with my come, pouring it out for her by the gallon. It was the only thing I could give her, aside from her papers and my nervous greeting.

She showed up every work day around eight, more predictable than the sun. Before her arrival, my heart slamming against my ribs, I kept my eyes on the crowded sidewalk, watching for the first glimpse of her curvy form coming up Lexington. After she left, I'd replay the memories: the twinkle in her eyes, her throaty laugh as she bid me good day. Had she been a bit more friendly today? Had she smiled more warmly, lingered a bit longer than usual? She hurried off to what must be some important job, maybe down on Wall Street, leaving me aching but happy.

Weekends and holidays, without my daily dose of her magic, I was miserable. Then I had to remind myself how lucky I was to be in the city at all.

Two years before, back in Santo Domingo, I killed a man. It was an accident. I was drunk. He was drunk. Before I knew what I was doing, there were knives, screams, blood pooling on the floor of the bar. My parents scraped together enough cash to get me to America. Their savings and the remains of my college tuition account went for fake papers and a one-way air ticket. It was risky, but the alternative was worse. If I stayed in DR I might rot in prison for decades.

My cousin Julio gave me a place to sleep. A friend of a friend got me the newspaper job. After my shift on the curb, I had another gig as a cleaner inside the terminal. It was hard, but I was surviving. In a few months, I'd have enough for the deposit on a room of my own.

I actually liked being a janitor. Something about Grand Central gave me hope. The first time I stood looking up at the star-studded blue vault soaring over my head, it was like being in church. I felt tiny, yet protected. The guilt that I'd been hauling around with me since I left home eased. We were in the same boat, me and all the crazy humans scurrying around me like ants. Maybe we had sinned, but there was always the possibility of forgiveness. When I finally lowered my head and rubbed at my stiff neck, I discovered tears in my eyes.

I never got tired of the place. The marble archways and grand staircases whispered of wealth, power and pleasure.

And of course, it was her temple. The gateway to her world. I wondered, if she happened on me scrubbing the floor in my orange coveralls, whether she'd recognize the shy *cabron* who provided her morning news.

Fantasy is no substitute for reality, but it's better than nothing. In the mornings, I had her smile. At night, she kept me company as I jacked off. I could at least relieve the physical need. Every time I came, though, I wanted her more.

Through summer and winter and back to spring, I offered my secret love the morning papers and my heart. Then came the day that changed everything.

It was a Tuesday, overcast and threatening rain. She was late. Eight-thirty, quarter to nine, and she still hadn't shown. My stomach twisted into knots of barbed wire. Maybe she was ill. Maybe, *Dios no lo quiera*, she had left the city.

Then I saw her, trudging along, staring down at the sidewalk. I could hardly believe that it was the same woman.

She wore a skirt and blouse of drab grey. She had the same juicy body, the perfect ebony skin, the fountain of black braids cascading down her back. But the energy that had danced through her was gone. As she plodded past me, I searched her face. Her forehead creased into a frown. Her lips pressed together as though she was struggling keep something inside. Her cheeks were wet with tears.

She didn't stop. I was suddenly desperate.

'Miss? Your papers, miss ...' I blocked her path, holding out her newspapers, which I had wrapped in plastic as protection from the weather. 'Here you are.'

She seemed dazed. It took a moment for her to focus on me. I saw gradual recognition, but no smile. 'Oh ... sorry. Never mind. I don't need them.'

'Please. Take them. You might change your mind later.'

Like a robot, she accepted the packet. She paused, looking confused. Pain sliced through my chest, echoing the pain I saw in her eyes.

'Don't ... don't worry, you can pay me tomorrow,' I stammered. 'You're late.'

A ghost of her normal smile flitted across her features. 'Yes. Yes, I'm very late. But he probably won't even notice.' A sob shook her. She forced the next one down.

'I'm sorry. Thank you.' She scanned my face as though trying to imprint it on her memory. 'After all this time, I don't know your name.'

'I'm Miguel.' My heart leaped into my throat. I 'Are you going to be all right?'

'It doesn't matter,' she whispered. I had to bend close to hear her. Her perfume swirled around me. My dick swelled inside my jeans.

'It matters to me.' My hand hovered above her shoulder. I wanted to pull her into my arms, right there on the street. I could barely resist. My imagination showed me what it would be like, to feel her melting against my body. I'd stroke her hair, comfort her, gently press my lips to hers ...

I reached for her. She was gone. While my mind was

spinning fantasies, she had disappeared into the bowels of the terminal.

No! I couldn't let her leave. She needed me. I threw a plastic tarp over the piles of newsprint and sprinted to the entrance. Pushing my way through the crowd, I hurried down the passage past the ticket machines and the fancy shops and into the concourse.

Morning in Manhattan. Thousands, maybe millions, of commuters filed back and forth through the vast hall, rushing to catch their trains or make their appointments. How could I expect to find one woman in this crush? Yet there she was, stock still near the information booth, looking lost. The tides of humanity flowed around her.

I raced over and grabbed her hand. 'Come on,' I urged. 'I know a place.' My queen followed me like a docile child. I led her through the Vanderbilt Hall to one of the side passages. The hum of voices died away. I sat her down on a marble bench in one of the arched alcoves. At one time, this corridor probably led to an exit, but now it was a dead end. Settling beside her, I dug in my pocket for a handkerchief. As she used it to wipe her eyes, I saw how I'd cherish the scrap of cotton forever.

'Don't cry, lady. I can't stand to see you so sad.' I put my arm around her shoulder, trying to ignore my throbbing dick. 'A beautiful woman like you should always be smiling.'

'Not beautiful enough for him.'

'Who? What are you talking about?'

My angel's laugh had a bitter edge. 'My boss. My married boss who told me again and again that he was going to leave his wife for me. The bastard has been lying to me for eight months. He'd promise anything, just to get into my pants.'

I could identify. My need for her was agony.

'Today I got the invitation. Next month they're renewing their vows! How could he be so stupid, to include me on the guest list? Hell, how could I be so stupid, thinking that I

193

could trust him?'

'You should forget him.' I watched her chest rise and fall as she breathed. The fine silk of her blouse hid nothing. 'Find yourself a man who appreciates you.' Open your eyes, I added silently. He's right in front of you.

'I can't.' Her eyes glistened with fresh tears. 'I love him. In spite of it all. I'm so pathetic. I can't help myself. I can't live without him ...' Her voice trailed off into a wail. She buried her face in my shoulder, and I held her tight. Her gardenia scent made me dizzy with lust. I didn't dare move.

My dreams had never been like this. I wanted her, but even more, I wanted to erase the sorrow that had quenched her glorious smile.

I was frozen. I had no idea what to do or say. If I shifted position, even a little bit, my *pinga* was going to spurt right inside my pants.

She was the one who made the decision. She raised her tear-stained face to mine and gave me a little grin. 'Thanks for listening, Miguel.' She added my name as though trying to fix it in her mind. Then she kissed me.

Her lips were as soft. Her tongue was as bold. She tasted like coffee, strong and black. She left me breathless.

She gripped my shoulders and mashed her pillowy breasts into my chest. Awkward, sure that I'd shoot in the next instant, I stroked her back with trembling hands. The thin fabric stretched across her shoulders was like a second skin. My fingers caught on the clasp of her bra. White lace fluttered in my mind. I could unhook the thing through her clothing if I wanted, if I dared. She moaned and tightened her arms around me.

I let myself wander further, to her waist and over her hips. Her abundant flesh made my palms tingle. Her skirt was made of denser stuff than her top, with a pebbly texture, but if I applied a bit of pressure, I could feel the elastic band of her panties hugging her body. I traced the line across the small of her back. Amazed at my own courage, I slipped my hands down to cup her butt, massaging her ripeness. She writhed in my arms. My dick surged inside my jeans as I struggled for control.

Her kiss became frantic. She sucked at my mouth as if she wanted to swallow me whole. Her teeth battered my lips. I tasted blood. I didn't care. Whatever she wanted, I was ready to give.

A breath of hot musk teased my nostrils. Groping, I discovered that she had spread her thighs. I rested my hand just above her knee, feeling her heat through the taut nylon. In my mind, I was trailing my fingers up the inside of her leg then sinking them into her wet centre. In the real world, I didn't dare move.

'Please,' she moaned, finally breaking the kiss. 'Touch me.' She pulled my hand under her skirt. I had a confused impression of bare skin and damp satin. My thumb brushed over a ridge of elastic running down her thigh. She was wearing an old-fashioned garter belt. White? My dirty mind painted a picture of her standing over me, bare-breasted, a black tangle of curls framed by the band of pearly satin and the pale suspenders stretched over her ebony flesh.

She pressed my palm against her soaked, satin-covered *chucha*. The wet heat shattered my image, bringing me back to the present. She opened to give me access. I stroked a fingertip along the crevice dividing her lower lips, scarcely daring to breathe. She squirmed under my touch. 'More,' she sighed. 'Harder ...'

I wriggled my hand under the elastic and burrowed through her pussy hair. Working blind, I found my way between her slick lips and finally, to the hard knot of her clit. She gasped and fell back onto the bench, eyes closed, shuddering each time I touched that magic bud.

'Oh ... oh, yes ...'

I pushed one finger into her cleft, rubbing her clit all the while with my thumb. She clenched her muscles, straining against me. I added a second finger and she arched up, forcing me deeper. My balls were tight and my cock ached, but I pushed those sensations away, wanting to concentrate on my lady's pleasure. Her ripe lips were drawn back from her teeth. Her forehead gleamed with sweat. She clutched at her breasts through her blouse, pinching her nipples. *Santos*, I wanted to do that, too, but I was fully occupied with her pussy.

It was awkward, sitting beside her. My arm was starting to cramp. Without removing my fingers from her sex, I slipped to the floor. Kneeling between her thighs, I used my free hand to force her skirt up. She raised her buttocks from the bench so that I could crumple the garment around her waist, out of the way. Now she could spread her legs wide. I could see her in all her glory.

My dick leaped inside my shorts. My heart slammed against my ribs. Her lingerie was as snowy as I dreamed, but her panties, pulled to one side, were dark with her juices. Her untrimmed bush glistened with her juices. Peaking out from that wiry thicket, her cunt lips were a dusky rose, much lighter than her thighs. My own brown hand was busy among those folds. I grazed my thumb over her clit and watched her writhe.

She smelled like the ocean back home. The rich, fertile aroma mingled with her floral perfume, light and dark together, driving me crazy. I had to taste her. When my fingers slipped out of her pussy, she cried out her frustration. I dove headfirst into her pussy, turning the cry into a moan.

My woman in white grabbed my head and pulled me deeper into her crotch. I worked my tongue over her flesh, drowning in her scent. I was drunk on her juices. Giddy, I speared her hole then backed off to circle the hot little nob of her clit. She was so sensitive, the barest touch made her vibrate with pleasure. I flicked at it, teasing, then caught it between my lips. A tremor shook her frame.

Her rough fingers dug into my scalp. My nose flatted against her pubic bone. I licked, probed, suckled, feeling her tension mount, reading her body like I'd known her for ever. Power raged through me. She was close. I knew I could

196

make her come. I retreated just enough to get my fingers into her, then pressed my mouth back against her pussy, sucking hard.

She arched up, grinding against me. I pumped three fingers in her clinging channel. Cradling her clit between my lips, I rocked it with my tongue. A stillness seized her, like the sea retreating before a tidal wave. I knew what she needed. I bared my teeth and nipped gently. The sea came roaring in.

My beauty's wail echoed through the marble vaults. Fresh moisture gushed from her. She thrashed underneath me as I continued to lick her sweet pussy. I was happier than I had been since I'd left home. Maybe happier than I'd ever been in my life.

Her cries died away to whimpers and then to silence. She slumped against the wall, breathing heavily, her eyes closed. A satisfied smile played on her lips.

I was panting, too. My knees felt bruised by the stone floor as I pulled myself to my feet. My face was smeared and sticky. I felt a silly grin stretching my cheeks. My lungs were full of helium.

My dick strained against my fly, demanding my attention. I glanced around, fearful that her cries might have caught someone's attention, but we still seemed to be alone. Tearing open my zipper, I freed my swollen cock. It throbbed in my fingers, hungry, angry at being ignored for so long.

My companion was still sprawled on the bench with her legs spread wide, looking wanton and inviting. I could take her now, I thought, slide my cock into her wetness and ride her to another climax. We could come together, the way I'd dreamed, her pussy clutching at my rod as I burst inside her. It would be so easy.

Something stopped me. For one thing, I didn't have a condom. I felt like I knew her, but to her I was a stranger. It wouldn't be right, to take her that way, rough and hurried, with no protection, pressed against the hard, cold marble.

When I made love to my goddess, I wanted it to be perfect.

Carajo! How I wanted her! It was like I'd never come before. Months', no, years' worth of come swelled my prick. I jerked my fist up and down, watching her face, until the pressure became unbearable. I let go at last.

The come churned up my stalk and exploded into the air. Bursts of pleasure chained my spine like a string of firecrackers, one igniting the next. I must have closed my eyes. I saw wheels of colour spinning in the darkness, blooming with each spurt then fading away.

I opened my eyes and stumbled against the wall. She stared at me, looking confused and a bit wary. I noticed that some of my spunk had landed on her blouse. My cheeks burned.

'Oh ... *perdóname* ... I'm so sorry ...' I took the handkerchief she'd used to wipe her tears and swabbed at the white puddles on the gray silk. Her nipples made visible peaks despite her bra. I started to get hard again.

'Never mind.' Her voice was cold. She pulled away from me. Standing, she hauled her skirt down and tried to brush away the wrinkles. 'Forget it.'

I stood there gaping at her like a clown, my half-erect dick hanging out of my pants. She picked up her purse and briefcase. 'I've got to go. I'm really late.'

'Wait! *Por favor* ...' Desperate, I clutched at her sleeve. The silk slithered out of my grasp.

'I'm sorry, Miguel.' A thrill shot through me, just to hear her voice saying my name. She was not smiling, though. 'I'm sorry for everything.'

'*Querida mia.* Just a moment, please.' But she was already gone, her heels clicking on the well-worn stone.

I sat on the bench like some stupid turd, not believing, not understanding. Finally, I stuffed my *bicho* back into my pants and returned to my newspapers. A chill drizzle dampened the sidewalks. The pavement was a sea of black umbrellas. I put on my slicker then crouched on my milk crate, fishing out papers from under the tarp and handing

198

them to customers like a robot.

I'd touched my angel. I'd tasted her. I'd made her come. Something was wrong, though. I'd seen it in her face, once her pleasure faded. Worry wound itself around my throat, choking me.

By the time evening came, I was feeling better. I dropped by El Malécon after my cleaning shift for the two beers I allowed myself and some conversation. I don't drink anything harder; not any more. But the bit of alcohol made me more hopeful. Probably there was some misunderstanding. Or perhaps my lady was embarrassed by her randy behaviour. I would see her the next day, and we could work it out. Maybe I could even take her for a coffee.

I had to jack off twice before I could sleep. Images of my woman's rosy pussy and sleek thighs filled my dreams.

I wore my best jeans to work the next day, and an ironed shirt. I was excited as a school kid. But she didn't show up. Thursday and Friday passed, endless, without any sign of her.

Where was she? What had I done? Every day was torture. I was like the sinner who had been shown a glimpse of heaven then cast into hell.

I couldn't sleep. My fantasies kept me awake. Now that I'd seen my lady's charms, the images were filthier than ever. I saw myself feeding her my cock, forcing it down her throat. At the last minute I'd yank it out and spray her face with my come. I saw her on her hands and knees, reaching behind to spread her plump butt cheeks. In that sultry voice, she'd beg me to ram my dick into her rear hole. I imagined how it would feel, the tightness gripping my cock. I imagined her whimpers as I exploded in her ass.

It all left me unsatisfied.

I began spending the money I should have been saving on girly magazines. Stretched out on my cot with a flashlight, I'd leaf through the pages, searching for big, black women with melon tits and come-hither smiles. None of them looked much like my woman in white; they were coarse and common by comparison. Even sprawled on that bench, limp and sticky, with her thighs splayed and her *coño* exposed to any passer-by, my lady was special. I longed for her grace almost as much as I craved her scent and her taste.

Little by little, I gave up hope. I'd never see her again. I tried to recapture my old attitude of acceptance, my silent worship of her image, without success. A touch of reality had soured the fantasy.

I started to think about going home despite the risk. I had nearly enough for a ticket. The thing was, everything about the city reminded me of her. The click of a woman's heels on the sidewalk. The scent of gardenia trailing from a florist's shop. Especially, the false heavens of Grand Central, arching over me as I pushed my mop. I'd glance over at the brass clock and think that I saw her there, waiting for me. I couldn't bear to clean the side passage where we'd touched. I traded assignments with one of the other guy, even though that gave me both the basement and ground floor toilets.

Returning to Santo Domingo might mean jail. But I felt like I was already in prison.

November came. I bundled up in the morning, stamping my feet and breathing on my hands as I distributed the papers. I dreamed of Dominica's warm breezes. The memory of my woman in white had grown as cold and brittle as the city.

I was swabbing the floor in the main concourse, around six p.m. Something made me look up. I scanned the blue vault, looking for that old sense of peace. All I felt was weariness.

As my eyes returned to my work, a figure on the Metrazur balcony caught my attention: a woman in a white dress.

Ignore it, I told myself. Don't give in. I moved closer, though, pushing my mop in front of me. The commuters flowed around me as if I didn't exist. I stood at the foot of the winding stairs that led up to the bar, no more than twenty feet from her.

Her back was to me. She rested against the railing, a martini glass poised in her elegant black fingers. A man stood beside her, some *papi shampoo* white guy wearing an expensive suit. He leaned toward her, laughing, a hand on her shoulder. As if he owned her.

Her jet hair was coiled on top of her head. Her neck was slender and strong. Her arms as she gestured were unerringly grateful.

She turned to look out over the concourse, and my heart turned over in my chest.

After all this time.

She was as gorgeous as ever. Her pale dress flowed around her when she moved like an angel's robe. I could almost see her smile; the one she gave her companion.

I gripped the mop handle until my knuckles hurt. At last! I wanted to rush up the stairs, take her in my arms, cover her with kisses. I needed to fall to my knees and beg her forgiveness for whatever I'd done that day to drive her away.

Instead, I stood completely still for the next half hour while the rush-hour crowd thinned, watching her incline her head toward the other man, laugh at his jokes, touch his face with obvious affection. You'd think that someone would have noticed, a man dressed in fluorescent orange coveralls frozen in the middle of the concourse, staring like a maniac. But people like me are invisible.

I didn't move until she picked up her coat and took the arm of her companion to help her down the stairs. They headed across the concourse toward the Lexington exit. Without thinking, I dropped the mop and hurried after them.

It was easy to keep them in sight. Her white coat shone like a beacon in the November gloom. I expected they'd flag a cab but instead they crossed 42nd Street and strolled down Lex, stopping to gaze into the shop windows in the Chanin Building. Most of the people on the sidewalk scurried by, collars up against the bitter wind, but she and her partner didn't seem to feel the cold. They were in a different world. They walked slowly, his arm around her shoulders. Every now and then they'd stop for a quick kiss. Jealousy burned in my gut like hot acid. The heat distracted me from the wind, which sliced through the nylon of my uniform as though it was paper.

I followed them for a few blocks, forcing myself to stay far enough back that they wouldn't notice. I didn't know why. I had no plan. I just couldn't bear the thought of losing sight of her.

At 38th they crossed Lexington and walked down to Third. Waiting for the light on the corner, I right stood behind them, close enough that I could smell her perfume. She didn't turn around.

They entered a high rise building halfway down the block. I was close enough behind to hear the doorman greet her, in a heavy Russian accent. 'Good evening, Miss Abernathy.' My heart danced. Now I knew her last name, at least. My heavenly Miss Abernathy.

The elevator faced the street. I watched the floor numbers rise, then stop at seven. My lucky number. I peered through the glass at the burly doorman. His attention was focused on a portable TV, but I knew there was no way I'd get past him, especially dressed in my day-glo coveralls.

On the other side of the building, further down 38th, an iron gate protected the trash bins. It was open. I let myself in. I stripped off the uniform, stuffing it into the prickly hedge that ran on either side of the gate. Underneath I wore my usual jeans. It was colder than ever without the extra layer.

A narrow path smelling of garbage led to the back of the building. There it was, a steel-clad service door not visible from the street. Let it be unlocked, I prayed. I didn't really expect an answer. When I pulled, though, the door opened onto a concrete passage that led me down into the basement. From there I found the fire stairs. I climbed the eight flights. My heart pounded in my ears, from excitement, not exertion.

A window in the fire door let me survey the empty corridor. There were six apartments on her floor. The fire door was at one end of the hall, the elevator at the other, so I had a clear view. I slumped against the door, sweating from my climb, and waited.

My mind was empty of every thought but her. My old memories of her smell and taste, came rushing back, given new life by the sight of her. She was in there with him, her boss, that *pinchero* who had made her cry. I hated the thought of him touching her, but my dick got hard anyway when I imagined them together. I wanted to break down her door, to rush in and pull him off her. I could feel the rage simmering underneath my lust. It was lucky that I didn't know which door was hers.

I waited, supported by some strange faith. She was meant to be mine. That was my only certainty. I would find a way.

I don't know how long I stood there in the stairwell, gazing out through that square of glass, daydreaming about my lady. A stir in the hall grabbed my attention. That *pendejo* slipped out the door directly to my right, closing it behind him. My angel was nowhere to be seen. I waited for my rival to disappear into the elevator, then rushed out and tried her door. Locked, as any sensible door in the city should be. But perhaps not double-locked.

I rummaged in my wallet and found the promotional calendar card I had picked up from Hudson News. I'd learned a few things from Julio's friends. I slipped it into the crack between door and frame and wiggled. The soft click made me smile.

The hinges were silent. I shut the door behind me, throwing the deadbolt. Her living room was empty. The polished wood floor was scattered with discarded clothing, marking a trail to her bedroom. I picked up a piece of peach-coloured silk – her bra – and held it to my face for a moment. Her scent swam around me, gardenia and musk intermingled. It made me dizzy. I stuffed the garment into my pocket and followed the path she had left.

The bedroom reeked of sex. Like a dark comma, she curled naked on the pale, rumpled sheets. I marvelled at the pure expanse of her back, split by the march of her vertebrae down to her swelling rump. Her knees were drawn to her chest. From where I stood, I couldn't see her breasts, but the flowing line of her raised hip filled me with awe.

I had the urge to sink to my knees but actually the only part of me that moved was my dick. It pulsed and strained inside my shorts, protesting its confinement. I caught the sound of her breathing, low and regular. Was she asleep? I took a careful step closer to the bed, then another. Now I could see her forearms crossed over her luscious breasts and a few dark curls peeking out from between her clenched thighs. Her eyes were closed. Thick lashes caressed her cheekbones. Her velvet skin was damp with tears.

Pain arced through me, followed by a thunderclap of desire. My poor darling. I would soothe her sorrow with my joy. I was convinced that I had been brought to her bedside in order to love her. The power of my adoration had overcome all obstacles.

As quietly as I could, I unbuttoned my shirt and pulled off my jeans. I would stretch out beside her and wake her with a kiss. Then I would slide my cock into her welcoming pussy, and we would finally be whole.

Despite my care, my belt buckle gave a soft clank as it hit the floor. My angel's eyes flew open. I saw fear in their depths, not the welcome I had imagined. Her scream drove my naked body away from the bed like a physical blow.

'Don't be afraid, *querida*. '

'Get away from me!' She huddled against the headboard, a tangle of perfect limbs, trying to put as much distance as possible between us.

'It's me. Miguel. Don't you remember? I won't hurt you. I love you.' I reached for her. She cringed. My fingers stopped inches from her face. She dashed them away.

'Forget that. It was nothing. Comfort, revenge. Nothing! You took advantage.'

'No.'

'Get out of here or I'll call the police,' she yelled. 'I'll bet you've been stalking me ever since that day.'

'No, no, it's not like that! But I missed seeing you.'

'Get out!!' She threw a pillow. I batted it to the floor. She glared at me. Unshed tears made a lump in my throat. How could I convince her?

My cock screamed for my attention. It reared up from my crotch, red and angry. I realized that I could take her, if I wanted to. She was tall and strong, but no match for me. I could hold her tight and slide into that channel of delight I'd briefly visited, months ago. The pleasure would win her over. Once we were joined, she would understand.

She lunged across the bed and grabbed the cell phone lying on the opposite table. 'Fuck off, shitface,' she hissed, flipping it open. 'Before it's too late.'

Her curses drove me out, not any fear of the law. I gathered my clothes and ran into the hall, fleeing from the terrible truth. She didn't want me. She had never wanted me.

It's a kind of miracle that I didn't break my neck, hurtling down the stairs. I dragged my coveralls from their hiding place and pulled them on over my naked limbs.

When the nylon brushed my swollen cock, I exploded. Even despair couldn't drown my desire.

I quit both my jobs. I couldn't stand to be anywhere near Grand Central. I hung out around that building on East 38th, day and night, praying for one more glimpse of her. I never saw her again. Julio got one of his *compinches* to pose as a delivery man. The doorman said that Miss Abernathy didn't live there any more.

I toss down my tequila and order another. The merengue

is almost loud enough to drown out my heart. I leave tomorrow morning. Whatever waits for me in Santa Domingo can't be worse than the nightmare of my life here.

I feel in my jacket pocket for the tattered scrap of lace-trimmed silk. I've tried to throw it away many times. I know now that I'll be taking it back with me. It's all that I have left of my woman in white.

About the Story

EIGHT YEARS AGO I got a temporary consulting job in Stamford, Connecticut. My husband and I decided to rent an apartment in Manhattan; it was no cheaper in Stamford, and obviously living in New York would be far more exciting. We found a studio on East 38th Street that was just about big enough for the two of us and our cats.

Every morning I would walk four blocks uptown to Grand Central Terminal to catch the 8:03 Metro North train to Stamford. Every day I'd buy a New York Times from the black vendor who crouched on his plastic milk crate outside the entrance to the station. Sun, rain, sleet or snow, he was always there, surrounded by stacks of newsprint. In the evening, when I returned home, he was gone.

I wondered about the man who sold me my daily paper. What did he do after rush hour ended? What did he think about? What did he desire?

When I saw the call for *Sex in the City*, I was reminded of this nameless individual whose path intersected mine so reliably. That was the genesis of *Woman in White*.

Other experiences from that nine-month sojourn in the Big Apple also fed into the story, particularly the proud and stunningly beautiful black women I'd see on the street. With their elaborate braids and their golden bangles, they were the epitome of sexiness, without looking cheap. The story also tries to capture my persistent wonder at Grand Central's magnificence and the thrill I felt pondering its history. Finally, one of my co-workers during that period was Dominican. Knowing him gave me a bit of insight into that culture.

I've never had any sexual adventures in Grand Central. But I've often considered the possibilities.

Manhattan Booty Call
by Thomas S. Roche

THE BEAUMONT FIFTH AVENUE reputedly has the best mojitos in midtown; open any number of recent fine-dining, living-the-good-life guidebooks or in-flight magazines and you can read an interview with the place's unbelievably pretentious bartender, a guy named Spike; some shit about fresh mint properly bruised, single-origin cane sugar and single-origin Dominican lime juice, *locovores* be damned. He'll also hold forth on which rum he 'always' uses, which has changed three times in three years based on which distiller has paid for his celebrity endorsement.

The damn things also cost more than Meadow's Prius; but then, Jeanette was paying, so who gave a fuck?

At the time the topic of Dr Jerome Cosgrove came up, it was seven hours after the seminar ended and Meadow and Jeanette were well in their cups. Jeanette had put away five of those top-notch mojitos, commenting each time on how exceptional they were and how single-origin lime juice was really the best, and Meadow was nursing her fourth and thinking, 'single origin lime juice?' But she had to admit the drinks were pretty damn good, if you liked that sort of thing, and to Meadow the company (Jeanette) was barely tolerable for the moment

Jeanette Parnell had been Meadow's boss for the last nine months and a major player in the pharmaceutical communications industry for almost two decades. Jeanette was a Certified Meeting Planner and certifiable lunatic.

From a hip home office in a converted San Francisco live-work loft, Jeanette hired an endless parade of female *apprentice* meeting planners fresh out of Berkeley, Davis, or USF, and with her magnanimous tyranny of *mentoring*, turned them into shuddering traumatized husks of human beings, miserable empty shells primed for careers at Starbucks or as much graduate school as their hapless parents would pay for.

Jeanette saw herself as a den mother to a small cadre of elite feminine commandos in the cut-throat world of pharmaceutical communications, except that no one in their right mind ever seemed to *apprentice* to her for longer than six months before saying 'Welcome to Cinnabon, how may I help you' all day seemed like a great fucking idea. 'It's so hard to get good help!' Jeanette was fond of observing, having, apparently, no idea what a total bitch she was.

Meadow was, by her own internal yardstick, not in her right mind. She had made it nine months, longer than about two-thirds of the apprentice meeting planners in Jeanette's past. Her employment history had prepared her for some challenging situations.

After a four-day industry-thought-leaders' round-table discussion on Developing Modalities in Recombinant Supportive Care for Colorectal Cancer – the only example of which happened to be manufactured by the event's big-ticket pharmaceutical sponsor, a Japanese giant with a name Meadow still couldn't pronounce – Meadow figured she deserved a couple drinks. In fact if Jeanette hadn't been buying, Meadow probably would have been putting away minibar scotch in her room on the 10th floor while waiting for 9:30 to roll around.

Nine-thirty: that was the time Meadow hoped to be doing something filthy.

'One more mojito, Meads?' said Jeanette, waving the waitress over. Jeanette always insisted on calling Meadow 'Meads,' which was far from her most annoying affectation.

'I'm still nursing this one,' Meadow sighed with extreme

patience. Jeanette was a lush, and disapproved of women in her employee ever turning down a drink under any circumstances.

'Just one more for the road,' pleaded Jeanette with a bestial passive-aggressive growl lurking under her whine; Jeanette the den mother baring the fangs of the were-grizzly.

'For the road? I'm not going anywhere,' observed Meadow.

'I am,' Jeanette said. 'Ugh, don't remind me,' she added, which Meadow had not; Jeanette had reminded herself. 'I fucking hate late-night flights. I'm flying into San Jose. It's, like, a hundred dollar cab ride. It was the only flight out tonight for under $500.' Jeanette looked Meadow up and down. 'You get to stay the night, you lucky dog. Order porno on cable or something.'

'Jeanette!' snapped Meadow, doing her best to imitate either offence or embarrassment; she was never that good at understanding the difference between the two. She almost said, 'I would never!' but she figured that might lead to a discussion of Jeanette's porn-viewing habits, which was the absolute last topic she wanted to get into at the moment. So, instead, 'When's your flight?' she asked mildly.

'Ten-twenty. What is it now, about eight o'clock?'

'Um ... nine,' said Meadow. 'You'd better go.'

'Bullshit.' Jeanette waved her hand dismissively. She was known for pushing every trip to the airport till the last possible moment, and claimed, in almost twenty years in the meeting planning industry, to have never missed a flight. ('Caught the last flight out of Kennedy before 9/11; got the first one out of Denver when it was all over!' she'd been known to brag, no doubt hyperbolically.)

Jeanette made a '2' sign with her fingers, which Meadow mused looked like a peace sign or the V for victory. The waitress had the drinks there inside a minute, not even bothering to clear the table littered with empties. They were apparently stacking up mojitos behind the bar, even though Jeanette and Meadow were the only patrons in residence: it was the Sunday night slowdown.

Jeanette sipped her fifth (or was it sixth?) mojito and shot Meadow a grin so lascivious it might have gotten her slapped by a less patient friend.

Then she said it: 'So how 'bout that Dr Cosgrove?'

Meadow felt a wave of meeting planner panic: in an instant, she saw Dr Cosgrove not as the hot doctor she had been flirting with, but as a name on an Excel spreadsheet, with arrival dates and times, Towncar pickups and SURF & TURF under the meal column. Dr Cosgrove's departure tomorrow morning was the whole reason Meadow was staying in New York overnight; Jeanette was so anal retentive she wanted every single VIP out of the hotel before her last employee vacated the premises, *in case anything goes wrong*.

The information came out of Meadow's mouth in a rush, as if it had been rehearsed a hundred times: 'Dr Cosgrove departs for ASO at 5:07; room service has coffee and rolls scheduled for 2:30; Towncar pickup at three.' She exhaled.

ASO was the American Society for Oncology, the next place Dr Jerome Cosgrove had a presentation scheduled. It had been Meadow's job to set up all the travel arrangements for the VIPs on this trip, and Cosgrove, the last to leave, was no exception.

'Bell desk?' Jeanette growled.

'They'll be there at two-fifty-five,' said Meadow.

Meadow thought her voice sounded savagely deceptive, as if her nose ought to be growing.

'Departure gift?' snapped Jeanette, a sudden unexpected challenge.

'Four Roses 20 Year bourbon,' bleated Meadow, heart pounding.

'Sex?' said Jeanette.

Meadow stared blankly. 'Excuse me?'

'Sex,' said Jeanette. 'Is he sleeping alone tonight?'

'Jeanette!' said Meadow. 'How ... should I know?' She'd had to work at it to not say 'How *the fuck*.' Since starting this job, Meadow was trying not to say the F-word constantly, since Jeanette seemed to think she was bloody innocent; and that could prove useful.

'He was flirting with you at the faculty dinner.'

Jeanette, 'He's, like, forty!' She tried to seem offended.

'Closer to fifty! And I'm, like, forty,' barked Jeanette angrily. 'How old are you, anyway, pipsqueak, twenty-eight?'

Meadow choked, gasped, sputtered.

'Ooops,' said Jeanette.

'Twenty-three,' said Meadow through gritted teeth.

Jeanette shrugged. 'Well, Dr Cosgrove was definitely interested, and it's been known to happen,' said Jeanette.

'You'd fire me,' smiled Meadow mildly.

'Not if you give me all the details,' purred Jeanette, her voice like melted chocolate. 'He's from New York originally.' Jeanette said those words as if she were telling Meadow the guy had a twelve-inch penis.

'Oh, he's from New York?'

Jeanette smiled savagely.

'You've never been with a New Yorker?'

Meadow had been with about a dozen. In fact, one guy had once flown her out here; oh, that one was a story, all right.

But Jeanette didn't need to know that, so Meadow shrugged, shook her head, and said 'No.'

Jeanette looked Meadow up and down like she was appraising a side of beef found of substandard quality. She sipped mojito and chuckled knowingly.

Meadow thought, *Christ, is this woman the biggest cunt in the world?*

Jeanette, a Long Island native, had been a meeting planner for the largest firm in New York for ten years before leaving to start her own firm in San Francisco, servicing west coast and Asian pharmaceutical companies.

Every chance she got, Jeanette would hold forth to anyone who was listening on how much better everything in

213

NYC was compared to San Francisco. The food, cabs, the hotels, the nightlife, the museums, the liquor, the wine bars, the cocaine, but most of all the men, whom Jeanette often bragged of sampling with phenomenal appetite during her ten years here. 'Get enough cocaine in me,' she'd been known to brag, 'and, whoo! Studio 54 was a sex central back then!' Jeanette was 42, so Studio 54 had closed when she was 16, but she never let reality get in the way of a good story, which was why she was so good at pharmaceutical marketing.

'What time is it?' asked Jeanette.

'Nine-fifteen,' said Meadow brightly, feeling a sense of accomplishment.

Jeanette waved obnoxiously for the check and drained the last mojito. The waitress brought the check; Meadow caught a glimpse of it: $120 plus tip, *holy crap*! Jeanette signed with a flourish, practically stiffing the waitress.

Jeanette stood, bent low, kissed Meadow on the forehead, and said 'Be good.'

'I will,' said Meadow.

Jeanette cackled evilly.

'Yeah, I know you will, you little librarian.'

Meadow glared.

Jeanette turned, swayed drunkenly out to the bell desk. The bellman had her luggage ready. Jeanette stumbled out to the hotel turnaround. Meadow looked at the signed-off check again, stared at the waitress sadly, opened out her purse and got a twenty. She left it smooth and crisp on the table and planted a bleeding mojito glass atop it so it wouldn't blow away.

Meadow was not as drunk as Jeanette, but she was quite considerably less than sober. Nonetheless, she managed to keep it together as she slung her purse over her shoulder and trotted to the doorway between the bar and the lobby.

Meadow lurked in the shadows, watching Jeanette wait for her cab to the airport. A garish pink monstrosity pulled up; the trunk popped. A uniformed valet held the door and

214

Jeanette poured herself into the back seat. The bellman hefted Jeanette's enormous overstuffed Rollaboard; it took about seven tries as traffic crept by on Fifth Avenue, headlights glinting off every silvered surface. Jeanette stuck her head out the window and gave him a glare. What the fuck was in that thing? A suitcase full of tiny minibar liquor bottles, no doubt, charges ready for pass-through to the Japanese client. The bellman finally got Jeanette's suitcase in the trunk and slammed the lid with an angry CHUNK that Meadow could hear through the Beaumont's airtight doors.

The hot pink cab peeled out and raced out onto 5th Ave, evoking a chorus of loud honks. Meadow let out a sigh as her boss disappeared from her life. She stretched languidly, looking around at the opulent lobby; the Beaumont had four stars, going on five. She took in a deep draught of the fresh flowers that endowed the lobby, year round; with Jeanette finally gone, Meadow felt like she'd just smelled flowers for the very first time.

She glanced at the clock: 9:20. She stood there with the tension flowing out of her, nervously waiting for Jeanette's cab to race back into the turnaround; she might have 'forgotten something.'

When five minutes had passed, Meadow decided her boss was not coming back. It was 9:25. She took a deep breath and walked into the lobby ladies' room, surrounded by opulent floral scents and glistening golden surfaces. Meadow looked into the mirror with mild approval; after four days of hell, she didn't look that good. She could have gone up to her own room on the tenth floor, but if she did that she'd be late. Instead, she opened her purse and touched up her make-up a little, smoothed down the front of her businesslike blue skirt, checked the hang of her white silk blouse, adjusted her navy blazer. She unfastened one more button. Nice. She turned and went into a stall.

Meadow took her panties off.

The VIP floors had an express elevator. Meadow took out

Dr Cosgrove's glistening black key card; nowadays hotel keys were midway between a library card and American Express. She had to ease the black VIP card into the slot before '35' lit up and the bright brass doors slid shut, showing her a perfect, luscious image of herself.

She fluffed her meeting-rumpled silken curtain of blonde hair, ran her hand down her silken blouse where the firm peaks of her nipples tented the diaphanous fabric, and thought:

That is one damn fine piece of ass. I would fucking pay for that.

Her stomach dropped away, and she rocketed to Heaven.

The whole way up – thirty-five floors, like half a minute or so – Meadow was thinking, *I'm about to turn a trick. I'm about to get paid for sex. I'm about to fuck this unbelievably hot guy I barely know and get paid for it. Why did I ever get this stupid fucking day job again?*

How exactly Jeanette had decided that her apprentice was a naïve librarian type, Meadow couldn't fathom. There *was* the degree in Library and Information Sciences, but Meadow couldn't possibly be the first LIS major who was a total slut. Probably not even the first one who had sex for money. But then, role-playing had always rather been Meadow's forte, and it appeared she did it pretty fucking well. Walking in to the interview with Jeanette nine months before, she'd played it completely innocent. Isn't that what you're supposed to do in job interviews when you've spent a year being a whore?

For the purposes of the job interview, Meadow had spent that year since college *travelling*. She'd pieced together moments from her year abroad in Hungary with crap she'd read from tattered Bill Bryson books and Wikitravel. Asked if she liked European men, Meadow said innocently, "Oh, they seemed nice enough." Jeanette bought it hook, line and sinker.

In reality, Meadow had spent the twelve months between

college and Parnell Communications working three to five days a week in a moderately classy Upper Market Street brothel called Luxury. It was the best job she'd ever had by a factor of about ten zillion. Why she'd decided to leave it for the corporate world ... Meadow occasionally groped after a reason, but lately could never seem to remember, especially when Jeanette was being a raging bitch.

That disconnect had seemed suddenly more acute to her when, at the faculty dinner, the six-foot-four, lantern-jawed, salt-and-pepper-haired, devastatingly handsome and powerfully charming New York native, now Chicago-based Jeremy Cosgrove, MD, and one of the 'thought leaders' at the meeting, had slyly manipulated the seating chart so he could sit next to Meadow.

She'd been staring at him dreamily the whole weekend.

Dr Cosgrove said to her, midway through the appetizer course: 'Is this just a sideline, or did you retire from your other work?'

She just barely didn't pass out in her crab cakes. 'Have we met?' she asked, puzzled.

'To my endless regret, no,' he said, speaking softly so that no one else could hear. 'I booked an appointment once, but I had to cancel my trip to San Francisco that week.'

Meadow was still trying to grasp the import of the revelation. God, he had the most amazing eyes. Meadow liked brown eyes. She liked tall men. She liked doctors. She liked, in fact, just about everything about Jerome Cosgrove.

Her eyes did filthy things to him, and she smiled wryly.

'That,' she said, 'is really too bad. *Really* too bad.'

'You're not still seeing clients?'

It all came together in a rush: her photo on the website was password-protected; you had to buy a membership even to see her. He really was a Luxury client.

Truth be told, she'd been coming on to him, not fishing for a client. But at that moment, Meadow didn't care how she got Dr Cosgrove into bed; just *that* she did.

So she'd said, 'I might be persuaded.'

217

'Are you staying Sunday night?

Meadow had nodded.

'I can never sleep before a morning flight,' he said.

Meadow had done some quick maths in her head: faculty flights, Towncar pickups, Jeanette's ride to the airport.

'Nine-thirty?' she had asked.

Cosgrove toasted her.

At the end of the meal, she'd found a shiny black key card tucked under her dessert plate. The guy had a surgeon's hands.

'VIP,' the key card said in raised gold letters.

The weird thing is, when she was a prostitute, she'd always kept a clear line between clients and dates; she would never, ever have seen a client outside of Luxury or taken money from someone she met elsewhere. But Dr Cosgrove, she would have eagerly done for free without thinking twice. It had been most of a year since she'd gotten any, and she was vastly more than horny.

So, she asked herself, *is this a client or a booty call*?

The elevator dinged at the thirty-fifth floor.

Meadow undid another button on her blouse in the instant before the bright brass doors slid open.

Booty call, she thought, and almost sprinted.

It would have been polite to knock, but not as slutty. Not nearly as hot.

She slid the black key home and watched the light blink red-to-green. She entered, breathing deeply, trying not to feel her heart pound. She used to do this sort of thing all the time, but it had been too fucking long.

She entered the room. She could smell the soft ripe aroma of a fresh shower on the air. She could also scent his body; she reacted instantly. It had been too fucking long.

The mammoth room was dark, cavernous. It was a corner suite: much of one wall was taken up by a picture window, beyond which blinked the million lights of Manhattan. Great skyscrapers crowded beneath them; below those the bright rivers of headlights and taillights headed uptown, downtown, uptown, downtown. Lady Liberty in the distance was illuminated by lights below, the moon above. Outlined against the skyline was Dr Jerome Cosgrove, six-foot-four and suit-clad, sipping at a highball glass.

Meadow came toward him. He turned slowly. He looked good in silhouette.

'Care for a drink?' he asked.

'I guess,' she said. 'Thanks.'

'Bourbon OK?'

Meadow felt her Meeting Planning self suddenly return. 'Is that the Four Roses?'

'Twenty year,' said Cosgrove.

She cleared her throat.

'You know that's ...'

'Expensive?'

'I was going to say 'gourmet'.'

'Like so many things I'm partial to,' he said with an up-down look so filthy Meadow could feel the heat inside her.

Cosgrove's glance toward the opulent antique sideboard was barely discernible, but Meadow got it; he had done this a lot. Even in the darkness, she knew it was there; she could smell the money.

Tucked beneath the $120 bottle of bourbon was a sheaf of bills. She'd gotten very good at fanning, rolling and counting without looking like she was counting; there were ten Ben Franklins stacked, and it was all Meadow could do to keep her cool.

That was a lot of fucking money; more than she'd ever made from a client.

'Thank you,' she smiled.

'Don't mention it.'

She tucked the roll into her purse, zipped, wrapped the shoulder strap around the purse and tucked it on the sideboard, feeling the hum of money, the potential energy now in her possession like a big fat chunk of nuclear material waiting to go fucking critical.

Now that that was finished, she felt like she could forget about the small talk. After four days of making nice with medical VIPs from all over the world, she felt very ready to shut up and fuck.

Meadow fished out ice, poured bourbon, and went to the window. She melted into Dr Cosgrove's warmth. She could feel his body heat, smell his freshly-showered body.

He put on a suit for me, she thought. His arms went around her. He kissed her; his hand went into her hair and she shivered as he pulled it gently.

'What do I call you?' he asked. 'Misty or Meadow?'

Misty had been her whore name, emblazoned in pink girly script beneath her photo on the cheesy 'Mcct our hostesses' page at the Luxury website. She hadn't heard it in a year. The fact that he'd remembered it was hot and somewhat frightening. But mostly it was flattering.

The word seemed to set her off, making her remember how fucking good she'd been at this.

'Meadow,' she said. 'And you're 'Dr Cosgrove.''

'Or Jerome,' he said. 'If you like.'

Meadow smiled wickedly and shook her head. 'You know, 'Dr Cosgrove' is kind of kinky.'

She arched her back, her breasts just touching him; her nipples, hard, brushed his chest.

She didn't sip; she gulped. Ice tinkled in the glass. She set it on the windowsill.

'How do you want me?' she said in her dirty voice.

His eyes went wide. Her eyes went languid; bedroom.

'Up against the window,' he said.

'Really?' she asked.

'Isn't that on your web page?' he said.

She felt a hot rush of mingled excitement, embarrassment, shame, pride, arousal. Yeah, that was on her web page, or it had been, when she worked at Luxury:

FAVOURITE POSITION: Bent over and taken from behind, against a window on the top floor of a high rise, looking at the gorgeous City skyline.

Something that had never happened; it had just sounded good at the time, and guys always seemed to like the idea of it. But that didn't mean it wasn't fucking hot. Which made Meadow remember something else on that stupid profile page, which she'd written before she'd ever turned a trick:

TURN-ONS: When you fuck me from behind and pull my hair.

'You've got quite a memory,' she said.

She put her hands on the broad windowsill. She tucked her ass back against Jerome Cosgrove, the moderately short businesslike navy skirt riding high, her abject lack of underwear feeling suddenly shameless, blatant, wicked, brazen.

He came up behind her and kissed her neck. His arms went around her.

His fingers found buttons. He undid her blouse.

He peeled back the silk, not even bothering with the jacket first. He was hungry for her, and tall enough that when she tipped her head back he could kiss her hard, his tongue feeling alternately rough and slick, upside-down as he opened her blouse and his strong surgeon's fingers traced belly-to-breasts, teasing her breasts out of the lace-top bra. He fingered her nipples, feeling them hard; he unfastened her front-clasp bra, peeled the lace over her tits, eased her blouse back, took it all away in a tangle with the blazer. He tossed it unceremoniously somewhere, far away. She was naked from the waist up. His hand went into her mussed jumble of blonde hair; he gripped it tight but tipped her head gently forward. She caught her breath; she fucking loved it when guys pulled her hair. But only if they knew how to fucking do it ... and Dr Cosgrove had a surgeon's hands.

He began to kiss her neck.

Her eyes fluttered closed, open, closed, open, closed,

open; the cool glass of the window close to her face, with Manhattan brilliant beneath them, alternately in focus and out of focus as her eyes went swimming in cascading waves of pleasure. She loved this more than almost anything, more than fucking, more than getting head: kisses on the back of her neck. She could almost fucking *come* from this; sometimes she thought she would, and this was one of those glorious times. Her eyes opened wide and she gazed out into the sky of Manhattan, luxuriating in the feel of his full, wet lips on the back of her neck, his teeth just grazing, his hand in her hair, tight, holding her, while his other hand went up under her skirt and found her bare, naked, smooth shorn, shaved. And fucking wet.

He started fingering her.

God, he had fucking incredible hands. There was a special way really good fingers felt going into her; an expert's fingers. Cosgrove was trained at Mount Sinai to do something very different from this, but sometimes knowledge translates. Apparently surgical instruments and Meadow's cunt had more in common than she ever would have guessed.

He didn't linger on her clit, at first; he just went right inside, fucked her with two fingers, curving in and touching the slowly swelling firmness of her G-spot while his mouth kept working on the back of her neck. She moaned. She moaned louder. He eased his fingers out of her smooth-shaved cunt, dripping with her juice. He brought them to her clit. He started rubbing. She slumped forward, hands flat against the window sill, face against the glass. Manhattan far beneath, an ocean of lights. His fingers moved in circles. She surged against the glass, against his body, her ass wriggling on his cock as it tented the slacks of his Armani. His fingers went from clit to cunt, then clit again, circles, strokes, circles, strokes, unpredictable and teasing. Meadow cried out. He slowed, stopped, eased his fingers out of her.

He brought his fingers to her mouth; they always did that. She always licked them eagerly, or 'eagerly', but she had to be really fucking turned on before her cunt actually tasted good to her, before the musky flavour of her juices on a man's fingers or cock actually sent her into overdrive, made her dizzy with wanting it.

She had never tasted so good.

He slipped his fingers deep into her mouth and she sucked, slurped, moaned, wanting more. It wouldn't have been quite so fucking hot if he hadn't kept his other hand in Meadow's hair while he fed her her cunt; he gripped it, pulled it just a little, not enough to hurt, quite, not really, but enough to make her melt inside and slurp his fingers deeper. He watched her with a growing rapture, and when his fingers came out they were glistening, a faint string of spittle snapping in the city-light from far below.

Cosgrove's cunt-wet, spit-wet hand went down to her skirt again, this time not under it but to its side; he took her zipper down like the professional he was. The businesslike skirt pooled around her ankles, shrouding her high-heeled shoes. She stepped out, kicked it away, and spread her legs.

She bent far over, pressing her face against the cool window. She could see the shadow-reflection of Jerome Cosgrove behind her, tall and glorious, and looking out at the glittering lights

Her cunt was naked, its wet and tight potential energy tucked in the exquisite frame of her most expensive garter belt, the lace tops of the white stockings with their saucy little red slutty schoolgirl bows on front and back. She'd shaved and dressed for him this morning; she'd spent the whole day with this juicy package hidden under the businesslike skirt. His hand slid up her thigh and over her ass, caressing, feeling the contour, the swell and dip of the sweet spot. She wondered if he liked to spank.

Playfully, he drew back and gave her a sharp smack; enough to send a shiver through her.

Check, she thought, going wet to the knees. *Mister fucking Right*.

His hand went around her and he began to caress her

223

again, sliding exquisitely manicured fingers from her clit to her cunt, fingering, rubbing, building her closer, his hand moving up every half-minute or so to caress her perfect tits and gently pinch her nipples. He was teasing her until she couldn't fucking stand it. Most guys would have been finished twenty minutes before, but Jerome didn't seem ready to stop any time soon; he already had her at his mercy. She needed to come so bad she could scream.

He put his fingers deep into her again, pulled her hair, kissed her neck, leaned warm and tight against her as she blinked out into the blackness and the lights, and Lady Liberty glowing like a lascivious beacon. Cosgrove kept fingering her.

As he did, his other hand stayed in her hair, tight, and his lips worked against the back of her neck. She leaned forward against the window and lifted her ass for him; he followed her every move. She reached back and groped for his belt. She couldn't see what she was doing; it wasn't easy, but he didn't move to help her. He was too busy with her sex, her hair, her neck. She got his belt open and her hand on his cock. She could feel the outline through his boxers. It was good-sized, smooth, and thick-headed. She swooned.

She had to work, to grope, to stretch and arch her back and press her ass against him to get the necessary purchase to bring his boxers down over his balls. She brought his cockhead up between the swollen, shaved lips of her cunt, and he met her there. His hand guided him in.

She moaned and shuddered as he entered her.

She straightened and lifted her ass, pressing as much of her body back against him as she could. Perched on the moderately high heels of her businesslike pumps she felt unsteady without the hard press of Jerome's firm body against her. He kept holding her hair and his other hand roved across her body: tits, belly, neck, thighs, clit, belly, tits, clit, the tight-stretched place where he was fucking her, his cock sliding smoothly into her in a rhythm that left juices sheened on her lips and dripping down her thighs. He tipped her head back, still holding her hair, and kissed her hard; tongues always felt rough and strange upside-down, but the taste of him set her off: salt, spit, bourbon.

He put his hand on her clit while he fucked her, and she understood at once that he intended to make her come.

She hadn't come but, maybe, once, in this position, or a position like it; she loved it, but it was always so fucking hard to come while standing. Whenever she tried it with a client, she always ended up faking.

This time, though, she went off like fireworks.

She came so hard she surged forward against the window and the whole thing shuddered; she froze, terrified she was going to break it. Then all of a sudden she was soaring on a hot rush of pleasure coursing through her naked body, rhythmic pleasure in her cunt clenching tight around Jerome's cock and coaxing him to fuck her harder. She came hard, fast, white-hot flashes suffusing her body as she looked out through the window, saw Manhattan, saw the rivers and seas of lights; still panting from her come, she turned, pulling against his hand tight in her hair. She looked at Jerome and told him, 'Come for me.'

He stroked in deep; she moaned and lifted her ass, and he fucked her with a steadily mounting rhythm.

It was always different, once a man knew you had come and was fucking just to finish or maybe for the pleasure of the moment, the soft slick bliss of every stroke. It's a different kind of fuck; a different depth, a different angle, a different motion entirely. Meadow fucking loved it, and it made her pussy spasm all over again. She let him fuck her till he cried out; she moaned with him, watching as he shuddered, as his face was glossed with bliss. Then she was slick with him, and he slid out, half-soft and spent.

He let his hand out of her hair; he pulled back just enough that she could turn and put her arms around him.

He was panting.

She had been so deliciously lost in getting fucked that

she had no idea how much time had passed. She felt a sudden stab of anxiety.

'What time is it?' she asked softly.

Still breathing hard, Jerome said: 'Why, is my hour up?'

It was almost like a slap in the face. If Meadow had let herself, she would have been pissed at that; instead, she just frowned sourly and said: 'That is totally uncalled for.'

'Sorry,' he said.

'I'm a meeting planner first, a whore second. I'm not leaving you until you get in that Towncar at three. What time is it?'

Cosgrove kissed the tangled mop of blonde hair he had just all but ruined by pulling it repeatedly.

He glanced at the softly glowing dial of his watch and said, 'About eleven.'

'Care to go to bed, then?' she asked.

'I never can sleep –'

She put her finger across his lips.

'Don't insult me,' she sighed.

As they slid between the clean, starched sheets, naked bodies fitting together like pieces of a puzzle, Meadow mused to herself: *That was a lie. I'm barely even a meeting planner. And I'm definitely a whore first.*

In fact, she was starting to think it might be time for another career change.

About the Story

I'VE ALWAYS BEEN FASCINATED by people with a *secret life*, an avocation or profession that presents a very different side to what people think of them. New York suggests such secret lives at every turn, perhaps because there are so many universes coexisting there: Wall Street, 42nd Street, the East Village, immigrant communities; it's a city of hidden realities.

Since I haven't ever lived there, when I think of New York, I think of hotels and hostels, airports and redeyes, intercity trains, the subway and crashing on peoples' couches. Put the irrepressible energy of the town into that mix, and it's all a recipe for rampant misbehaviour.

I always feel like I should be cautious when writing about call girls, because that profession has been misused in literature, film and made-for-Skinemax-movies to reflect the sexual fantasies of the voyeuristic bourgeoisie.

But, that said, I know just enough call girls that I can't not write about them. The ones who enjoy their work, at least, are among the most puzzling, fascinating, and erotic women I've ever known. When a call girl character suggests herself, I'm always aware that I'm writing a fantasy, not reflecting reality, but that's true of whatever I'm writing unless it's an essay or memoir. The best I can do is try to make her on some level a real person – to me, if not to anyone else. The best I can do is try to make her on some level a whole person, to the best of my meagre abilities, and to base what I write about her not entirely on stereotypes but at least partially on what I know about the real world. But that, too, is true of any character, whether she's a call girl, cop or construction worker.

Mojitos often seem to get thrown into the mix lately

when I'm writing about misbehaviour; these were phenomenally trendy in San Francisco a few years back when I was going through a calculated promiscuous period, and so in fictional terms lime juice, mint and cane sugar will always show a natural affinity for me with round-heeled characters of several genders.

All these things collided to build the fantasy in *Manhattan Booty Call*: a story about which I'm very fond, with characters I hope to see again.

New York Electric
by Cara Bruce

I GOT MY VERY first real job before I even graduated from college. I was excited, thrilled even. I was supposed to start right after school ended and I couldn't wait. This was the way it was supposed to be: you went to school and got a job. I believed that my life was about to finally begin. I had new grown-up clothes which made me feel fabulously chic, even though looking back now they were cheap and plain, like playing dress up, and not even very well. That first job was in white-bred Connecticut, proofreading science journals. It was horrible, tedious work. I had to sit in a room, stark white and empty except for a single table which held an imposing stack of reference books, each of them thicker than the last. By the end of the day my head would be swimming with words, thousands and thousands of words, like tiny black ants, marching to a militant beat across my brain. It was boring, and I dreaded it more and more each day. After the first day my eyes were tired and after the first week I was depressed. I could hardly stand it. I felt trapped; walking into that blank white room was akin to suffocating. It didn't take long until I knew without a shadow of a doubt that this wasn't for me.

Each new day sucked another piece of life from me. I couldn't understand why people fought for jobs like this, how they could give forty hours of their lives each week to doing tasks that would only make someone else money. How they could give their lives to doing something they didn't care about, to go through life not creating something, not feeling passionate about something, not loving every moment of every day. I watched them hurry to the bars as soon as five o'clock hit. I questioned a society where alcohol was the biggest thing people had to look forward to; a society where boredom and unhappiness were so accepted – even fought for and sought after.

I suffered through it for almost a full month. I longed to be back in school and missed the freedom of being encouraged to follow creative and artistic pursuits. I already knew that parts of me would die if I continued along this route. And then one glorious day, my friend Dee called. She had been my film partner in college. We had made three movies together, two narratives and a documentary. She called to tell me that she had gotten a job as a Production Assistant on a movie set and she was sure that if I came to New York to join her that I could get one too. It sounded like a great idea and even though I wouldn't be paid I had some money saved and Dee and I would share a room and all of our costs. But the best part was that it was outside. It might not have been the most intellectual work, at least not on paper, but I had already discovered intellectual work that looked good on paper could be incredibly boring. And more than anything, that monotonous month had shown me that I hated to be bored.

So I told her I was coming and I quickly gave my notice and packed my things. The next day I took the train back to my parent's house in Virginia to drop off my work clothes and get clothes proper for unpaid grunt work. Dee and I didn't have a place to live yet, but we did have a few weeks until the movie started. I borrowed my parent's car, a crappy Chevy Celebrity, and drove by myself into New York City. This time I was convinced that my life was finally going to begin. No more false starts, even if this didn't work out at least it would be something worth remembering.

Dee and I got every paper and made call after call, searching for a suitable place to live. We walked for miles, up and down the city, checking out each and every room, of which there were few. We talked up bartenders and waitresses, college students and professors; we woke up at 5 a.m. to be on the street when the *Village Voice* was dropped off, we tried begging and bribery, and we finally got a few leads on possible places for rent. We saw an efficiency apartment in Hell's Kitchen that had the bathtub in the kitchen. It wasn't even big enough for us to be in the same room at the same time. To get any privacy one of us would have to stay in the bathroom, a tiny room with just a toilet, to wash your hands you also had to use the kitchen. But even in the bathroom you weren't actually alone, cockroaches scattered each time the single yellow light bulb was turned on and something scurried across the floor each time it was shut off.

We saw a five floor walk up railroad apartment in the Lower East Side. Our lungs and sides stabbing with pain by the time we reached the top floor apartment but we still considered taking it. At least until we went out that night, walking out of the building we were caught in a fluid stream of junkies. It was like a zombie film, but instead of brains they were searching for dope. Winding lines formed at burned out buildings. A burly man in a worn leather jacket stood guard at every corner; crossing guards directing the dope fiends to the proper spot, to their own personal place of safety. You got into line, then when you made it to the front you handed one guy your money and he passed it off to another kid, then he would jerk a hanging rope, the amount of yanks told the boy above what you were supposed to receive. The rope was attached to a can which was hoisted up to the second or third floor, they put the glassine baggies of dope, marked with stamps or skulls or names like Redrum, into the can and lowered it back down. Even the drug dealers understood branding. They were marketers as savvy as Pepsi or Coca-Cola, an old drug for a new generation.

We watched as the drug addicts pushed up their sleeves

to show their track marks, proof that they weren't cops, desperate badges of tainted honour. We also watched them scatter like rats in the light whenever the cops did appear. Rumour was that once in a while the police would load up all of the junkies into a wagon and drive them around until they were sick or drop them far uptown in Harlem or the Bronx. It was probably true; there wouldn't have been enough room in the Tombs to hold them all.

We watched them slink into abandoned, boarded-up buildings after they scored in dirty shooting galleries where diseases spread like rumours in a high school. It was a bit scary and depressing but it was also strangely thrilling. Simply walking through those night-time streets was a rush of crazy adrenaline, a drug in itself. I remembered books like Burroughs *Junkie* and I wondered if he too had walked these streets, scored in these same buildings, and in a sad, twisted way, it was almost glamorous to me. Of course I didn't know the truth, couldn't know the truth. That would come years later.

But when we went to look at our apartment we saw rats, large and fierce, crawling out of a gigantic hole in the foundation of the building. We saw a woman, skinny as a rail, her jutting hipbones and pointed elbows poking out of her, squatting on the sidewalk and taking a shit right in front of our front door. We hesitated, but after speaking to a weathered man who perched like a gargoyle on the front steps and learning that the apartments were robbed almost weekly, we finally decided against renting it.

We were staying at Dee's grandmother's apartment, all the way up the east side at 90th and York. It was a typical older woman's apartment. The plastic-covered couch folded out and we shared it, by morning we both had rolled into the crack, stuck together in the heat. She had a window air conditioner unit that she refused to use; instead she preferred shaking her head and complaining about those crooks at Con Ed. We stayed there for a few weeks until a friend of mine from back home called and said she'd heard I needed a place to stay. She lived in a studio apartment in the East Village, right on St. Mark's Place between 2nd and 3rd Avenues. We walked all the way downtown and met her that evening. An hour later we had signed her sublet lease and made plans to move in. For almost two weeks we shared a studio apartment on St. Marks. It was a very close fit. Lou Reed used to live in our building and every Saturday morning tour buses would pull up out front and the entire bus would empty, necks tilting, cameras clicking and the entire crowd collectively oohing and aahing, between asking each other who this Lou Reed had been, and if he was famous.

We would sit on the balcony and throw extra eggrolls at the punk rock bouncer of Coney Island High. I loved that apartment. New York in the early 1990s was a much different place to what it is now. It was dirty, gritty, real. Today you will see well-dressed people eating at chic cafes, but back then it was homeless kids and heroin addicts, artists and beautiful androgynous boys and girls. It was alive; the very streets pulsed with danger. Every night was like dipping your toe in quicksand, a little too far and you could feel how easy it would be for it to suck you in, warm and smooth, enveloping you like a fleece blanket, seducing you deeper and deeper. We weren't there long. During that second week her other roommate came back from her European vacation months early and we were, once again, homeless.

Finally, we lucked into a two-bedroom apartment on 7th and D when two junkies overdosed and died, their bodies undiscovered and decomposing around the stained vinyl kitchen table. At one point it had been a bright and cheery yellow, the top was now nicked and scarred, gouges had been violently spooned out of it. We got the apartment for a great price, an amazing price actually, and all we had to do was clean out all the shit they left behind; including a drawer full of used hypodermic needles and a closet floor of clothes that stuck together and smelled as if they had never been washed.

Dee and I moved in before the place was completely clean. We found old letters, photographs, and a large, brown spatter of old blood behind the bed. Underneath the bed frame was a collection of dried boogers. Rotting food made opening the refrigerator more a dare than a domestic event. It was depressing and disgusting; I had done heroin but not like this. I had snorted a bit here and there, but I had never shot up and didn't understand what really being a junkie actually meant. This apartment was my first taste of the reality of that lifestyle, and even with the evidence surrounding me I still neglected to accept it.

Dee and I had already started working on our first film set. Not Hollywood film sets, but independent guerrilla-style film sets, the kind with no money. These are the people you see running from transit cops and using stolen shopping carts as dollies. It was guerilla film-making at its finest. To a girl fresh out of college, not yet skilled in the ways of the world or the ways of men or love, it was incredibly romantic.

Just as Dee had promised, the first job we got was as Production Assistants or P.A.s. We worked our asses off for no money, just paper plates groaning under the weight of all the carb-heavy food from the craft services table. But we had an idea, we would specialize, learn a skill. So Dee attached herself to the Grips, putting together scaffolding, and building things, and I began training as an electrician. I loved it. There was a beautiful, tall, thin, mulatto boy named John who wore T-shirts boasting little-known punk bands and shorts with combat boots. It took me just a week to convince him that I was worth keeping around, that I could do the job. Finally, he took me under his wing.

He taught me how to put up scaffolding, how to adjust lights, how to create shadows. He taught me how to tie in to live power lines and steal electricity. This was the biggest rush. You attached metal alligator clips onto live electric wires. You were supposed to stand on a rubber mat while someone stood behind you with a thick, heavy wooden board. If you were sucked into the power current they would have to hit you really hard and knock you out of it. I got shocked a few times, but I never had to be whacked across the back with that impending piece of plywood.

My hands were small and I was unafraid. Back then I wasn't afraid of anything. I would walk into the heart of Alphabet City at any time by myself and buy whatever illegal substance I wanted or thought that I needed. I did things that now make me cringe with fear and self-awareness. I climbed down an elevator shaft to lay cables, mice and rats crawling over my feet. I hung off of a broken statue with one hand twenty feet in the air to hide the thick, black cable. I didn't care. Every day was an adventure, and every new experience a dare to be accomplished.

Strangers pointed at the tiny girl buckling under the weight of the bulky, heavy lights. I squeezed through chained doors and cracked windows to get into locked rooms with beckoning electrical boxes. Often I was the only one who could fit. People were impressed by my fearlessness, my ability to take everything in stride. I used to have dreams, night after night, about winding cable, feet and feet of black cable, rolling it around my arm until it was a huge, thick roll of dead power.

There was something thrilling about working with electricity. It was alive, dangerous. Electricity always has to be balanced. You have to measure, to make sure that one part of the set wasn't using more than the other. That meant you had to lay cable evenly, plug the right paddle cords into the right boxes. If the balance was off you could end up with a power overload, and either no power at all or a fire: the type of fire that wasn't even afraid of water.

Making a movie is all about light. It's about capturing light, manipulating light. You use light to suggest what time of day it is, to set ambiance and feeling. Lights on a film set are huge and bulky. They're heavy; you put them on stands and point them at anything that needs to be illuminated, uncovered. Once they are set you can place barn doors on them, a metal box with doors so you can close them to cut the light, or keep it from shining on a certain part of the set. Scrims are also used to cut the light, different size scrims allow you to control how much light you cut. Gels are used to change the colours, blues and oranges to create day and night. I'd put on my heavy, insulated work gloves and eagerly climb up the metal scaffolding. I'd be sitting on top, queen of the city, waiting to make the adjustments to my big light as soon as the Director of Photography, or John, was ready to instruct me.

I also drove the film truck, packed with expensive equipment because no one else wanted to. It was hard driving a big rig through a crowded city, making wide right turns and avoiding pedestrians. Road construction was an especially irritating and terrifying event.

I was the only girl electrician most of the other Grips, Gaffers, and crew hands had seen. They laughed at me, running around making sure everything was in place, but they stopped laughing when I lifted 40 pound lights and placed them expertly on top of a stand the size of my finger, or moved around a hundred degree light with my bare hands because the Director couldn't wait. I impressed them all, but the only one I really cared about was John.

On a typical film we'd work three weeks of days and one week of nights. Each day was twelve to sixteen hours of work. We worked all summer, sweating under the hot sun and even hotter lamps. I'd get home and wash off a thick, black layer of dirt and grime, the city itself having transferred to my skin. I hated getting stuck sitting on a set when the cameras started rolling because you'd have to be perfectly quiet. It sounds glamorous but it was horrible. If you were stuck in a squat, then in a squat you'd stay, whether your legs began to ache before falling asleep or not. We'd stumble home, backs bent and shoulders burning, shuffling our feet all the way to our beds. Then we'd wake up at 4 or 5 a.m. and do it all over again. Leaving our apartment in the thin darkness of the morning and returning in the thicker, blacker darkness of night. Our lives were nothing but the film. Films we would never see, films almost no one would ever see. The crew members became family, the actors distant cousins that made you slightly uncomfortable every time they walked into the room.

On the weeks that we worked nights it was a mad hurry of doing laundry, going to the bank, and it was the one week that we actually had to buy groceries. The rest of the time we'd simply fill our backpacks and Tupperware containers with lasagna, baked ziti, and everything else in the pasta family that the creative craft services could think of to feed us. We'd say to ourselves that we would have time to spend with ourselves, that we would go to museums, get some culture, read a book, but usually, starting around two in the afternoon, we'd find our way to the Holiday Cocktail Lounge.

The Holiday was the diviest of dive bars. It was always dark in the Holiday, no matter what time it was. Sad, dingy Christmas lights hung year-round over the big mirror behind the bar, plastic palm trees from a celebration that was long since forgotten were still pasted on that mirror, their corners lazily peeling off over the years. The big oak bar took up the entire right side of the establishment, a few cocktail tables littered the left, and, in the back, were two tattered red vinyl booths, and a jukebox. The same people sat at the bar day after day, lonely men and women who were older than they looked, hands shaking as they lifted that first blessed drink of the day, extras from a Bukowski book, perfectly cast for their own never-ending dramas. The bartender was nice enough; he looked the part with his shocking white hair, passing his days polishing glasses.

John and I would duck in, a dark respite from the brutal heat of a summer in the city. It was always cool in the Holiday, in here, time crawled. We'd stop at the bar to order

$2 watered down vodka cranberries in tall, thin glasses with even thinner straws. We'd stand side by side at the bar, our shoulders touching, and even that faintest touch bringing back the electricity. Then we'd head to the back, again side by side, and each time our legs touched it was a surprise. John would play the jukebox, the same songs over and over. *Satellite of Love* by Lou Reed and *Blank Generation* by Richard Hell were my favourites and to this day they both take me back there.

We'd talk and laugh and make plans for the next movie we'd work on, John always promised to take me with him. It was in the Holiday that we first kissed. John took my hand, running his thumb back and forth over my palm, his touch inspiring me. He pulled my hand close to him and leaned in and kissed me. His lips were strong and his breath tasted faintly acidic like cranberries. We held that kiss for as long as we could and when it was over he pulled back and we looked at each other. We had wanted this for so long, skirted around it for so many days until the tension itself had become palpable, sexy. I bit my lip and lowered my eyes and he lifted my chin with his hand. He smiled at me and we kissed again before we were interrupted by Dee and two brothers, Jorge and Mikey, who worked with her as grips. They slid into the booth with us, unaware of what had just happened.

We were all excited, that night we were shooting on top of the Brooklyn Bridge. I had never been up there and couldn't wait to see a new view of the city. John and I had to pick up the generators so we took off early. Once we had them we met everyone at the staging location at the base of the bridge. It was a strange day, the air was quivering with tension, in California they would have called it earthquake weather but in New York it is a rare feeling for summer. It was more like Halloween; that spooky impending feeling you can't explain yet you can't shake.

The entire crew and all of the actors started walking up the ramp to the bridge two by two, like the animals ascending into Noah's ark or little children attached by that invisible bond of the buddy system. Low conversations drifted back to John and me as we pushed the generators ahead of us. Dee and Mikey each took a corner and laughing we made it up the ramp, calves aching as we pushed one leg in front of the other. Finally we made it to the top. New York, alive and buzzing, a million lights each promising a million stories shone back at us, on the other side was Brooklyn, darker, it appeared almost naked – the strong silent type compared with its dazzling show-offy sister.

Like the starter pistol at a race, or the quick snap of a finger, the director clapped and off we went, struggling to get light stands and lights set up, an impromptu make-up station and the director began preparing the actors. John and I were working as one, passing tools back and forth without asking, exchanging meaningful glances and laughing at nothing. When you work together in a situation like this, where every second counts, and often where one of you can't move, it's important that your partner feels confident that if he asks you to do something it will get done. We had that relationship. We depended on each other implicitly.

We had gotten off the first shot when the rain started. It was a light drizzle at first, nothing more than a fine mist. By the time we had set up the second shot the sky opened and the world began to cry. It sobbed, bawled and with the first huge crack of thunder, it was as if Zeus himself was shaking a gigantic rattle in the holiest of temper tantrums. We were out in the open; there was nowhere to go, nowhere to hide. People were screaming, panicking, worried about getting a little wet but John and I were the ones dealing with live electricity. There is nothing like the heaven-splitting strike of that first lightning when you are high above a dark body of water, hundreds of cars racing right beneath you, and live wires at your feet. The director, producer and P.A.s began ushering people off the bridge. John and I started taking down the lights. The thunder and lightning were getting closer together, and we were moving as fast as we could.

Other people were taking our disassembled lights and stacking them on dollies, like lined of dismembered heads on gurneys. I ran over to unplug that last cable and the largest bolt of lightning I had ever witnessed crashed across the sky. The hairs all over my body stood up and I could feel the shock passing through me. It wasn't bad, I was lucky, but I still felt it. I pulled my hand back and John was right behind me, holding my arms. I turned to him, shaking and he kissed me, hard.

'We need to get these generators out of here,' he said, stroking my hair.

I nodded but pulled his head back toward mine. John and I were the only two left on the bridge and we were already soaked; my T-shirt was stuck like a second skin, my nipples were hard. It was thrilling; kissing on the top of the Brooklyn Bridge, John pushed me down and rolled over on me. We were kissing as raindrops rolled down my face like tears. With one hand he reached up and held my face, he slid the other hand up my shirt, lightly rolling my nipple between his fingers. I moaned and arched my spine. I put my hands on his strong back and pulled him down closer. He pushed his leg between mine, applying pressure on my cunt. I wanted him, wanted him inside me, filling me, completing me.

The thunder, lightning and rain kept coming. A boat blew its horn, the low and terrible moan of a lost and tortured ghost and the rushing cars blended into the frantic wind. There was something otherworldly about it all. Something so far from normal. I hurried to unhook his belt and pulled down his shorts. His dick was hard, rock hard. I wrapped my hand around it and stroked it, over and over. He unbuttoned my shorts and pulled them the rest of the way down.

I pushed him down on his back and kissed a soft line down his chest to his stomach. He shivered beneath my gentle kisses, slightly arching his back up to meet me. I continued down, breathing hot breath against his crotch, I kissed the inside of his thighs, lightly, and was answered with a happy moan. I kissed up the shaft of his cock, kissing the head before taking it in my mouth. I sucked it long and hard as his feet clenched and his body tightened. He leaned over, trying to yank down my shorts without interrupting my mouth. I helped him, getting my shorts and panties down. His finger found my clit, circling it faster and faster, I could feel my pussy dripping as my body responded to his attention. I pulled my mouth up and slid my hot, wet pussy down on his dick.

'You're so tight,' he moaned as I began pushing myself up and down, faster and harder. He reached up and pinched my nipple, twisting it until I felt the most exquisite pain. Then he flipped me over so he was on top, expertly he moved me around until I was kneeling and he was behind me, his hand snaked in front to tease my clit.

'Yes,' I groaned, 'harder, fuck me harder.'

He did, he was pounding his cock into me, and his finger was working diligently, moving faster and faster until I felt myself beginning to come. My body was tightening, my cunt squeezing and contracting around him. He pulled my hair back, pulling my head up; I opened my eyes and saw the blood-black water beneath me and all of New York before me. It was beautiful, being up so high, the entire world laid out beneath us. I wanted to hold on. I didn't want him to stop but I couldn't take it any more. I pushed back against him. 'I think I'm coming,' I said. 'Don't stop.'

He pushed into me harder and faster until I let go, my body exploding into spasms, he pushed once more, deep, and I felt his body go tight before he stopped, collapsing onto my back. We stayed like that for a moment, connected.

We lay naked on top of the Brooklyn Bridge, the rain pouring over us. He took my hand and held it for a moment. Another bolt of lightning shocked the life back into us.

'We should go,' he said, then rolled over and kissed me.

We got up and began pulling on our wet clothes. There is almost nothing worse than putting on clothes that are already soaked. The temperature had dropped drastically. It was now freezing and I shivered each time a new breeze blew. We pushed our generators down the ramp, careful not to let them go too fast or too far ahead of us.

When we finally got down to the bottom Dee and Mikey were there waiting. 'Oh, thank God you're okay,' Dee said. 'We thought you might have been electrocuted.'

John and I exchanged smug looks. 'Then why didn't you come to help us?' I asked.

She shrugged. 'If you had been and there was still live electricity we could have gotten electrocuted just walking up there.'

We all laughed because she was right; there was no point to all of us dying. Not when there was the promise of so much light.

About the Story

PARTS OF THIS STORY are true and writing it brought up many memories, both good and bad. The true parts include: having so much trouble actually finding an apartment and the horrific apartments that we did find; working as an electrician's assistant on independent films in New York in the mid 1990s; pushing a generator up the Brooklyn Bridge for a film shoot and being up there during a spectacular thunderstorm. Most of the characters and the sex were fiction.

To me, New York is a city of life. It's the energy: the desires, ambitions, hopes and dreams of the people who live there. When I lived in the East Village and Lower East Side it was full of junkies, impoverished people, squatters, and punk rockers. I remember going to work in the early dawn, and seeing it as a city of living ghosts. The longer the day went on, the more alive the city became. However, the New York I know has changed and I was shocked when I went back recently. The entire city has been cleansed; it's brighter, shinier and more hopeful. Some of the places I remember are still there, but most of them have been replaced with trendier restaurants, gourmet grocery stores and chic cafés.

To me, New York represents a time in my life; a time of beginnings and new discoveries; including discovering who I was meant to be. It was the first time I was on my own, the first place I moved by myself, the first apartment I had with my name on the lease. It was also the first time I was mugged and had a car stolen; my first-time experiences encompassing a darker, more violent, side of life. But most importantly, I met new people, inspiring people doing innovative and artistic things. Overall, it was an exciting time in my life and, because of that, New

York will always represent the frenetic energy of change and exploration, the breathtaking wonder of possibilities, and the overwhelming sense of limitless freedom.

Cell
by Ira Miller

I'M THE KIND OF girl boys don't keep. Pretty face. Thick, dark hair. Decent curves, in a full-figured sort of way. Smart enough to want the best out of life. Demanding enough not to *settle*. Attractive enough so that men consistently try to pick me up at a club, or on vacation, but not traditionally alluring enough so they want to stay for breakfast. Truth is, I look a lot like Monica Lewinsky.

I sit in *Au Bar*, or *Au Club*, or *Au Pair* for all I know, one of the latest, trendy, places young, Manhattan, professional singles go to for drinks after work. My best friend, Chloe, sits next to me on a couch. Her role has been to discover places like these and talk me into going. My role has been to resist, to trash them, to complain about all the phonies, wannabees, momma's boys, players, and lawyers who come to places like these. But I always go. She knows I will go. The last five men I dated I met in a place like this. It beats staying home alone and being depressed … just barely.

There is a nearly imperceptible rise to Chloe's chin, which causes her nose to point towards the corner of the north bar. There is a group of four men: one sitting with his back to the bar, the other three standing around him. I understand that Chloe is pointing specifically to the man sitting. He has the light around him, is the one the friends seem keen on impressing: black, shiny hair combed straight back in one thick wave, expensive suit, tie already loosened, muscular, athletic body balanced perfectly on the bar stool, gestures comfortable and fluid, drink in his hand as he points to one friend and laughs. My nod is as imperceptible as Chloe's rise of the chin, but it communicates just as much: yes, our type, which is rarely good news.

It is later, after Chloe orders drinks for the second time by the corner of the north bar and is finally able to strike up a conversation with Mr Big and his buddies – and I am debating as to whether I will get up from the couch if Chloe waves me over – when a voice by my left ear says, 'Come here a lot?'

I turn. It is a woman, now on the couch behind me. I laugh and say, 'Bet you hear that one a lot.'

'Actually,' she says, 'I use it a lot and I do.'

'What?'

'Come here a lot.'

I take her in full for the first time and realize there is something about her that is quite striking, exotic. She has thick blonde hair, cut short, parted to the side. Her teeth are perfectly straight and brilliantly white. It could be the high cheekbones and the boyish smile, Brad Pitt sort of cheekbones and smile when he was skinny and muscled in *Thelma and Louise*. Then I realize what it is. Though she is all young woman, probably early to mid-twenties, just a few years younger than me, and nothing specific about her is actually masculine, one could almost think one is looking at a very pretty boy.

'I'm here on a blind date,' she says. 'It sucks. *She's* in the bathroom.'

'I'm here with my friend,' I answer.

'She seems to be making headway.' We both look over at Chloe, who is in the middle of buying the next round for her new buddies. 'Can I get your number?' She glances quickly towards the back bathroom, a bit of urgency in her voice, the return of her blind date surely imminent.

'Chloe is just a friend,' is all I can say.

'I know,' she says. She looks over at the bathroom again and we both see her date heading this way. She discreetly presses something into my hand. I look down. It is a silver cell phone. 'I'll call you.'

'No, really.' I try to give it back. But she is already a step away, heading back to her couch.

It is not much later – the mystery girl and her date gone – when I am doing my own chuckling and drink buying with the group at the north bar. Not Mr Big, but the one who seems like the second lieutenant, graduated from Brown as well, just a year ahead of me. It makes the evening go smoother; whenever an awkward lull threatens, one of us asks if we know so-and-so.

Chloe and I share a cab home. The lieutenant's number is in my bag next to the silver cell phone. I tell Chloe the mystery girl story and she laughs, soundly drunk, and mumbles, 'Only in New York'.

I fall asleep in my bed wondering if second lieutenant is any different from the last few guys I met. I leave the girl's cell phone on, in my bag on the floor. If she calls, it will be awkward again, but I feel obligated to leave open the possibility of returning the phone.

It is deep into what remains of the night when the silver phone rings in my bag. Dazed, harpooned back to semi-consciousness, I crawl along the floor on my hands and knees, find the bag, the phone, flip it open, say hello.

'Sammi there?'

'No, he's not. I think you have the wrong number.'

'Sammi, two m's and an i. She's right next to you isn't she? The bitch.' Then she laughs, says good-naturedly, 'Did she do that thing with the tongue twist and fingers?' Her voice is suddenly all rapture. 'Damn, I miss her. Tell that boi Loriel called.'

Confused, still half-asleep, I mumble, 'Thought you said Sammi's a girl?'

'B-o-i. Did you just get off the boat?'

I flip the lid closed, back track to bed, drift into slumber, no motivation at all to figure out tonight's spelling lesson. It is very early in the morning, a Saturday morning, when the silver menace rings again.

'Hi, sweetie,' an older woman's voice says to me.

'It's not Sammi.'

'Who is it?'

'Who's this?'

'Sammi's mother.'

'Sammi's not here. She, uh, lent me her phone.'

'She's always doing stuff like that. Gave away everything as a child. Please tell her Mom called. I need her help again at the house.'

Mmmm, a generous hottie who dotes on her mother. If only the second lieutenant showed some of these qualities.

My one-bedroom apartment is already filling with morning light and I can't go back to sleep. I look at the face of the cell phone and see there is barely one bar of charge left. I push buttons and phone number after phone number pops up, each with a girl's name next to it. Sammi gets around. Sammi likes to keep her names straight. Sammi better call soon or this cell phone is going into the trash.

I'm in the shower stall, drying myself, when the phone rings again. I reach onto the counter of the sink. 'Hope I'm not calling too early, didn't remember how much charge was left.'

'Sammi?'

'You know my name?'

'Loriel and your mother want you to call. Your mother needs help at the house.'

'Kitchen faucet must be leaking again.'

'You're handy?'

'A plumber. By trade.'

'If you give me a minute I will get your address so I can send the phone back.'

'What's your name?'

'Zoë.'

'Like *Franny and Zoe*?'

'That's *Zooey*. But I'm glad you are well read. It's Zoë as in Chloe, the friend I was with. Just a *friend*, like I said. I don't think you and I play on the same team.'

'Always thought being on a team was rather limiting.'

'Are you a good plumber?' I slosh out of my shower stall, my feet slimy and wet, the greyish water at the base of the stall barely draining.

'Very good.'

'Do you work on Saturdays?'

'You have a problem?'

'My pipes are backed up.'

'I'll give you a special rate.'

'I'll give you back your phone.'

It is less than an hour later when Sammi is on her knees in my bathroom, hunched over my shower stall. I stand behind her. She is wearing greased-stained khakis and a short, tight tee. There is a tattoo of an elegant spider web at the base of her spine. She leans into the stall with serious intent, working a long metal device she calls a snake into my clogged pipe. This is the first time I've seen plumber ass crack topped off by a V-shaped thong.

Despite never having had sex with a woman, I can see why Sammi is so popular. She has a fantastic body, her crack as deep and dimply as any super model ass cleavage. Her khakis are hiked up a bit and I see her muscular calves, just above rolled up sweat socks wrapped in tight construction shoes; not manly, just sexy, curvy, tight woman's calves. I like her confidence as well, the ease in which she approached me at the bar, the intense way she works the pipe.

Done, Sammi takes care to scrub her hands clean in my bathroom faucet. She demonstrates, with a long hard spray from the shower spigot, that my pipes are as good as new. In the kitchen I dig out my checkbook from a basket of bills.

'So what do you do?' she asks.

'Interior designer.'

'Like a decorator?'

'We prefer *designer*.'

'Sounds boring.'

249

I laugh, say lightly, 'Well most of my friends, and my mom, think I have an absolutely fab career.'

'Is that what you always wanted to do?'

I finish writing the check. 'Actually, I always wanted to be a singer. No one famous. Just someone with a sweet, bluesy voice who could hold the attention of a room full of people, at least for an evening.'

'Sweet,' she says, finally impressed. 'There's more light in your eyes when you talk about singing.' I hand her the check. She seems ready to leave. I invite her to stay for lunch.

It is before lunch is over, I am at a cabinet reaching for tea bags, when she turns me around and kisses me. It is an aggressive kiss, like a man's, only her lips are terribly sweet and soft. Absent is even the hint of abrasion a man's moustache or shadow can cause. Though aggressive, also absent is the wild entering of tongue those poor stupid boys are so prone to do after a night of drinking as they say goodbye at the doorway, hoping to be asked up. She is taller than me, something I did not realize at first.

Expertly, she kisses and explores, guides me to the bed in complete context of what we are doing. As with her work, Sammi pays particular attention to detail. Though I could never imagine complete fulfilment with a woman, I always suspected that this might be something interesting: the exotic meal, the off-the-beaten-path vacation, the surprisingly moving moment at some alternative theatre.

It goes on for what seems like hours. I am hungry again and in need of another shower. But then Sammi surprises me once more. She goes into the bathroom and I hear her fumbling around in her tool bag. She returns, still naked, her breasts a perfect size, two sturdy coconuts that felt pleasant in my mouth, her hips curvy, but somewhat boyish, a cock, quite hard, strapped-on between her legs.

She approaches the bed and tells me to suck her. I find it touching that she thinks I need this as well. Not sure what the goal would be, but as I've already proven I am quite

250

game today, I begin a gentle sucking. The taste is startling, sweet; she literally has coated herself with honey. I close my eyes, go to work, hungry for her, soon lost in the sucking, aroused supremely again at the idea not of sucking a man's cock, but of sucking Sammi's cock.

Then she pulls me up, leads me to the large windows overlooking the street twelve stories below. She pulls the shade up. She faces me against the window. She grasps a wrist in each hand and places my hands above me, against the left and right side of the pane.

From behind she enters me slowly with her perfect, wet, sweet cock.

'The stage is dark,' she whispers. 'You wear a beautiful, long sequined dress, thin straps at the shoulders. Your hair is done up perfectly. Just one tunnel of light appears, on you. The room is full of people sitting at tables. They can't take their eyes off you, you are so beautiful. I am behind you, your dress hiked up so discreetly no one can tell. I am inside you, still, letting you feel, letting you get used to my hardness. Then you begin ...'

And she begins, going in and out with her hard honeyed cock, the lining of my vagina velvet with moist desire.

'Your voice starts low and soft and you know you have everyone's attention. You have my attention. All of it. You add energy and power and you attack your song and they are all mesmerized, men, women. You find the real you. You feel the beauty within you begin to grow, to rise up in your voice and reach out to the audience like a caressing hand.' Her hands caress my breasts, my belly. Her cock goes in and out in the exact rhythm, with the exact strength of her words. 'Your song arouses everyone in the room. The men are hard, the women wet. The power of your voice is so strong they cannot help touching themselves.' Like a conductor, baton in hand, she makes me sing. It is not exactly words, but there is a sound, a melodic tone rising within me. Though my eyes are closed, seeing everything she asks me to imagine, I do sense the openness of the street

251

below me – my erect nipples against the glass – that there may be people below, or in the buildings across the way, who are watching.

She convinces me they are, that everyone is watching and that my voice is the prettiest they've heard. Deeper, deeper with her pressure, her penetration, as she quickens, as she tells me my song is near its climax, though I don't need her to tell me as I feel it all, see it all so perfectly.

She makes me come. She tells me that, at the same time, I am making every man and woman in the room come. We all come. We all sing together. She fucks me hard and furiously until the song is done, until everyone is spent, including Sammi, though her cock is far from flaccid.

I have the urge to collapse to the floor, but she leads me back to the bed. In one swift motion she removes the cock and drops it to the floor. We both lie on our backs.

This is a moment I have learned to fight. In my early twenties I let it swarm over me and carry me into a grateful rush during the times a boy got it right, or the chemistry seemed to be there, or my feelings were just too strong. But I've learned. After the fuck can be danger time. After the fuck is when you find out what really went on. So I've learned to check the feelings after I've left my guard down during the lovemaking, when the rare man has touched me the way Sammi has. I let the man take the lead, try to intuit as quickly as possible if I have a *Harry Met Sally* morning-after on my hands, if it even lasts to morning.

She reaches for me. She holds me. She kisses me. She stays the rest of the day and all of Sunday: breakfast, lunch, and dinner. On Monday morning we both go to work and I feel changed, recharged, renewed ... and sore. It seems so obvious I am sure everyone can tell.

When I arrive home from work, I notice her silver cell phone on my kitchen counter next to the basket of bills. The battery is dead. I take it to an electronics store and buy the appropriate charger. I charge the phone up, wait for her call. I acknowledge that Sammi never did say she would call me, which I see as a positive, as that farewell cliché is usually an automatic indicator that an encounter is, indeed, a one night stand, or in this case two.

I carry the fully charged phone around in my bag all week, charging it up in the evening, but leaving it on through the night. I chastise myself for not offering to call her before she left on Monday, but I've learned what a turn-off that can be for guys. I push buttons on the face of the phone in an effort to find the number she called me from last Saturday morning, but it is a blocked number. I toy with the idea of calling some of the numbers in the directory to see if I can get a number for Sammi, but don't want to sound like another desperate Loriel. I would even welcome an early morning call from Mom.

I can't help but be depressed as next Friday comes around and I still haven't heard. Against my better judgment, I tell Chloe we should try *Au Bar* or *Au Club* or *Au Pair*, again. We sit on the same couch. Chloe says I am unusually quiet. About a half hour after we arrive Sammi does come in with a date. I hunker down so she doesn't see me. I remember her hands, her mouth, her tongue, her breasts, her deep inside me. Later, Sammi's date gets up to go to the bathroom. To my utter horror, Sammi goes over to talk to a woman who is with a guy who just left her to go to the bar for drinks. The girl laughs awkwardly and shakes her head. I don't know why I am surprised, but I am. Just before both their companions return, Sammi slips the woman a cell phone, which she awkwardly puts away.

Now let's see; I have been with a married guy who presented himself as divorced. I briefly lived with a man who stole money from me. There are the standards, the ones who try to come off as film producers, surgeons, investors, when at best they are paper pushers for some low level investment firm. I have met ones who use flowers, jewellery, even one who sent me a new dress for our first date to get what they wanted, but even they never wanted to keep me.

I know this is stupid, but I really was moved by Sammi, so I couldn't help going over. I shouldn't even have come back to the bar. I was content to give Sammi the benefit of the doubt when she didn't call. But now I am so blind with anger I put her in the category of the men who get great pleasure out of leaving the bar with a pick-up, their buddies left behind smiling with envy, who, once out of the bar, don't even want to have sex, but go through it anyway because they've gone this far and feel obligated and want to make sure they have something to tell their buddies during the next day's recap. But Sammi seems to have her own particular fetish: seducing straight girls. Once again, I should've known better.

I approach Sammi at the couch, ignoring everyone and everything, even the date at her side. I say, 'Were the phone calls from Loriel and your mom even real, or was that staged, too, to help show what a sexy, well-rounded person you are?'

'Hi, Zoë, this is my friend, Nina.'

'I don't need to meet your friend.'

'Hey, calm down. Look, we had an awesome time, can't you just leave it at that. I never made any promises.' I half-expected some more of the classics: 'Let's be friends,' or 'It's me who is fucked up, not you,' but she came up with one I hadn't heard before: 'Look, you got topped. Enjoy it. Get over it. I'll never settle down.' Then, delivered with a bluntness only the largest of assholes have used, she added, 'Just basically someone who likes to get her dick sucked.'

There is a line I've often thought of delivering to some of the men when they turned a cold shoulder or gave me the old heave-ho. It seems especially appropriate at this moment and I deliver it with the panache of someone who feels free, speaking to someone so locked into a lifestyle she may never grow up. 'You may have a dick, but you have no balls ...'

With that, I go back to the couch, grab my purse, tell Chloe I'm leaving, and hail a cab uptown.

It's while sitting alone in a cab with cracked leather seats, moving quietly through traffic, when I realize the freedom I allowed to creep into my voice had been false. And that perhaps she didn't deserve the anger I keep buried, caused by so many other men. She had been better than most. She had stayed. She took the time to touch me, to pay attention to the light in my eyes. I sink lower into the seat, causing an ancient spring to moan. Perhaps it is me who is locked in, jailed, perhaps more so than Sammi. She, at the very least, knows her strengths and limitations. There are plenty of men out there besides the phonies, wannabees, momma's boys, players, and lawyers. Decent men. Kind men. To my great self-disgust I have never been attracted to one unless he had the look, the cockiness, the arrogance, the muscular body, the near-perfect features. The times I have gone out with the easy-going, shy, less confident, less than perfectly fit, plain man (ones in their own way mirror images of me) I haven't felt even a spark. 'We're doomed to love the bad boys,' Chloe once said as we vented over another frustration.

In the back seat of the cab, I do what I do too often. Nevertheless it does provide some comfort. I cry.

I HAVE BEEN WORKING on my short story collection, *Sex and Love*, for a number of years. These erotic stories deal with characters ranging from their early twenties to late fifties; men, women, some single, some married, some gay, some straight. Everyone is missing something from their lives and all of their conflicts derive from their search for sex, love, or both. One of the stories I had already written, *Lonely Man*, was also set in New York City and showed how even in a city of millions one can feel isolated and lonely, especially if a pattern of poor choices doesn't change. I was looking to do a companion to the story from a woman's point of view.

My sister, who is single and lives in Manhattan, told me the story of a man on a date who tried to pick up a friend of hers in a bar while his girl friend went to the bathroom. With no time to get her phone number, he slipped her a cell phone and said he would call. I had also read an article about the *boi* lesbian culture in New York; lesbians who took pride in loving and leaving women in the same aloof fashion typically associated with men. I had these story elements in my head for about a year, but was still searching for the story. One day the first line popped into my head – *I'm the type of girl boys don't keep* – and it fell into place. How big a dose of reality is it for Zoë (a straight girl) to fall for a girl (*boi*) who is exactly like all the boys she ends up getting burned by?

The last piece of the puzzle was the narrator's voice. My second novel, *Whipped*, is written from a woman's point of view, but in the third person. I had never written anything in the first person from a woman's point of view. However, the confessional tone of *Cell*, along with the dramatic dose of reality that hits Zoë as she sits in a New York City taxi cab, alone among millions, seemed much more powerful in the first person. Man or woman, you know what she is feeling.

Author Biographies

Donna George Storey can't seem to write anything that doesn't have a lot of sex in it. Most of her adults-only tales are set in the world's great cities, but New York definitely takes first place as the scene of her edgiest erotic exploits. Her short fiction has appeared in numerous journals and anthologies including *The Mammoth Book of Best New Erotica*, *Best Women's Erotica*, *Best American Erotica*, *Penthouse*, *Scarlet Magazine*, *Ultimate Burlesque*, and *Ultimate Decadence*, along with broad-minded literary journals like *Prairie Schooner* and *The Gettysburg Review*. Her first novel, *Amorous Woman* (Neon/Orion 2007), the story of an American woman's steamy love affair with Japan, was also based on her own experiences teaching English in Kyoto. She currently writes a column for the Erotica Readers and Writers Association called *Cooking up a Storey*, that focuses on all of her favourite topics: delicious sex, well-crafted food, and mind-blowing writing. She also loves to read – or rather, purr – her stories aloud and is producing a series of erotic podcasts. Read more of her work at *www.DonnaGeorgeStorey.com*.

Maxim Jakubowski is a twice award-winning British writer, editor, critic, lecturer, ex-publisher and ex-bookshop owner. He shares his time between the wonderfully dubious shores of erotica and the perilous beaches of crime and mystery fiction. He is responsible for the *Mammoth Book of Erotica* series and the *Mammoth Book of Best British Crime* series, is editor of over 75 anthologies and counting, as well as being the author of two handfuls of novels and short story collections. He was crime reviewer for *Time Out London* and then the *Guardian* for nearly twenty years, and also makes regular appearances on radio and television. He also co-directs Crime Scene, London's annual crime and mystery film and literature festival, and runs the MaXcrime imprint. *I Was Waiting For You* is his latest novel.

Though based in London, he has been known to travel and frequent hotel rooms with depressing regularity, which no doubt inspired his *London Noir*, *Paris Noir* and *Rome Noir* collections, as well as the *Sex in the City* series. He has lived in, or regularly visited, every city featured in the *Sex in the City* titles published so far. When not writing, he collects books, CDs and DVDs with alarming haste.

Polly Frost is an author, journalist and playwright known for both humour and erotica. *Deep Inside*, her collection of satirical erotic horror and sci-fi stories, was published by Tor in 2007. *Deep Inside* has been written about and reviewed over fifty times, including praise from porn legend Ron Jeremy and Rachel Kramer Bussel, who listed it as one of the ten best erotica books in *Time Out New York*. Stories from *Sex Scenes* and *Deep Inside* have been included in Maxim Jakubowski's *Mammoth Books of Best Erotica*.

Polly's humour has been published in *The New Yorker, The Atlantic, The New York Times, Scene4, Identity Theory, Exquisite Corpse, Art Design Cafe and Narrative Magazine*. Her humour has frequently been anthologized, including *The New Yorker Best of* collections *Fierce Pajamas* and *Disquiet, Please*, and the upcoming *Ecco Anthology of Contemporary Humor* edited by Ian Frazier.

She is married to Ray Sawhill and they are frequent creative collaborators. They co-wrote, directed and produced *Sex Scenes*, a comic and erotic theatre project which was performed regularly at the Cornelia Street Cafe. In 2007, they performed *Sex Scenes* in nine cities across the country, then recorded it, using the voices of thirty-three top NYC actors. It's available as a download and CD from *http://rapturehouse.com*. Together with Matt Lambert, Polly and Ray co-created the sci-fi burlesque web series *The Fold*, which was compared to early Pedro Almodovar by film critic David Chute.

Polly and Ray co-wrote the play *The Last Artist in New York City* which was performed in May 2009 at PS122 as part of Theatre Askew's *Avant Garde Arama*. *The Last Artist in New York City* was selected for *Best American Short Plays 2008-2009* published by Applause.

Jeremy Edwards is the author of the eroto-comedic novel *Rock My Socks Off* (Xcite Books). His short stories have appeared in over forty anthologies offered by Xcite, Cleis Press, and other publishers, including three volumes in the *Mammoth Book of Best New Erotica* series; and his libidinous literary efforts are also well represented at quality online magazines such as *Clean Sheets, Fishnet, Good Vibrations, Oysters & Chocolate*, and *The Erotic Woman*.

As a guest on the Web circuit, Jeremy has been seen or heard at *Erotica Readers & Writers Association, Lust Bites, LoveHoney, Dr. Dick's Sex Advice*, and *Cult of Gracie Radio*. In the non-virtual world, he has read his work at the *In the Flesh* series in New York, the Erotic Literary Salon in Philadelphia, and (via telephone) *In the Flesh: L.A.* He has been featured in the literary showcase of the Seattle Erotic Art Festival and is a frequent contributor to *Scarlet* and *Forum* (UK) magazines.

Jeremy's greatest goal in life is to be sexy and witty at the same moment – ideally in lighting that flatters his profile. Readers can drop in on him unannounced (and thereby catch him in his underwear) at *www.jeremyedwardserotica.com* .

Tsaurah Litzky writes erotica because she believes in the ardent ascent of astonishment and getting it up one more time. She hopes her erotic writing contributes to taking sex off the leash and many, many simultaneous orgasms. Her erotic stories have appeared in over eighty publications including *Best American Erotica* (eight times), two volumes of *Mammoth Book Of Best New Erotica, Bitten, X-The Erotic Treasury, Sex for America, Penthouse, The Urban Bizarre, Politically Inspired, Blacklisted Journalist* and *Dirty Girls*. Tsaurah's erotic novella, *The Motion Of The Ocean,* was published as part of *Three The Hard Way*, a series of erotic novellas edited by Susie Bright. Tsaurah has taught erotic writing at the New School and erotic poetry as the Bowery Poetry Club, both in Manhattan. She has just compiled a collection of her erotic short stories titled *End Of The World Sex*. From the windows of Tsaurah's apartment on the Brooklyn waterfront she can see the Statue of Liberty, icon of free women everywhere.

Shanna Germain lived in New York until she was twenty-two, but doesn't have an accent. Now, she spends her summers on a wild isle off the coast of Scotland, where she walks in the rain, laments the lack of coffee shops and wonders why she doesn't own wellies and a kilt.

Shanna (pronounced like 'Shaun' with a sigh of pleasure at the end) also claims the titles of (in no particular order): girl geek, lust/slut, wanderlust-er, avid walker and biker, tree kisser, knife licker, steak-maker, book-nerd and She Who Fears Spiders Ticks. Her work has appeared in places like *Absinthe Literary Review, Best American Erotica, Best Gay Romance, Best Lesbian Erotica, Blood Fruit: Queer Horror, Hint Fiction*, and more. Travel to her world at
http://yearofthebooks.wordpress.com/

Thom Gautier lives in New York City, where he was born. His fiction has won him fellowship awards from The National Endowment for the Arts and The Bronx Council on the Arts, and his stories have appeared in print and online magazines in the UK and USA. He is also a widely published poet and translator whose work has appeared *in Modern Painters, Circumference, Shenandoah and Denver Quarterly*, among many other publications. His erotic short stories have appeared *in Clean Sheets, Lucrezia Magazine, Oysters & Chocolate and Sliptongue*. His story *The Bet* appears in *Mammoth Book of Best New Erotica Vol 9*. You can visit him online at *http://thomgautier.blogspot.com/*

D. L. King is a New Yorker with a passion for roasted chestnuts sold on the street and a penchant for writing smut. She lives somewhere between the Wonder Wheel at Coney Island and the Chrysler Building.

The editor of *The Sweetest Kiss: Ravishing Vampire Erotica* and *Where the Girls Are: Urban Lesbian Erotica*, both from Cleis Press, she is also the publisher and editor of the book review site, *Erotica Revealed*. Her short stories can be found in anthologies such as *The Mammoth Book of Best New Erotica, Volumes 8* and *9, Best Women's Erotica 09, Best Lesbian Erotica 08 and 10, Please, Ma'am, Girl Crazy, Broadly Bound, Swing!, Frenzy, Yes, Sir and Yes, Ma'am* among others. She is the author of two novels of female domination and male submission, *The Melinoe Project* and *The Art of Melinoe*. Find out more about D. L. King on her website, *dlkingerotica.com*.

Michael Hemmingson wrote the independent film, *The Watermelon*, and has a few other movies in the works, including the film version of his 2002 novel, *The Dress,* which was also published in truncated form in Maxim Jakubowski's 1998 groundbreaking *The Mammoth Book of New Erotica*. Recent books include a collection, *Sexy Strumpets and Troublesome Trollops* (Wildside Press) and a crime noir, *The Trouble with Tramps* (Black Mask Books).

Ten years ago **Lisabet Sarai** experienced a serendipitous fusion of her love of writing and her fascination with sex.

Since then she has published six erotic novels including the BDSM classic *Raw Silk* and two collections of short stories, *Fire* and *Rough Caress*. Her shorter works have appeared in more than two dozen print and ebook anthologies edited by erotica luminaries such as Rachel Kramer Bussel, Alison Tyler, M. Christian, and Maxim Jakubowski, including four straight volumes of *The Mammoth Book Of Best New Erotica*.

As an editor, Lisabet is responsible for the anthology *Sacred Exchange* (with S.F. Mayfair) and well as the acclaimed *Cream: The Best Of The Erotica Readers & Writers Association*. She also edits the single-author branch of the Coming Together altruistic erotica imprint, and will be bringing out volumes by three top erotica writers in the first half of 2010.

Lisabet holds more degrees than anyone would consider reasonable, from prestigious universities who would most likely be embarrassed by her literary endeavours. Although she grew up in New England, Lisabet loves to travel, and many of her tales are set in foreign locales. She currently resides in Southeast Asia with her long-suffering husband and spoiled felines. For more information on Lisabet and her writing visit Lisabet Sarai's Fantasy Factory
http://www.lisabetsarai.com
or her Beyond Romance blog
http://lisabetsarai.blogspot.com.

Thomas S. Roche's several hundred published short stories include work in the fields of horror, crime fiction, science fiction, and fantasy, but he is best known for his erotic short stories and for his sex-related nonfiction. His work has appeared multiple times in both Susie Bright's *Best American Erotica* series and Maxim Jakubowski's *Best New Erotica* series. Roche's own published book projects have included three volumes of the *Noirotica* anthology series (which blended erotica and queer fiction with hardboiled crime-noir), *Sons of Darkness* and *Brothers of the Night* (two volumes of queer-themed horror stories), *In the Shadow of the Gargoyle* and *Graven Images* (two mainstream horror-fantasy anthologies), and *Dark Matter*, a collection of his early short stories. He collaborated with Alison Tyler on *His and Hers*, two books of short stories intended for couples. A longtime spoken word performer at underground, queer and sex-positive events in San Francisco, Roche has performed more than 100 of his stories before audiences. He can be found at *http://www.thomasroche.com*.

Cara Bruce is the editor of *Viscera, Best Bisexual Women's Erotica and Best Fetish Erotica*. She is the co-author, with Lisa Montanarelli, of *The First Year-Hepatitis C*, and the co-author of *Horny? San Francisco*. Her short fiction has appeared in many anthologies including *Pills, Thrills, Chills & Heartbreak, Public House, Best American Erotica 2001, Best Women's Erotica 2000-2004, Best of Best Women's Erotica, Necrologue, Mammoth Book of Best New Erotica 1 & 2, The Unmade Bed, The Oy of Sex, Uniform Sex, Of the Flesh, Starfucker, Best Bondage Erotica* and many more. She has written for *The San Francisco Bay Guardian, While You Were Sleeping, GettingIt.com, Playgirl, On Our Backs, Girlfriends, Salon.com, Young Money* magazine, the *McClathy-Tribune*, and more.

She is currently co-teaching online writing workshops with author Shawna Kenney. They are co-editing a series of anthologies: *Robot Hearts: Twisted and True Tales of Seeking Love in the Digital Age, Tarnished: True Tales of Innocence Lost, Caught: True and Twisted Crime Stories,* and *Grounded: True Stories about Nature.*

Ira Miller's first novel, *Seesaw*, was published in the U.S. in hardcover by St. Martin's Press and in paperback by Bantam. It went through four printings in paperback and sold over 132,000 copies. There was also a German and Spanish edition, and a book club sale. His second novel, *Whipped*, was published by Xlibris. It was also published in

German by Wilhelm Heyne verlag, a division of Random House. Both the first and second novels remain on sale today in Germany under the titles *Die Gelehrige Schulerin* and *Die Herrin*, respectively.

Mr Miller was also a screenwriting fellow at the American Film Institute, where he had two short films produced. He has taught screenwriting at Hofstra University and creative writing at Fairleigh Dickinson University. He has had numerous magazine articles published and short story called *Writerhampton* appeared in the 1998 book anthology *Hampton Shorts*. *Cell* is part of the current collection of erotic short stories he is preparing for publication called *Sex and Love*.

More titles in the Sex in the City Range

Sex in the City – London
ISBN 9781907106226 £7.99

Sex in the City – Paris
ISBN 9781907106257 £7.99

Sex in the City – Dublin
ISBN 9781907106233 £7.99

www.xcitebooks.com